Unbearable
LOSSES

Jennifer L. Jordan

Spinsters Ink
2006

Spinsters Ink, Inc.
P.O. Box 242
Midway, FL 32343

Printed in the United States of America on acid-free paper
First Edition

Editor: Catherine Harold
Cover designer: LA Callaghan

ISBN 1-883523-68-0

For Georgine

About the Author

Jennifer L. Jordan is the author of *A Safe Place To Sleep*, *Existing Solutions*, and *Commitment To Die* (a Lambda Award Finalist), all mysteries in the Kristin Ashe series. Visit her Web site at JenniferLJordan.com.

Prologue

I had never felt so cold in my life.

Here I lay, three days before Christmas, on an elf stakeout, the only dark spot among 25,000 twinkling lights.

If I'd thought to dress for the elements, lying in the bushes wouldn't have felt so painful. But who knew? Earlier in the day, I'd worn a windbreaker on an afternoon bike ride. Four hours later, a cold front had moved in, the temperature had dropped thirty degrees, and I'd started to have serious doubts about this assignment.

Two weeks earlier, the case had looked simple when the Crumpler sisters had hired me to find out who was filching from their Christmas display.

A couple of munchkins had been stolen, plus Mrs. Claus. And okay, baby Jesus, too. Yet, that evening, as two buses and a steady stream of cars had pulled up to the holiday extravaganza, none of the sightseers had seemed to miss what was missing.

How could they—they still had Santa and his reindeer on the roof, dozens of oversized candy canes, an army of snowmen, five circling trains, a flock of angels in the trees, and three nativity scenes.

Not to mention the continuous loop of holiday tunes. If Santa Claus came to town one more time or another chestnut roasted on an open fire, I knew I'd lose it.

As I fidgeted on the frozen ground, I thought I couldn't possibly experience any deeper misery when the cell phone in my pocket began to vibrate.

Holding the plastic away from my numb ear, I whispered, "Hello."

The response came in a chilling wail, "Kris, she's gone!"

Chapter 1

The whole mess began on December 7, the morning Fran Green talked me into solving "The Case of the Missing Christmas Decorations," as she called it.

Fran convinced me to meet that evening with the Crumplers, two elderly sisters whose award-winning display had started to shrink. Even as the ladies added new figurines, lights, and cut-outs, mean-spirited holiday vandals made off with a few pieces each year, and the twin sisters were fed up.

As I organized files on my desk at work, Fran explained all this over the phone, between loud bites of Grape Nuts and crisp toast, which she enjoyed from the comforts of her apartment.

I suppose I agreed to take on the Christmas case for three reasons.

First, I rarely found the words to say no to Fran Green. An ex-nun thirty years my senior, she had a way of shaming me into accordance.

Second, I was in the thick of a pre-holiday stupor, the likes of which only a post-holiday depression could rival, if this year unfolded as most before it had.

Probably, though, I agreed to care about a garish light display because Fran was the main source of referrals for my part-time detective business.

In fact, she'd put me in touch with Lori Parks, the head of the Children's Academy, the most elite daycare center in the Denver metro area. From what scant information Fran had revealed, the director's quandary promised to be a challenging one.

I had to offer a rushed good-bye to Fran when I saw a late-model Volvo station wagon pull up in front of my office.

Unaware of me watching, Lori Parks exited the car, looking as if she had flown in from New York. While most of us slog through Colorado winters in hiking boots and parkas, this woman had selected an entirely different look with a black overcoat, cream wool scarf, and conservative heels.

I rose to greet her as she stepped into the office. "Hi, I'm Kristin Ashe."

"Lori Parks."

After she peeled off leather gloves, we shook hands.

"It smells like snow, doesn't it?" I said conversationally.

She looked at me quizzically. "You smell it? I used to be able to, but I haven't in a long time."

I nodded. "Something's in the air."

"They haven't forecast any storms."

"It's coming," I said, as I placed her coat and scarf on the rack next to the door.

She moved to tidy the garments, absentmindedly patting the fabric of her coat.

Throughout most of Lori Parks' life, she probably had turned heads, men's and women's, with her tall, shapely figure. Her broad forehead complimented round eyes and thick lashes, and her cheekbones were prominent enough to render the spaces below them concave. In her younger years, her cascading hair—now stiffened with dye and spray to reach the desired "natural" effect of flowing, auburn hair—had probably been her trademark feature. She still took pride in it, if her frequent, reflexive ministrations were any indication.

She wore a charcoal gray business suit, a white scoop-neck shell, black hose, and pearls. Fran had told me Lori Parks was forty, but light make-up couldn't conceal years spent outdoors. I made a mental note to start wearing more sunscreen, but I would have given anything for one full day of her unmistakable self-assurance.

As it was, I rose each morning and bemoaned a chest that was two cup sizes too large for my liking, bushy eyebrows I had to pluck into submission, and freckles that splayed all over my body in random patterns. On my last birthday, my thirty-sixth, I'd added gray hair to my list of woes. While only a few were scattered among otherwise dark-brown short hair, their numbers had grown beyond what I could realistically pull.

On the plus side, I could have answered honestly a "weight-in-proportion-to-height" ad, my eyes were an unusual shade of blue when caught in the right light, and my cut calves could have qualified as models for a Title 9 clothing catalogue. Title 9, Eddie Bauer, Land's End—these were my main sources for clothes. That day, in jeans, turtleneck, and fleece vest, I hoped Lori Parks wouldn't notice the loafers with no socks.

I led her down a short hall, invited her into my private office, and offered up the couch across from my desk. "Can I get you anything? Coffee?"

"No, thank you. I've had a pot already."

"You must get up early or drink fast," I said, taking a seat across from her on my favorite well-worn chair that swiveled.

She pinched a half-smile. "Both."

"So, your partner Donna is a friend of Fran Green's?" I said, in hopes of easing the tension I could see in her eyes.

"Friends might be overstating it. Donna and Fran met in a women's snowboarding class four weeks ago. Donna's instructing on weekends, at Loveland. As she tells it, Fran's a natural."

"Hmm," I said. When Fran had announced her latest passion, my vision included more of a crab crawl across the mountain. The helmet, hockey pants, knee pads, and wrist guards she wore to protect her short, compact body completed the mental picture. This new information didn't compute. "She's that good?"

Lori must have heard the skepticism in my voice, because she smiled ruefully. "According to Donna. Who would have guessed a lady in her sixties could impress my forty-year-old athletic partner?"

"Don't let Fran's age fool you. She's sixty-six going on twenty."

"Donna's quite taken with Fran," Lori said, almost snidely. "In fact, she can't stop talking about her."

"Have you met her?"

"Only by phone, but Donna's planning a get-together sometime soon. Off the slopes."

"You don't snowboard?"

She shook her head. "I had my fill of cold-weather sports growing up."

"Did you ski?"

"A bit when I was younger."

"Cross-country or downhill?"

"Both."

"Were you any good?"

A shadow crossed her features. "Quite, but none of that mattered when . . ." Her voice cracked and she paused. "It was a long time ago. Could we please address my issues with the Academy?"

"Of course. Right away," I stammered, aware I'd touched a nerve but unsure why. "Fran hasn't told me much, only that strange things have happened. How about filling me in from the beginning?"

Lori took a deep breath. "First, I need your assurance that this won't go any farther. I can't afford to let word leak to the media. Last year, *USA Today* featured the Children's Academy in an article, and this year, we celebrated our fifteen-year anniversary."

"I'll be discreet, and Fran is my only associate."

Lori's shoulders relaxed. "At any rate, I don't think what's happened amounts to anything more than pranks. The first occurred about two months ago, in October."

I pulled a pad from the top drawer of my desk and began to take notes. "What time of day?"

"Around five o'clock in the morning. I was coming into work, and as I crossed the playground, I saw clothing strewn about. I brought them inside before anyone could notice."

"How did you notice them in the dark?"

"Floodlights surround the building and grounds."

"What kind of clothes did you pick up?"

"All outerwear. A coat, snow pants, mittens, a scarf, a hat."

"New or used?"

"Used. Some a little torn."

"Dirty or clean."

"Clean and organized. An outfit. Not matching exactly, but complementary colors."

"What size?"

"Adult medium, I suppose."

"Where were they on the playground?"

"All around. At the bottom of the slide, on the merry-go-round, on the bars of the climbing gym."

I dutifully recorded the facts. "Is the playground locked at night?"

"No. It's fenced but never locked."

"What was the weather like?"

Lori Parks paused to reflect. "It must have been warm, because I remember thinking there was no need for winter garments. The children hadn't begun to wear coats to school yet."

"What did you do with the clothes?"

"I put them in a box in our lost and found, hoping someone would claim them. Thus far, no one has."

"Are you always the first to arrive in the morning?"

"Yes."

"So someone may have directed this at you?"

"Possibly," she said carefully. "But the next incident makes even less sense."

"What happened?"

"About a week ago, I came to work and found a picture taped to the front door."

"A drawing?"

"A photograph. A black and white snapshot of a young girl."

"How old is she?"

"About three or four."

"And the era of the photo?"

"The sixties or seventies, I'd guess."

"Did you recognize the girl?"

Lori hesitated. "No."

"You're sure?"

"Something struck me on an intuitive level when I saw her smile, but no, I couldn't place her."

"Was she posed in winter clothes?"

"No, more of an Easter outfit."

"By herself?"

"Yes."

"Anything in the background?"

"Part of a brick home, but nothing distinguishable."

"Did you keep the photo?"

"Yes," she said, reaching into her purse. "But it's a bit marred. Ink from the back bled through to the girl's dress on the front."

I raised both eyebrows. "Something is inscribed on the back?"

"If you could call it that, scrawled in block letters."

"What's written?"

Lori Parks retrieved the photograph and read from the back, methodically, as if announcing the winner of a prize. "Still, you believe no harm will ever come to your children . . ."

Chapter 2

Was this woman in denial, or what?

This case should have gone straight to the police, not to me and my amateur helper, Fran Green. Clothes scattered across a playground, an ominous note accompanying an innocent picture. What more did Lori Parks need—a dead body?

I felt queasy agreeing to help, but it fell to me or no one. Lori Parks remained adamant about that when I urged her to call the authorities.

After all, she announced, she dealt with children.

Not any children, mind you. Sons and daughters of the wealthiest families in Denver, the most valuable assets of the scions of society. At the first whisper of impropriety, she'd lose every client, and she wasn't about to risk that.

Lori Parks had founded the Children's Academy shortly after earning a doctorate degree in languages. The start-up funds came as a graduation present from her father, a man eager to see her open the business of her choice.

She had selected daycare, or at least that's the industry category she fit into, but I'd never heard of a daycare program like it in the country.

From the beginning, the Children's Academy had specialized in infants and toddlers. The first five years of a child's life were a "window of opportunity" for development, which set the groundwork for entrance into elite primary and secondary schools. These in turn represented the most likely path to Ivy League colleges, prestigious graduate schools, and prosperous careers.

At the Children's Academy, a large staff worked with small groups of children, primarily one-on-one, to promote early childhood learning. The babies listened to classical music, while the toddlers played tennis and golf with whittled-down rackets and clubs. All children, as they learned the language of their parents, simultaneously studied at least two others. Mon dieu!

The going rate for this level of attention was $1,500 per month (give or take a few hundred depending on how many hours per day the child spent at the Academy), and Lori Parks had a one-year waiting list. Over the years, she'd added after-school care for children up to age twelve and renovated, moved, and expanded her facility five times. Her business had grown to include 100 employees who "expanded the minds" of 200 children.

No wonder my new client didn't want any bad publicity. By my rough calculations, she had a $3.6 million empire.

I felt like a slacker with my half-million dollar business. Then again, no one had bankrolled me.

Or so Fran Green reminded me a few hours later.

I'd started Marketing Consultants at the age of nineteen with $500 and now employed six women full-time, producing marketing materials for health care professionals.

Because business always lagged during the final weeks of the year, I gave my employees paid vacation from the week after Thanksgiving until the first business day of the new year. They loved that perk more than any other I could have offered.

The time alone benefited me, too. I looked forward to the break as a chance to catch up on details that slipped through the cracks throughout the year. The quiet gave me an uninterrupted opportunity to finish re-cordkeeping and forecasting, and most years, I also added a big project to my "to do" list. This year, I planned to update our dental library of four hundred articles.

I had almost finished editing, "Eight Great Reasons to Visit the Dentist," when Fran Green popped in, ostensibly to bring lunch, but really to get the scoop on the Lori Parks case.

Fran never had demonstrated a lot of patience.

In her years as a nun working for parishes across the Denver area, she'd put her agitation to good use, often rocking and ultimately changing systems or policies she viewed as inadequate. Fran and I had met a few years earlier, on a tricky adoption case I'd investigated, and we'd become fast friends and associates.

Known for her outlandish T-shirts, Fran didn't disappoint with that day's choice. Teal letters proclaimed "Betties Do It Better!" on a purple cotton version that fit snugly over her flat chest and slight belly. I guessed this alluded to a snowboarder's joke, but I'd learned not to ask. I swore Fran had half these works of poetry custom silk-screened, but she stead-fastly maintained they all came as gifts or off-the-rack purchases.

This one looked particularly good with her gray hair. It never would have occurred to this stalwart feminist to color her locks, even if some mistook her for a man. Forget coloring; some days she could barely take care to brush them straight up.

"You look a little stiff," I said as she tossed her coat three feet onto the rack.

With considerable effort, Fran took off her snow boots and placed them on the shelf she'd installed to protect the hardwood floors.

Somehow, my office had become Fran's home away from home.

I worked in the Washington Park neighborhood, in a one-story brick building that originally had housed a soda fountain. The space had been converted and now accommodated a chiropractor, an insurance agent, a hair salon, and my business.

After Fran straightened up, she turned her whole body to face me. "Neck's a little sore. Lower back has a few chinks. Left wrist and thumb slightly sprained. Nothing serious, except for the bruised tailbone. Check it out."

Before I could protest, she pulled down her sweats. I started in amazement, more at her blinding white butt than at the purple and green splotches. "You're sure you want to keep snowboarding?"

"Wouldn't give it up for anything. Took a couple hard spills Saturday. Nothing serious. Be healed by now if Ruth had helped me tie on some ice packs, but she refused. Another student in the class lent me a set of magnets. Been trying those out. Can't get too close to the fridge, though." She guffawed loudly.

When I didn't join in, she explained, "Or I'd stick to it."

I smiled on cue. "I got it the first time, Fran."

"Just seeing if you're awake."

We walked down the narrow hallway to the first glass-enclosed office, where Fran spread out lunch on my desk, oblivious to important papers, files, and equipment. A few minutes later, we settled in to eat. I sat behind my desk, and Fran lounged on the couch, resting against two pillows.

As I wolfed down the Chicago-style hot dog and chili fries Fran had purchased at Dawg's, a stand near the University of Denver campus, I marveled at how she'd managed all this on the bus. Apparently with a weathered backpack and a double layer of foil she'd brought from home, one we'd since split and converted into makeshift trays. Never having learned to drive, Fran made it around town by relying on her partner Ruth, Denver's woeful mass transit system, unpredictable cabs, and rides mooched from friends.

"What's your strategy?" Fran asked after I'd updated her on the details of my meeting with Lori Parks.

"I'm visiting the Children's Academy tomorrow. I'll know more after I see the place."

"Want company?" she asked, as she bit off a third of her hot dog.

I couldn't fathom Lori's reaction to Fran Green. "No, thanks. That might startle her."

"Don't like it, Kris. Has a bad feel to it," she said, wiping a brown-orange dribble from her chin.

"Me neither," I agreed, struggling to take a bite of hot dog without all the condiments plopping on my desk. "But what else can I do?"

"Better let me in if the coppers are cut out. Be happy to take on more responsibility. We'll be fine."

That's what I loved about Fran. She never suffered from a shortage of confidence. However, the statement, "We'll be fine," made me a shade uneasy.

With each detective case I'd undertaken, Fran had established her usefulness, allowing me to rely on her more and more. Still, I didn't want an associate, who, knowing her, would soon act like my boss. The day would come when I'd have to face the shifting patterns of our relationship, but I had no desire to do it today.

I promptly changed the subject. "Can I ask you something about Ruth?"

Fran and Ruth had met in the convent and fallen in love. Over several decades, they'd conducted their relationship in secret before leaving the church twelve years earlier.

"Shoot!" she said, collapsing a fry in her mouth.

I tried not to notice some potato had fallen to her chest. "How do you deal with her irritating qualities?"

Fran tracked down the spud and popped it between her lips. "This about Destiny? What's your honey done?"

"She woke me up at four in the morning to ask if I had food poisoning."

"And?"

I pushed my food to the side. "This is after we had split a burrito from a stand on Sixth Avenue. She fell right back to sleep, and I lay there waiting to throw up."

Fran shoveled a large bite of chili onto her plastic spoon. "You get sick?"

"No, but that's not the point."

"Worry too much, Kris. Like paying interest on a debt you may never owe. Plus, keep frowning like that, you'll have a permanent cross on your forehead."

Her warning only served to deepen my wrinkle. "Destiny sleeps soundly every night, and on a good night, I get a handful of ninety-minute naps, separated by rounds of tossing and turning."

"Can't begrudge someone her shut-eye."

"What about the toilet paper? With just ten squares left on the end, she doesn't change the roll. How inconsiderate is that?"

"Might be frugal. Only use six myself for liquid jobs."

"What about this holiday mess? She insists on being cheerful, and I barely can drag myself out of bed in December."

"Need to take up a winter sport, Kris. Get your mind off the darkness. Snowboarding'd give you something to look forward to. Could join me and Donna next week. Might have a little catching up to do, but I'd wait on you."

"Thanks, but could you focus on me and Destiny for a moment?"

Fran grinned sheepishly and brushed crumbs from her lap onto the midnight blue carpet. I forgave her the sloppiness, mainly because she was the only one who vacuumed the office. "Sorry."

"What's with you anyway? Did Destiny hire you to defend her?"

"Not on the payroll last time I checked."

Fran always had loved Destiny Greaves. Most people did. My lover had a charisma and grace that served her well in her position as director of the Lesbian Community Center. While some admired her tenacity and strength, more were struck by her generosity of spirit.

On top of it all, she was naturally good-looking with shoulder-length hair the color of the sun and penetrating green eyes. We were close in temperament and age (thirty-six, separated by only a few months). We laughed at the same things, could talk about any subject for hours, and served as each other's center of gravity.

How the hell could I complain?

I softened every time I saw her eyes crinkle when she smiled, and I still ached at the thought of her body lying naked next to mine, long limbs gently cradling me. Yet, I often felt uneasy and rarely seemed able to commit past the next month.

Right then, I felt pain of a different sort when I rolled back from my desk and knocked my knee on the edge. "Ouch. Being together fits Destiny. Sometimes, in the morning, she looks at me as if she's never been so happy, as if she's waited for this her whole life."

"Maybe she has."

"How? Why me? Why now? She tries to sneak kisses in public all the time."

"Sounds romantic."

"We could get killed!"

"Not a bad way to go, smooching in the arms of your lover."

"She wants to merge our finances," I said, disconsolate.

"You too cheap to share your high-powered wages?"

"Are you kidding? She has way more money than I'll ever see. Her family gave her a bunch, she invested it, and made tons more. Now she gives away most of it."

"Destiny ever use the money in a bad way, hold it over you? Strings attached?"

"Never," I said wearily.

"Merge away, I say." Fran patted my arm. "You two'll be fine. Only moved in together six months ago. Newlywed jitters. They'll pass."

"What if they don't? Destiny had an endless parade of women before we met. How can she make the transition so smoothly?"

"You asking me why she can or why you can't?"

I let out an exasperated sigh. "Have you heard a word I said?"

"Every one. Some twice," Fran said easily. "Got a rich girlfriend who adores you and wants to show it. Sleeps soundly and forgets to change the TP roll. I miss anything? Gotta ask—what's the problem?"

I shrugged.

"Kris, what's really causing the run on Tums?"

I let out a deep breath. "I don't know. She has her job, and I have my company and this investigative stuff. It seems like we never make us come first. What happened to the day we made love three times, and Destiny accidentally wore her shirt inside out to the grocery store. Why can't we stay there forever?"

"It can't be that far gone, kiddo. You've only known each other, what, a couple years?"

"Two and a half."

"All the more reason, can't let yourself lose it. Requires careful stoking."

"Stroking?"

"That, too, but I'm talkin' about stoking the fires. Ruth and I did it for years."

"Did it?"

Fran seemed startled by her own slip. "Have done it."

I looked at her sharply. "Is everything okay between you and Ruth?"

"Same old, same old," she said, a little too heartily.

•••

After lunch, Fran disappeared into one of the back rooms to make a flyer for her apartment building's holiday potluck. She liked to dabble in the graphic arts and often took advantage of our state-of-the-art computer, layout software, scanner, and printer.

Knowing that would occupy her for hours, I heeded her advice and called Destiny.

"Hi, honey," Destiny said before I could utter a word—thanks to caller ID.

"We need to have sex more often," I said brusquely.

"Okay." I could hear the smile in her reply. "Now?"

"Not now," I said, unprepared for the immediate acquiescence. "Fran's here."

"Later this afternoon?"

"I can't. I have to go meet the Crumpler sisters, that Christmas case I told you about."

"Oh, right," she said, her disappointment showing. "After that?"

"No, we're both too tired on Monday nights. Plus, we need more time."

"Really?" she said, dropping her voice seductively. "What did you have in mind?"

"Everything. How about Saturday?"

"Saturday would be perfect."

"We'll stay in bed all day, like we did when we first got together."

"I can't, not that day. I have a board meeting at noon."

"Sunday?"

I heard the sound of calendar pages flipping before she answered. "Done."

"Good. I'll see you tonight."

"Kris, wait! What brought this on?"

"I don't want to lose our passion."

"I haven't lost mine."

"I haven't either, but somehow we've lost it as a priority. We're both busy with work, and obligations, and, you know . . ."

"You want to start scheduling sex?"

"Maybe. Not as an obligation, but as something to look forward to."

"I'll start anticipating now. While I'm raising money and lobbying legislators and meeting with community leaders, I'll think about all the things I'm going to do to your luscious body."

"I'm serious, Destiny," I said, hurt.

"I am, too. I think about you all the time."

"You do?"

"Of course. I especially like to imagine—" A series of clicks interrupted Destiny's revelations. "Damn, Kris, I have to take this call."

"Sunday," I reminded her. "All day."

"Every minute of it," she said quickly.

"We'll have sex until we're raw," I said quietly.

In the pause, I thought Destiny had already hung up. But then, in a trembling voice that gave me chills, she said, "It's on my schedule."

Chapter 3

Fran did linger a few more hours before announcing she had to run. As she gingerly put on her coat and boots, she outlined her pressing plans. At her next stop, a sporting goods store, she intended to purchase a new snowboarding outfit.

"No one's wearing neon anymore," she solemnly informed me.

I could have guessed that, and I hadn't skied since junior high.

She insisted she needed to discard her pink ski suit in order to gain respect from shredders. This marked a milestone for frugal Fran. Usually, she held on to items until they wore out or came back in style.

Shortly after she departed, large flakes began to descend in a gentle shower. By the time I left at six to begin my investigation of the missing Christmas decorations, about an inch of snow had accumulated on grassy areas.

Taking no chances, I drove slowly to the Crumpler sisters' home in Observatory Park, one of Denver's older, affluent neighborhoods. On the trek, I thought about how much I hated the holidays.

If I could have, I would have erased them from the calendar.

Thanksgiving was harmless enough, but it marked the beginning of the staging of Christmas, and the days between the two celebrations dragged interminably. The malls, the frenzy, the falsity, the wretched gifts, the overstuffed food, the obligatory gatherings, I couldn't stand any of it.

Clearly, however, I was in the minority.

On the ten-minute journey, I passed countless lit-up houses, most with a sprinkling of lights, a row of candles in the window, or a blow-up decoration on the lawn, some with more intricate displays.

But none came close to the brilliance of the Crumpler showcase.

Fran had warned the extravaganza was a bit over the top, but nothing could have prepared me for what I saw.

My shock began at the sheer volume and brightness. White flashing lights draped nearly every inch of the house, and blue ones choked the wrought-iron fence surrounding the half-acre lot.

Santa was everywhere. He and his full ensemble of reindeer launched from the roof of the two-story mansion, while another look-alike in a red suit struggled to exit the chimney. He also toiled in a workshop on the north corner of the property and managed a union of elves in the "Snow Village" at the back.

If that wasn't enough, giant letters blinked "Merry Christmas," a band of carolers serenaded six bears skating around a miniature rink, and a platoon of elves climbed a candy cane jungle to the rhythmic beating of a man-sized drummer boy.

Almost as an afterthought, three nativity scenes were wedged among the remaining choirs, snowflakes, and toy soldiers.

I had never seen anything like it!

I couldn't find a space near the Crumpler house and had to park two blocks away and backtrack through the throng of cars and pedestrians clogging the street. When I arrived at the gate, I pushed my way past a family of four, grabbed a complimentary candy cane from a decorated garbage can, and hurried up the winding sidewalk.

Wiping my feet on the penguin-adorned mat, I rang the bell and prayed someone would hear it over the blare of loudspeakers. I clapped my hands together and stomped my feet to regain sensation.

Fortunately, someone answered my call. Two someones, in fact. The giant oak door opened, and two ladies appeared before me. Had they been stacked on top of each other, the two seemed like they wouldn't have cleared the height of one NBA player. They had identical hairstyles (neatly permed, coifed, gloss black hair), glasses (large, gold, octagonal frames), and handshakes (soft, fingers-only). They also shared the same facial features: thin lips painted in bright pink lipstick, miniature teeth, and penciled-in brows. Never before had proof of a split egg appeared as vividly. Identical except for their attire, they greeted me in stereo and ushered me into a massive marble foyer. My first apartment would have fit in the entryway, with room to spare.

Clad in a red sweater adorned with an embroidered white snowflake, Clarice Crumpler took my jacket, which she hung in a large wardrobe. Eunice, dressed more conservatively in dark blue pants and a green blouse, asked me to remove my loafers, which she laid carefully on a brass shelf next to the door.

Interrupting each other, Eunice and Clarice inquired about the roads, which I assured them remained dry despite the steady fall of snowflakes. Eunice had posed her question out of solicitude for my safe return home; Clarice's interest revolved around the continued transport of gawkers to their display.

I downplayed both concerns and expressed delight at their two Christmas trees, one covered in faux candles, the other adorned with red, sparkling balls, Clarice led me to the living room, while Eunice excused herself to prepare refreshments.

Minutes later, as I sat awkwardly on an antique sofa, my attention flitted between two more trees. None of these natural wonders would have fit inside or on top of any family vehicle. A flatbed must have delivered them, and not from a corner lot. In their fullness, freshness, and symmetry, they put the Charlie Brown stragglers of my childhood to shame.

The sisters, oblivious to wood-burning restrictions in effect that day, had a blaze roaring in the stone fireplace. Not gas or Duraflame, but a good, old-fashioned burn with logs that warmed the room. Two trees, one with glass angels and the other with gold crosses, flanked the floor-to-ceiling bay window that looked out onto the front lawn.

Without benefit of overhead lights or lamps, we sat in semi-darkness.

The smell of pine and homemade cookies, the crackling of the fire and soft sounds of Perry Como, and the intimate lighting and merry visuals all combined for an enchanting experience.

I could get used to this, I thought, as I nibbled on the leg of a warm gingerbread man.

"So," I said conversationally, "it's just the two of you."

"Two is enough, can't risk four, that's what Daddy used to say," Clarice replied. "Although, he might have preferred a son to help carry on our holiday tradition. I'm not sure he would have felt something this grand was fit for the weaker gender."

"He was a chauvinist," Eunice agreed. "He never did recover from the shock of my employment."

"Fran tells me someone has taken part of your display—"

"I'll leave you two," Eunice interrupted, without budging. "This is none of my business."

She and Clarice sat across from me, comfortably settled in overstuffed chairs with matching footstools. I could have used a little more padding in my sofa. I fidgeted as the sisters began to argue.

"Be gracious, Eunice, we haven't had a visitor in ages."

"Folks pass by every night."

"They're not proper guests, not like this young lady. Do you decorate for the holidays?" Clarice asked.

With zeal, I bit off the elbow of my gingerbread snack. "Not really."

"Do you live alone?" Eunice prodded.

"Er, no."

Clarice shook a finger at her sister. "Quit prying, Eunice. Kristin lives with her girlfriend Destiny Greaves, the one we see on the news all the time."

The admission didn't seem to faze Eunice. "It's nice to have someone you can count on. It's a long journey if you're lucky, not all of it pleasant."

"Stop with the melancholy, Eunice. You've led a charmed life. We both have."

"You do have a nice home," I said, bringing the china teacup to my lips to test the temperature of the spiced tea. Too hot. I blew on it, took a delicate sip, and singed my tongue.

"Thank you," Clarice replied. "We grew up here, but Eunice married a man in the service and moved away."

"To California."

"She recently returned."

"Ten years ago, after my husband Harry and my mother died in the same year."

"Around Christmas, our dear mother passed away," Clarice added, in a tone barely above a whisper.

"On Christmas Eve," Eunice felt compelled to add.

"Your display outside is," I paused, searching for the right word. "Ambitious. Where did you get everything?"

"Oh, from all over," Clarice said, eyes sparkling. "Daddy built most of it when we were girls. He liked to weld and work with wood. He would make the figures, and Eunice and Mother and I would sew costumes or decorate them with lights and garland. We looked forward to it every year. We wanted to start in the summer, but he made us wait until Halloween. Couldn't have Christmas all year, he'd say, or it wouldn't be Christmas."

"We started on All Souls Day," Eunice corrected.

"Right enough, November 1. Oh, how I loved that day, when Daddy would spring his new ideas on us."

"Most of which came to him during church services."

"Nice quiet place to think, he'd say. One year, we built the workshop, the next year the ice rink, and so forth. Every year, he would make new wooden cut-outs, and Eunice and Mother and I would paint them, oh, so carefully."

"It seems like a lot of work," I said mildly.

Clarice smiled. "When you enjoy something, it's no work at all."

"Time passes quickly when you're young," Eunice added.

"After Daddy died suddenly—"

"Thirty years ago," Eunice enhanced.

"Mother and I continued the tradition. He would have wanted that. Eunice joined in by sending ornamental art from her movie jobs."

"We had odds and ends lying around, and I couldn't bear to see them go to waste."

"What was your job?"

"I scouted movie locations for MGM."

"No kidding?"

Eunice began to show increased signs of liveliness. "It was demanding, but exhilarating. When we made Westerns, I traveled back and forth from California to Colorado."

"Travel wasn't easy then," Clarice chimed in.

"Quite disagreeable."

Cautiously, I took another sip of tea, this time without injury. "Has your display always been this big?"

"It gets larger every year and more expensive," Eunice answered, with a bit of the judgment I felt.

"After Mother died, we dedicated more time to the project."

"You did." Eunice looked at me, but pointed at her sister. "She spends all year on it."

"Mother would have liked that."

"I grew tired of it."

"Mother wouldn't have liked that."

"You became competitive with it," Eunice accused. "She wouldn't have appreciated that either."

"Perhaps not," Clarice said tartly, "but I couldn't help myself. Once we won the first award, we had to have another."

Not up-to-speed on the sport of holiday displays, I said, "What award?"

Eunice answered, "The best holiday lights. The newspaper features them every year."

"They used to bestow a city-wide honor. We won that nineteen times, not to mention seven years in a row."

"Then they broke Clarice's spirit by announcing winners by region. This house falls into the southeast Denver area, which she's won every year since."

"But it's not the same," Clarice pouted. "Traffic slowed when they began listing other houses. We don't pass out half as many candy canes."

"The first year of the change, she became so upset, she stopped handing out postcards."

I almost choked mid-sip. "Of what?"

"Of our house, of course," Clarice said with pride. "We had them printed each year, in full color. Daddy had a friend in the business. We liked people to have a souvenir to take home and enjoy year-round. Eunice is right, though, my heart hasn't been in it since the split."

"Your heart must be in it, somewhat," I observed.

"Oh, certainly."

"Is it expensive?"

"Not really."

"Stop fibbing," Eunice snapped. "You're using 130 extension cords and eighteen circuits, pulling a hundred amps. Don't show me the December electric bill."

"Well, it's worth it, and every night promptly at nine, we turn it off. No matter what!"

"If you didn't, I'd pull the plug."

Clarice ignored her sister. "Even when there's a busload of children outside, I dim the lights," she said, with a touch of regret.

"At that hour, kids should be in bed anyway," I offered.

"How right you are. We'll get along just fine I imagine. More tea?"

"No, thank you." I put my empty cup on the coffee table and tugged the afghan tighter around my legs. "You ladies look like you're in good health, but surely you don't set this up by yourselves."

"You're right about that." Eunice nodded. "I don't lift a finger."

"Sister lost interest after Mother died. She couldn't climb a ladder anymore anyway."

"I can still paint," Eunice protested.

"But you won't," Clarice said brightly. "I end up doing all the work with the help of our handyman Leonard. We purchase supplies year-round and start sketching the layout around Labor Day. If I see something that strikes my fancy, I'll buy it and put it in the garage, and no one sees it until after Halloween, especially Eunice."

"She won't let Leonard start working until November 1—"

Clarice interrupted. "It's tradition."

Not missing a beat, Eunice continued, "And the poor man moves so slowly, he could use six months."

"I like him," Clarice countered, "And he comes from Nebraska, where Eunice and I were born, so we had something in common right away. We must have lights on by the day after Thanksgiving."

"Most years, she ends up hiring day laborers to help Leonard. That must cost a pretty penny, but she never lets me see the bill."

"We have plenty of money," Clarice said stubbornly, "and there's no reason we shouldn't share with others who are less fortunate. It's our family's legacy."

"Those day workers don't need your job. You're not Roosevelt, for goodness sakes. Franklin or Eleanor."

"I was referring to the people who make visiting our house a part of their holiday tradition," Clarice responded haughtily. "Kristin, you should see the glow in the children's eyes, and in the seniors' too. This is a favorite stop for several nursing home buses. Strangers send thank you cards. It's a shame someone wants to ruin our happiness by stealing heirlooms."

"When did you first notice items missing?"

"Around the time Mother died."

"I seem to remember it was before then," Eunice interjected.

"No, it was the year you came back from California. I know because we started an inventory list. Mother used to keep track of it all in her head, but I never had her memory. I decided I'd better make a list. Leonard and I itemized everything as we unpacked the display. When we put it away, I saw discrepancies."

"What was missing?"

"Oh, I can't recall exactly. Nothing much, perhaps a snowman or two. Those first few years, I chalked up the differences to my own errors."

"You never were good at math."

Clarice must have heard the insult before, because she didn't flinch. "No, reading was more my love," she said, before expelling a squeal of delight. "Oh, there's another bus."

She shot from her chair and bounded across the room to the front window. She may as well have seen Santa himself, such was her delight. Eyes like gumballs, nose pressed to the window, she only betrayed her age by hanging on to the heavy curtain for support.

"That's three tonight and twenty-nine for the month. See, Eunice, I can count," she said without rancor, returning to her seat. "To get back to my story, I borrowed a calculator from Leonard, and we both counted and double-checked, and there was no question. Pieces were missing."

Eunice spoke for us both. "You certainly had enough to spare."

"But that wasn't the point, was it?" Clarice said sweetly. "For the next few years, I dismissed the losses. I attributed them to petty vandals, and I didn't care to worry."

"What changed?" I asked.

"This year, they took Mrs. Claus!" Eunice said, almost triumphantly.

"That's it! Eunice and I spent a long weekend painting her when we were in grammar school. She meant a lot to me, and I specifically had Leonard put Santa's workshop near the house, thinking she'd be safe from thievery."

Eunice read my mind. "But she wasn't."

"I considered ringing the police. You know, I've never involved them because I assume they have more important jobs to do with their limited resources."

"They certainly do," Eunice agreed.

"Luckily, I ran into Fran Green at the grocery store. When she asked about the lights, I told her about our dilemma. She suggested I call you. You're easy to work with and have had success helping other people, she said."

"Do you have any idea who might want to steal from you?"

"If you ask me, it's Mr. and Mrs. Claus," Eunice said.

"Pardon?"

"The couple across the street," Clarice clarified. "They dress up every night and pass out chocolate Santas. They certainly envy our display, but I don't believe they'd stoop to crime. Florence Bailey, now she's another story."

"Flo didn't take your trinkets," Eunice said irritably.

"She may have. She puts up a display of her own."

"She hasn't done that since her husband died and she changed churches. Her house has been dark for years, you know that," Eunice said matter-of-factly.

"I never look at it," her twin huffed.

"She's right next door. How can you miss it?"

"I choose not to see," Clarice said simply.

Eunice addressed me. "They were best friends for years. Now they don't speak."

"She's the one not speaking to us."

"She's friendly enough with me."

"You didn't argue about Nixon."

"I thought your squabble was over a recipe."

"That, too. She gave Mildred Vilicent my meatloaf recipe, as if it were her own. I wouldn't put it past her to dampen my holiday spirits. Perhaps you should talk to her first."

"Put the screws to Florence, and get back Clarice's kidnapped Claus," Eunice said, enjoying herself a little too much.

I concealed a laugh, at the same time as Clarice said, "You may find all this amusing, Eunice, but I don't. Mother would—"

Sensing a lecture coming, I hurriedly performed a bypass. "I'll go visit Florence and the couple across the street. What are their names?"

"Tony and Alison Pollard," Clarice offered. "But don't mention we sent you. I don't want them to think we suspect them of wrongdoing."

"Clarice, let the poor girl do her work."

"I'll tell them I'm investigating an outbreak of vandalism that's affected homes in the area," I said quickly. "How's that sound?"

"Splendid." Clarice beamed.

We chatted for another thirty minutes, and when they rose to walk me to the door, Clarice couldn't resist a few admonitions. "When you visit Florence, don't stop by before noon. She's a night owl and likes to sleep in late."

"She always did enjoy the wee hours," Eunice added.

"If you call, let the phone ring. She has trouble getting around and uses two canes, but she'll pick up. She's always home. And don't shake her hand, she suffers terribly from arthritis."

As I exited the Crumpler house, I waved to passing cars and grabbed a few more candy canes. I also made a point of checking out the Pollard home.

On any other block, the Pollards would have been champions of festivity. Here, their efforts bordered on simplistic when compared to the Crumplers' display.

As I munched on a cane, I wondered if that would be enough to provoke them to pilfer a few pieces.

Maybe, just maybe.

•••

That night, I went to sleep with Christmas tunes playing softly in my head.

My lighthearted mood continued the next morning as I drove to work on dry roads, under clear blue skies. I remained in a chipper mood at the office, right up until the moment Fran Green dropped by unexpectedly.

Her disheveled appearance and pale complexion caught me off guard. "Are you okay?"

"As well as can be expected, kiddo," Fran said in a lifeless tone. "Didn't catch a wink last night. Came home from the store yesterday, and Ruth told me to move out."

Chapter 4

"Out of where?" I asked, shocked, as I guided Fran to the couch. She shuffled along behind me at a fraction of her usual military march.

"Our apartment."

"For good?"

Fran didn't bother to remove her new black snowboarder's coat. She sat slumped, moving only enough to shrug. "For a good amount of time, according to her."

"Why?" I practically shrieked.

"Says we were supposed to grow old together—"

"And aren't you doing just that?" I cried. "You've been together thirty years."

"Thirty-three in January. Said as much. Know what she said?"

I shook my head in disbelief. Why was I so hysterical and Fran so calm? She had enormous bags, dark purple-black circles that surrounded bloodshot eyes. Her hair was limp, and there was no color to her lips. Skin hung loosely from her hands and neck, as if she'd shrunk overnight.

"Said—get this—'But you're not growing old.' Can you believe that? She accused me of playing golf all summer, Fantasy Football in the fall, helping you year-round. Final straw was the snowboarding. Never knew she resented my hobbies."

"Addictions," I corrected reflexively.

"Interests."

"Obsessions."

"No need to label 'em," Fran said with a shadow of a smile. "If they give me pleasure, what's the harm? If Ruth had her way, we'd watch the news all day. Six a.m., nine a.m., eleven a.m., noon, four, six, nine and ten. No point going out in the world if you can sit on your rump and watch bad news."

"Is that really what Ruth does?"

"Pretty near. Years ago, we talked about buying a diesel truck and a fifth wheel. Planned on touring the country RV-style. Never was my idea of a good time, but figured I'd humor her. She won't even consider that now." Forlorn, Fran grabbed her cheeks and ran one hand across her mouth.

"Why?"

"Too much road rage, she claims. Hell, she causes most of it. Uses her middle finger like a turn signal."

"Maybe she's not feeling well."

"My rear end! She's fine. Ought to be with her fifteen pills a day. Heart, thyroid, indigestion, depression, sleeping. You name it, she has a capsule for it in her daily slot. Spends more time organizing those pharmaceuticals than exercising. Her favorite time of the day comes when the UPS gal or the postman delivers a fresh stash of drugs. Don't dare ask how she feels—that's a solid hour lost. But somehow, she'll get it in anyway. Me, I never discuss health. Take my vitamins and supplements, that's it! Can't abide no doctor giving me a pill, then need another to counter the side effects, then another. Where does it end?"

Once Fran started on the medical establishment, there was no stopping her. I returned to our original track. "Ruth's been upset with you before."

"She ain't mad," Fran said, her voice creaking. "That's what's got my intestines braided. Cool and collected, like she's been sitting on this egg for a long time, ready for it to hatch."

"Is there . . ." I began delicately but couldn't complete the treacherous thought.

"Another filly? Can't imagine."

"What will you do?"

"Won't try to win her back, that's for sure. Too much pride to swallow. Never hear the end of it."

"Where will you stay?"

"Can bunk down at the Gertrude Center for a few days, just 'til I get my bearings."

Fran had founded the Gertrude Center years earlier as a private club for lesbians. Located in a two-story Victorian house in the Broadway Terrace neighborhood, the center served as a social base for hundreds of women. Members dropped by to play cards, read books, or partake in lively discussions on the main floor or wraparound porch. Upstairs, one bedroom housed a caretaker, and two others were available to members for short stays.

"Is there anything I can do to help? Maybe if I talked to Ruth?"

"Waste of time, but thanks for the offer."

"You'll have to dust off your sex toy collection," I chided, unable to absorb the gravity.

"Did that a long time ago," Fran said grimly. "Know what it's like to be desperate for sex, but can't let go?"

I couldn't answer that. "You're sure you can't patch it up?"

Fran sighed heavily. "More holes than rubber in this old tire, I'm afraid."

I couldn't get Fran and Ruth off my mind for the next few hours.

I tried to concentrate on various projects but overrode every pursuit with incessant recycling. I replayed my conversation with Fran and couldn't erase the vision of her stupefied expression as she conveyed the heartbreaking news. I relived my last encounters with Ruth, searching for answers. I even revisited my parents' divorce, an event that had occurred almost twenty years earlier. That one at least had made sense. My mother and father had barely liked each other, much less shared a deep, abiding love.

Fran and Ruth, on the other hand, they fit together. They seemed comfortable and companionable, respectful and loving, loyal and devoted. If two nuns couldn't make it work—talk about shared interests and values—what hope was there for the rest of us?

Fortunately, my appointment with Lori Parks brought an end to the perseverating.

Or rather, the hunt for the Children's Academy, situated in the Lowry neighborhood, distracted me. Lori had given explicit directions, but once I arrived in the general vicinity, I struggled to find the building.

Lowry, a former Air Force base, had developed into one of the crown jewels in central Denver, "developed" being the key word. Seemingly, every builder had swarmed to start a project on the newly-available land a few miles east of hoity-toity Cherry Creek and a short commute to downtown Denver.

Homeowners could choose from lofts, condos, attached townhomes, duplexes, and every size of single-family home. The appeal: modern amenities in structures meant to replicate ones built in the early years of the twentieth century. Lowry advertised that it offered charm equal to that of Denver's historical neighborhoods, with bonuses of great rooms, jetted tubs, walk-in closets, and state-of-the-art wiring.

True, master planners had hoisted trees and planted parkways, something few suburban enclaves bothered with. They also had dispatched scads of press releases extolling a modern neighborhood environment, one in which residents could decrease reliance on cars and stroll to nearby schools, stores, and activities.

Yet, funny how this "car-less" neighborhood had such a preponderance of garages as focal points, and the closer I looked, the more the area reminded me of Highlands Ranch. The suburb, twenty miles south of Denver, epitomized everything wrong with rampant growth. There and here, the houses stood too close together, and different shades of paint and trim did little to disguise a cookie-cutter approach.

Give me the Capitol Hill mansion Destiny and I shared any day. I wouldn't trade its division into apartments, funky plumbing, and antiquated furnace for any amount of alleged safety, friendliness, or carefree living.

Who said we neighbors in Capitol Hill weren't friendly? Any time we heard gunshots, we called 911 in unison. Graffiti, we took turns painting over, and we loved to compare notes on loud music, strange tenants, and abandoned vehicles. Our ongoing war to preserve the quality and diversity of our neighborhood bound us together in a way no marketing could duplicate.

Nonetheless, I understood why Lori had relocated her business five years earlier, fleeing the Golden Triangle area. That neighborhood, while more centrally located, had changed irrevocably when real estate prices had soared and high-rise condominiums, populated primarily by empty-nesters, had appeared on every corner.

At Lowry, the price of the land and buildings would have cost a fraction of her former digs, and conveniently, her target market of affluent parents and their overreaching children, surrounded her.

I could have presented a report on Lowry, because I saw nearly every structure before I managed to locate the Children's Academy on the end of a cul-de-sac.

By the looks of it, Denver's premier children's learning center now occupied what once had been a firehouse. A small sign, "Lowry Fire Station #1," testified to the building's heritage, and above the entry, a large banner announced the "Children's Academy" and proclaimed "Expanding Children's Minds for 15 Years."

Before I exited my car, I surveyed the grounds. I'd driven in through a large iron gate that, if closed, would have connected the black ornamental fence that surrounded the property. The circular driveway led to a parking lot on the north end and a playground on the south, with the facility as the centerpiece. Gorgeous landscaping connected the three areas, including lush sod (green in December), aspen trees, mature pines, and tall grasses.

I locked my car and walked into the building through double-glass doors. Inside, a rich, cultured look dominated, broken only by the whimsy of a fire pole that sliced through the main room. In a small circle below the pole, hardwood remained, surrounded by a sea of plush, dark green carpet.

The large room split naturally into sections, without walls or dividers. To the right were wingback chairs and twelve-foot bookshelves. Interestingly, the collection of books contained more classics than children's favorites. In the center of the room, small café tables and chairs surrounded a refreshment counter, which was stocked with self-serve coffee, tea, and pastries. I was about to help myself when a voice halted my beeline.

"May I help you with something?"

Sally Patterson (I guessed from the brass nameplate) beckoned from the left. A slight, sixty-something woman, she called to me from her cherry-wood fortress. Barricaded behind a desk, matching credenza, and filing cabinet, she looked diminutive.

"I'm here to see Lori Parks."

"Do you have an appointment?" she asked, casting an appraising glance at my "dress-up" outfit of pressed khaki pants, turtleneck, and wool sweater.

"For three o'clock. I'm Kristin Ashe."

She pointedly stared at the clock behind me, prompting me to add, "I would have been on time, but I've been driving around Lowry for the past fifteen minutes, lost."

"Apparently, you found your way."

"Eventually," I said, feeling oddly defensive. "Is Lori available?"

"Dr. Parks is expecting you. She's on a conference call but asked that you join her. Her office is at the end of the hall." Sally rose, pointed, and headed in the other direction, dismissing me without a word. As she strode off in knee-high black boots, I caught a glimpse of her sand fleece pullover with decorative yarn stitching. In the center of the back was a six-inch appliqué of a wildlife scene, a half-moon, a moose, and a pine tree. It complemented the three elk embroidered across the collar of her ruby turtleneck and her ankle-length tan skirt.

"Thanks," I called out.

I found Lori's office with ease but hesitated at the threshold until she gestured for me to enter and take a seat across from her.

There were only three pieces of furniture in the room: an oversized, distressed leather chair, a wooden banker's chair, and a Mission table that served as a desk. Southwestern art and Navajo rugs covered one wall, but the other three were bare. Lori's desk was empty except for a manila folder, a Montblanc pen, and a multi-line phone, to which she was tethered by a headset.

I sat in the leather chair.

Given it was in the middle of a school, the room was strangely quiet, except for an occasional squeak from Lori's chair and the faint sound of classical music being piped through speakers in the ceiling.

For the next thirty minutes, I had the dubious privilege of watching Lori Parks in action. From her side of the call, I gathered the Children's Academy had an upcoming fundraiser, a tour of a millionaire's house. Said millionaire had begun, belatedly, to balk at the thought of 600 strangers walking through his private space. For some reason, 450 hadn't concerned him (last year's ticket sales to his best friend's mansion), but these extra 150 had put him over the edge.

Lori pacified, cajoled, and bullied the man back into accordance, finally trumping with the words "breach of contract." Throughout the negotiations, only the constant twisting of her gold necklace and the intermittent rolling of her eyes betrayed any degree of discomfort or impatience. She looked sharp in a white V-neck shirt with darts, a red skirt with a narrow scroll-buckle belt, and a lightweight black leather jacket/sweater.

As soon as Lori brought the conversation to a close, she rose, strode across the room, and closed the door. Almost as an afterthought, on the way back to her desk, she shook my hand.

Her first words contained no apology. "I told the gentleman we'd have fifty volunteers guarding his possessions. Only thirty have signed up, but if we spread out, he shouldn't notice. If it snows, that will cut into not only our attendance, but also our volunteer commitments, but I can't control the weather. Are you free this Saturday? If so, I'd like you to be at the Baker-Brown house."

"To volunteer?"

"To pose as a volunteer. I'll pay for your time, of course," she replied coolly. "The event will provide an excellent opportunity for you to familiarize yourself with most of the staff and administrators, as well as many of our parents."

"I'll be there," I said, without hesitation. "Even if there's a blizzard."

"Excellent," she said, flashing me a bright smile. "What do you think of the Children's Academy?"

"It's impressive. I had no idea child care was this complex."

The flickering of her eyes reflected my inadvertent insult. "This is a learning institute, Kristin. Child development is not the same as child care. We're a cultural facility, not a babysitting service. Research over the past decade has repeatedly illustrated the importance of early education. This is a billion-dollar industry in Colorado alone, with 8,000 licensed providers. Of those, a recent report found 82% provided mediocre care and 11% provided poor care. Last year, an industry magazine ranked the Children's Academy number one." She paused for effect, before adding with practiced timing, "In the nation."

"That's impressive."

"All the more reason I won't have someone thwarting my plans. Next year, we're adding a building across the street."

"You need more space?"

"Desperately. We'll relocate our creative movement studio into the new building, which will free up space to house a full-time nutritionist and wellness instructor."

I couldn't hide my surprise. "Little kids need all that?"

"More than adults," Lori said somberly. "Do you have any idea how many children we could wean off Ritalin, the drug of choice for attention deficit disorder, if we could control their diet?"

She continued without waiting for my reply. Just as well, because I didn't have one.

"The wellness program would highlight Eastern culture and holistic teachings. We'd like to incorporate those into our children's Western upbringings."

"You'd teach toddlers yoga and meditation?" I joked.

"Exactly," she said enthusiastically. "Experts produce research every day extolling techniques for breathing, exercises for stretching, and tools for quieting the mind. If we can instill these values at a young age, the children can enjoy a lifetime of good health."

"You have ambition," I said grudgingly.

"That's only the beginning. We'll budget space for a small amphitheater where we can stage the children's productions, and we'll expand our music department. I'm currently in negotiations to bring in a Juilliard-trained opera singer. Our concierge made the introduction. I can't tell you the soprano's name at this preliminary juncture, but she's had the principal role in several Denver Opera productions. Her voice is exquisite, much like—"

I cut her short, still recovering from the shock of what she'd said a few sentences back. "You have a concierge?"

"Sally Patterson, stationed in our welcoming area. Didn't she greet you as you entered?"

"Older lady, frizzy hair, timid voice?"

"Precisely."

"I thought she was the receptionist."

Lori Parks let out a mirthless laugh. "Don't let her catch you saying that. We employ her to coordinate all our social outings."

"Field trips?"

"We rarely visit fields," she said reproachfully, "although the children do enjoy monthly treks to the botanic gardens. In addition, they travel to the aquarium, natural history museum, and butterfly pavilion, as well as theater, dance, ballet, art, and musical venues."

"You get preschoolers to sit through all that—" I barely swallowed my last word, "crap."

"We do. We model etiquette and decorum for the children and stress good manners."

"That works?"

"To be safe, we commission private performances, not open to the public," Lori said with a forced smile.

"Sally works full-time?"

"She does. Her duties include availability to our parents, as well as scheduling the Academy outings. She has contacts with every arts group and broker in town. At a moment's notice, she can procure tickets to any event."

"Bronco games?" I asked for purely selfish reasons.

Lori's thin smile reappeared to announce her condescension. "Anything cultural."

Never mind. "I can't believe you've taken it to this level," I said, embarrassed when the words came out coated in more scorn than admiration.

"It hasn't been easy," she said with a humility she must have practiced in copious interviews with the media. "The first years, I spent as much energy educating parents as I did children. They couldn't conceive of what I proposed. No one in the city, or country, had thought to delve this deeply into childhood enrichment."

"Have they today?"

"There are a handful of facilities on par with ours, mostly on the East coast, two in California."

"None in Denver?"

"Absolutely not," she said, offended.

"Who's the closest competitor?"

"The Learning Emporium would like to view themselves as such, but they can't compare."

"It's a—" I struggled to remember her preferred description, "learning institute?"

"More of an entertainment center, although they squeeze in conventional teaching between distractions. Parents tend to compare us because our prices are in the upper range. They connote high price with high quality, which they shouldn't."

"Where is it located?"

"They have five locations. Highlands Ranch, Denver Tech Center, East Aurora, Arvada, and Cherry Creek."

"Could the pranks have come from someone at the Learning Emporium?"

"That would surprise me. They're all branches, with corporate headquarters in Illinois. I can't imagine that any of their employees, especially top-level managers, care enough to harass us."

I considered the geography and chose the closest competitor. "When did the Cherry Creek branch open?"

"Six years ago."

"How's it doing?"

"Thriving. No one in this industry with facilities this size suffers. There's no shortage of business."

"They're probably not involved," I conceded, "but would you object to my visiting one of the Learning Emporiums?"

"I suppose not. Be discreet."

"Of course," I said. "I'm not sure—"

Lori silenced me by tapping her watch. "I have to cut this short. I have a meeting downtown."

"No problem," I said, rising. "I'd like to look around the Academy while I'm here, if you don't mind."

"Certainly. Sally can show you around."

"I'd rather go alone."

"That's impossible," she said curtly. "No one wanders around unescorted. Sally won't mind."

Before I could invent an excuse, Lori buzzed the outer room, and on speakerphone, we overheard Sally Patterson conversing with a young girl.

Using a much nicer tone than she'd employed with me, Sally said, "Your mom is with someone right now, and then she has a meeting to attend. But she wants you to start on your homework."

The young girl replied, "Shall I sit out here with you?"

"No, sweetie, we'd distract each other with all our giggling and wouldn't get anything accomplished. You'd better head to the homework lab. We'll have a nice talk on our way home."

Lori interrupted the congenial exchange with a brief, "Hello, Erica. Sally, I need to leave shortly. I'd like you to show Kristin the facility."

The girl answered enthusiastically, "Hi, Mom," and Sally muttered, "Certainly" with considerably less animation.

After Lori concluded the call, I must have looked perplexed, because she explained, "Erica is in second grade at Village Elementary. She comes here after school on our complimentary shuttle."

"She's your daughter?"

Lori's reply came as a hard stare, no blinking.

"Fran didn't mention you had children," I said, lamely. "Neither did you."

"A child."

"Are you the, er, mother, or is Donna?" I said, stumbling.

"I gave birth to Erica. While we're both her mothers, I prefer to keep information about my relationship with Donna private."

My jaw dropped. "No one knows about Donna?"

Lori's unflinching gaze challenged me. "Not at the Academy, with the exception of Sally, my administrative assistant, and my business manager."

"What do people think?"

"I'm sure the staff and parents presume I'm a single mother. I don't bother to contradict them."

I felt like shouting, but I dropped my voice to a whisper, "You'd rather look like a single mom than a lesbian with a partner?"

"In this business, yes," she said with deep feeling.

"How does Erica handle this?"

"Quite well. Most afternoons, she comes to the Academy if Donna's at her law office. Either Sally or I take her home, depending on my commitments. Her Village Elementary friends come to our house and meet us as a family. Her Academy friends are just that—friends while she's here at the Academy. The children of my clients. We don't mix the two."

"How does that work when—"

Lori didn't allow me to finish my sentence. "I have to go," she said irritably and left the room.

I chased her down the hall. "I'll walk you out."

"Fine," she said, her tone implying the opposite. She power-walked to her car, barely pausing in the front room to grab her coat and say goodbye to Sally.

I had to take two strides to keep up with one of hers, but I'd be damned if she'd outdistance me. "Now that you've had time to ponder, have you come up with any ideas about who might be behind the incidents?"

"I haven't," she said roughly.

"No one in the world would wish you harm?"

Lori pulled up, turned to look at me impassively, and said slowly and evenly, "No one I know."

"Not professionally? Not personally?"

She shook her head slightly.

"Nothing's happened to cause discord recently? Nothing in the past?"

"No clue," she said and added a little maliciously, "or I wouldn't have had to hire you."

With that, and without a hint of farewell, Lori crossed the last chunk of gravel driveway, punched her keyless remote, opened the Volvo door, and slid into the driver's seat. She started the engine and drove off without a backward glance.

Long after her car disappeared from view, I had a bad feeling. And not just because I'd supersized my fast food meal at lunch.

I'd known Lori Parks for less than thirty-six hours, yet I already distrusted her. Why?

Maybe because I suspected she would reveal what she wanted, when she wanted, to whom she wanted.

I could only hope for something pertinent, soon, to me.

What followed reinforced my discomfort.

Sally escorted me around the Children's Academy, and our time passed more agreeably than I'd anticipated. She proved to be an entertaining and illuminating tour guide, up on all the history and inner workings of the Academy, though she'd only joined the staff six months earlier.

Prior to my arrival, Lori had told her I was a family friend, interested in starting a learning institute in Minneapolis, and I maintained the cover with minimum effort and few lies. At the end of our rounds, I asked to use the restroom and prefaced my request with hints about digestive problems, correctly guessing Sally wouldn't dare follow or question the length of my stay.

Instead of going to the bathroom, I headed for the lost-and-found closet. In cramped quarters with low light, I examined every coat, glove, mitten, hat, and scarf. I had almost given up mining for clues when inside one of the last pieces I checked, I found something that made my stomach churn for real.

From a dark-blue mitten with white stripes, I pulled out a plain square of paper. In block letters, someone had printed, "You do try to prepare . . ."

Chapter 5

I hightailed it out of the lost-and-found closet, called out a hurried thanks to Sally Patterson, and drove to my office as fast as I could, oblivious to the nuisance of other cars and yellow lights.

From the top drawer of my desk, I retrieved the photo of the little girl, the one someone had taped to the front door of the Children's Academy.

My heart raced as I compared the block-letter handwriting (identical!) and pieced together the correct sequence.

The garments scattered around the playground had been the initial sign of mischief. Therefore, "You do try to prepare" should have been the first clue, but Lori Parks had missed it when she retrieved the clothes.

Weeks later came the photo, with the message about no harm ever coming to children.

Put them together: "You do try to prepare. Still, you believe no harm will ever come to your children."

But it will . . . it always does . . . the messenger may as well have added.

I left a message on Lori's private voice mail at work, apprising her of my recent find, and sat back to ponder the point of the notes.

Why had someone delivered the warnings in their respective forms? What did mittens, scarves, and hats represent? And why the black and white photo of a young girl in an Easter outfit? Who was she, and had Lori, contrary to her denial, recognized her?

I pondered this well into the evening hours, right up to the moment I picked up Destiny for dinner at our favorite pizza joint, Antonio's.

On one of our first dates, we'd discovered the restaurant on East Colfax and had frequented it almost every week since. Occasionally, we called for delivery or take-out, but most nights we walked the dozen blocks and enjoyed sightseeing through Denver's "red-light" district.

Tonight, we'd elected to drive. We found a parking space in front of the restaurant and hurried inside.

The front windows, steamed with condensation and plastered with hand-made signs about lunch and dinner specials, had blocked the view from the street. Only after entering could we see the patrons, which represented a cross-section of Capitol Hill's population. A table of six lesbians. Three prostitutes on stools at the bar. Two men from a nearby senior center. A middle-aged couple with young children. And the owner's girlfriend, Leah, a tattooed woman with a boa constrictor around her neck.

Destiny and I claimed our usual booth, fourth in the row to the right of the entrance, and before we could peel off our jackets, Carla, the owner's mother, had deposited our favorite drinks: iced tea, extra lemon and a straw, for Destiny; Dr Pepper, extra ice, for me.

We waved hello to Maria, the owner's grandmother. Maria always camped out in the corner booth, nearest the kitchen. In earlier visits, we'd sat closer to her, but her odd mannerisms had distracted us. Destiny cringed when Maria tipped the sugar dispenser for ten full seconds into each cup of coffee, and I had to look away when she dipped pizza crust into the coffee to soften it enough to gum it. Clearly, one habit had led to the other.

At different times, we'd dragged various friends to Antonio's, but only one seemed to enjoy the experience—Fran. Friends our age objected to the dated décor: pale yellow linoleum, silver chrome booths, and seats and backs that were one part turquoise vinyl, four parts duct tape. They also protested the menu. Maybe they wanted feta cheese, shrimp, or barbecued chicken as pizza toppings. No such luck. Destiny and I had simpler tastes, mushroom on her half, sausage on mine. And neither of us complained about the iceberg lettuce salad with shaved carrots and one tomato slice. We'd accepted the limited choices of Italian, Thousand Island, and French, but sometimes, to amuse ourselves, we smuggled in a packet of Ranch. If Carla noticed, she never commented.

Benefiting from the warmth of the pizza ovens, Destiny and I enjoyed a lovely dinner until I broke the news about Fran's break-up.

My girlfriend choked on her pizza and spent five minutes coughing, downing water, and visiting the restroom before she had recovered sufficiently to chew again. On me.

"I can't believe you didn't tell me before," Destiny said, on the verge of tears.

"I just found out this morning."

"You could have called."

"I knew we'd talk tonight," I said lightly.

"Kris, this is a disaster. Don't you take it seriously?"

"It's not as if I have any control over it."

"Couldn't you talk to her?"

My voice rose an octave when I replied, "Ruth?"

"Yes. Convince her she's made a mistake. Suggest a cooling-off period before she makes any more rash decisions." Destiny went on in a rush, "Refer them to a couples counselor—"

I dismissed these ideas with a grunt. "I barely know Ruth, and I'm not good at this."

"I could coach you, write a short script, to the point but persuasive."

I looked at Destiny in amazement. "This bothers you that much?"

"Of course it does! They have all those years invested, with no support from their families. At times like this, we have to offer it. We can't let this happen."

"I don't think we have a choice," I said reasonably.

"They're the only lesbian couple we know who have been together that long. Who will we use as role models?"

I sighed. "I don't know."

"How could Ruth do this to Fran now, around the holidays?"

"Is there a better time?"

"If they haven't reconciled by Christmas, we'll invite Fran over for dinner," Destiny declared, cheering herself slightly.

My mood darkened. "What dinner? You know I can't stand to celebrate Christmas."

"A simple meal. No gifts. You owe me one for skipping the Holiday Gala."

"You said you didn't mind," I protested, feeling betrayed.

After giving me permission to opt out, Destiny had attended a formal dinner the Saturday after Thanksgiving. At the time, she'd said she understood my dislike of large gatherings, especially those comprised almost exclusively of straight people. I'd dutifully attended the previous year's event and had held my tongue every time Destiny introduced me as her "partner," only to have the person reintroduce me moments later as a "friend" or "roommate."

First, I resented the immediate, if unconscious, demotion. Second, at the time, we didn't live together, so how could we qualify as roommates? Destiny had overlooked the mild affronts, but each slight had annoyed me.

Furthermore, I'd started my own company, in part, to avoid office Christmas parties, and this one qualified. Every non-profit in the city received an invitation to the Holiday Gala, and Destiny, like many other executive directors, looked forward to the evening as an opportunity to gossip and network, in that order.

Sensing my suspicion of a double-cross, Destiny's tone softened. "I didn't mind going alone, at least not until I saw how much fun everyone else had dancing with their spouses or significant others. And if you and I set up our lives separately, how can they not separate?"

Before I could answer, she continued, "As far as Christmas, I have to point out, we did what you wanted last year."

I smiled brightly and nodded. "Delivered Meals On Wheels in the morning, saw a movie in the afternoon, and ate dinner at the Manhattan Deli. Let's do it all again."

"Handing out meals depressed you—"

I interrupted with, "Okay, we'll skip that part."

"The movie was awful—"

"We'll make a better selection," I said hurriedly.

"And we had to wait an hour for a table at the deli."

"Take-out?"

"Kris, what's wrong with you? Why can't we enjoy a meal together, at home? With Fran, if she's available?"

I could tell I had no chance of winning this argument and decided to save my energy for a time with better odds. "No decorations?" I bargained.

"None," she said gleefully.

"I do like the cookies," I said begrudgingly.

Destiny leaned forward with excitement. "I'll make whatever you want. Snowballs, sugar cookies, toffee bars, spritz—"

"And I am getting used to the Christmas tunes," I admitted.

"Light music playing in the background. If it starts to affect you, we'll put on k.d. lang or Sheryl Crow."

"Maybe it will snow," I said, my spirits rising. "I love snow on Christmas."

"It might," Destiny said indulgently.

I lowered my voice. "I wish we could spend it alone."

"Talk to Ruth, and maybe we can," Destiny replied pointedly.

Later that night, as I tossed and turned well into my second hour of sleeplessness, I thought about the valid question Destiny had asked earlier. What the hell was wrong with me?

Why did I view a supposedly joyous time of year as such a hazard?

Maybe because the holiday had always represented more strife than celebration.

As I scanned my memories, a horrible one choked every pleasant one. The terror-inspiring uncle we saw once a year wiped out the stocking full of candy. The stultifying Mass obliterated the excitement of new toys. And the grandfather who had a heart attack one Christmas eve overpowered the delicious smells of baking.

Long ago, I'd given up on the prospect of holiday happiness. These days, I gave myself credit for merely surviving.

Just get through it alive—that was my main goal.

It seemed like a simple request, at the time.

•••

The next morning's blinding sunlight elevated my mood, and as soon as I arrived at the office, I plunged into a list of tasks.

Number one involved setting a late-afternoon appointment at the Learning Emporium in Cherry Creek. Posing as a prospective parent, I intended to check out Lori Parks' chief competitor.

Number two undertaking, I broke off mid-dial. Halfway through numbers I knew by heart, I replaced the receiver. I'd promised Destiny I'd try to reason with Ruth, but I felt wholly unprepared. We'd never had much of a relationship, and frankly, the domineering, seventy-one-year-old ex-nun scared me. I was not exactly anxious to renew our acquaintance, especially outside the company of Fran. I could postpone the outreach, I reasoned, for at least a few days. With any luck, long before I gathered the courage for such an unsavory calling, Fran and Ruth would have reconciled.

I spent the rest of the morning on the Internet, researching the eighty-five Learning Emporiums spread across the country.

At noon, I stopped for a rice bowl at Tokyo Joe's, which I ate while I read *Westword*, one of Denver's weekly rags. Shortly after one o'clock, I drove back to the Crumplers' block to secure an interview with Florence Bailey, the woman who allegedly had purloined a meatloaf recipe and defended Nixon.

In the light of day, the Crumplers' mammoth display had lost some of its charm but unfortunately, none of the gaudiness. However, I did appreciate the complimentary candy canes. I snatched three and headed toward Florence Bailey's. I had to tread carefully on a walk that hadn't been shoveled, and on the Bailey porch, I stepped on the "Happy Birthday, Jesus" mat and vigorously rubbed my feet dry.

I rang the bell and waited a solid five minutes for an answer. I had almost given up when the door opened a crack, and I saw a portion of Florence Bailey's nose and a wisp of her hair.

As soon as she heard my reason for coming, investigation of neighborhood vandalism, she invited me inside.

I followed Florence, consciously slowing my pace in order to avoid a rear-end collision, and silently cursed the waste of time. Florence's stooped posture barely permitted walking, much less stealth running while carrying a Christmas figurine.

Using two canes, she shuffled back to her seat on the sun porch off the living room. From this vantage point, she would have had a front-row view of the Crumpler holiday display, except for the eight-foot high brick wall.

Settled into my wicker chair on the sun porch, I inwardly cringed at Florence's choice of wall color: light blue. Next to her chair, she had a pink rotary phone and a basket full of mail and magazines. Across from her was a large console TV. Glancing around, I realized with a pang that this hundred-square-foot area probably represented most of her world.

Yet, she'd taken care in dressing as if the world might come to her. She wore black slacks, a gold turtleneck, a red button-down sweater, and white Keds. Reading glasses dangled from a silver chain around her neck and often collided with the large Christmas tree brooch she wore above her left breast. Her skin was shiny and remarkably unlined, and she reminded me of my grandma when she pulled a tissue out of her sleeve and dabbed at her nose.

Florence offered me a Coke (which I had to get myself) three times before I accepted, not because I felt thirsty, but because her persistence showed no signs of subsiding. On my way to the kitchen, at her request, I watered the Christmas tree in the living room and used a DustBuster to pick up dry needles. When I complimented her on the small but striking tree, she apologized for its sparse look and vowed to add more tinsel next year.

After I retrieved my soda and rejoined Florence, she commented, "Anita Barnes had a daughter named Kristin. You don't know her by chance, do you?"

Before I could reply tactfully that I hadn't yet met all the women in Denver who shared my first name, she added, "Boots McCray did, too. No, she was Christine. Still, a pretty name. She's long since dead, bless her soul. She gave me that doll."

Florence pointed to a two-foot tall figure sitting in a miniature rocking chair in the corner, and I feigned interest. When she threw in, "That's my hair, you know," I moved closer to take a look at the reddish-brown locks.

We covered many topics (her grocery store preferences, her sleeping patterns, and her religious conversion, among others) before I could wrestle the afternoon back to discussion of the disappearing Crumpler display. And when I did, I got an earful.

"Serves Clarice Crumpler right. Putting up that kind of fuss every year. She never did have an interest in marriage, or men for that matter."

Following that non sequitur, I struggled to grab a thread of the conversation. Fortunately, the subject changed again.

"I saw someone over there," she said offhandedly. "But I won't say who when I can't prove anything. I'm not one to accuse someone without cause, unlike other people with whom I've been acquainted."

I smiled politely. "Anything you know would be helpful."

She clenched and released her fingers repeatedly. "I'm not a busybody who butts into other people's business. And if Clarice Crumpler is missing a few Christmas decorations, it's for the best."

"Why do you say that?"

Florence's nose wrinkled. "Before her mother died, she had a lovely display. These last years, she's turned into someone I don't know. Two years ago, the neighbors threatened to sue when she expressed an interest in buying the house on the other side and expanding into that yard. She'll never get this house. My daughter knows my wishes."

"Eunice told me you used to decorate. What did your house look like at Christmas time?"

"It was beautiful. I must say, our display was always tasteful. A thousand lights on the ten evergreens in front of the house, that was work enough. Earl would rent a lift to reach the tops of the trees."

"When did you stop decorating?"

"Some years ago. When I changed churches. I realized this wasn't the proper way to celebrate the birth of Christ. I suppose, too, after my husband died, it didn't seem appropriate. It was more his calling than mine."

Florence slowed down only long enough to draw a breath as I enjoyed a deep swig of Coke.

"Not that something such as that would stop Clarice Crumpler. She turned out the lights for one night in memory of her mother, but then back to business as usual. I'll tell you this, Clarice and Eunice fought like cats and dogs when Eunice came back from California. Eunice didn't think it proper to continue with the lights while they were in mourning. I heard them raise their voices on more than one occasion."

I suppressed a belch. "That's the only time they missed a night?"

"One other time, in 1984, they blew a transformer, which, I might add, didn't merely inconvenience their family on a cold winter night. Many of us went without electricity. The neighbors certainly didn't appreciate that. Nor were they pleased in 1993 when Clarice erected her blinking, 'Honk if you have hope for the New Year' sign. That came down faster than it went up."

"Are any neighbors in particular put off by the display?"

"Not really. Some are perturbed, but most seem to enjoy it." Florence looked at me shrewdly. "By the by, you're not really snooping around for the neighborhood, are you? I have a feeling Clarice Crumpler sent you."

"Well, yes," I said, collapsing at the slightest prompting. "But not because she suspects you. She and Eunice thought you might have seen something because you're next door."

"If I had, I surely would have informed Clarice."

"She implied you're not talking."

Florence raised both eyebrows. "What else did Clarice say?"

"She said you had been friends. I think she misses seeing you."

"It's true enough we used to enjoy each other's company. Did she bother to mention why *she* stopped speaking to *me*?"

"She thinks you stopped speaking to her over a mix-up with a recipe."

Red splotches on Florence's face telegraphed her indignation. "Well, I never! She accused me of taking credit for her meatloaf. As if I would! She should look into the mirror sometime and see what's facing her. As for those missing decorations, it wouldn't surprise me a bit if you found them in the basement. Those Crumplers never throw out anything. Last time I was down there, they had enough canned goods to survive two more wars."

"Do you miss Clarice and Eunice?"

Florence's eyes narrowed for a moment. "I wave to Eunice when I see her."

"And Clarice?"

Florence dropped my gaze. "Not particularly, but I do miss her pickles. If you're in the basement, fetch me a jar, if it's not too much trouble."

I smiled, assured her I'd try, and rose to make my exit. She wanted to see me out and strained to catapult herself upright, but I gestured for her to stay in the chair. Against Clarice's advice, I couldn't resist touching Florence in farewell.

As I gently cradled her arthritic hand in mine, she said in a low, conspiratorial voice, "Go talk to the Pollards. That young lady spends far too much time at home for someone her age. She comes across the street to visit me, and bless her heart for trying, but I'd rather sit here peacefully by myself."

Before I could murmur an assent, she tugged at my sleeve and continued in a whisper, "You know, it's common knowledge they were asked to leave their last neighborhood."

Florence Bailey punctuated this remark with such an obvious wink, I almost laughed.

Chapter 6

Thirty minutes later, I managed to get to my car, after having shouted an inventory of everything in the refrigerator to Florence in order for her to compile a shopping list. On my way out, I'd also paused to add a slice of coffee cake to the tin in the front yard and moved it under the pine tree, in case of snow. By the size of the squirrels I saw frolicking, none of them needed any more Sara Lee, but I dutifully dropped the snack.

Until I caught sight of the clock on my dashboard, I hadn't realized how close I'd cut it with back-to-back appointments. I had about fifteen minutes to traverse five miles through the side streets of Denver. Enough travel time, but I would have preferred a few more quiet moments to rehearse for my upcoming role as a parent.

En route to the Learning Emporium, I lost precious "method acting" moments when I had to fumble to answer my cell phone. Months ago, Destiny had given me a headset, which I'd safely stowed in the glove compartment.

I struggled to shift, steer, and hold the phone to my ear. "Hello."

"Fran Green here."

"How are you doing?" I said cheerfully. "You sound good."

"Hanging in there."

"Has Ruth changed her mind?"

"Who cares?" Fran bellowed. "Loving my time at the Gertrude Center. Don't know what I'd do without the gals. Old Fran should be back in no time."

Despite my relief, her miraculous recovery concerned me. If she could forget Ruth in less than forty-eight hours, what did that say about their commitment? "Don't you miss her at all?" I said, stricken.

"This morning, did see a woman smoking in her car at K-Mart. Takin' frantic puffs, all the windows rolled up. Made me think of Ruth."

I hadn't managed to concoct an appropriate response when she added with forced heartiness, "Enough about me. What gives with the cases?"

I started to update her on developments at the Children's Academy and the Crumplers' Christmas extravaganza but had to cut short the call when I pulled into the parking lot of the Cherry Creek Learning Emporium.

Fran didn't seem to mind the brevity. She informed me that a hot game of lesbian trivia was underway in the library at the Gertrude Center. Fran never missed an opportunity to recount the title of Cris Williamson's first hit ("The Changer and the Changed") or the controversy that led to lesbian sex therapist JoAnn Loulan's fall from grace (intercourse with a man).

After we disconnected, I gathered my file folders and notebook and focused on the Learning Emporium.

What a spectacle!

From the outside, the Learning Emporium looked as if it belonged in Disneyland, with its bright purple, red, green, and yellow walls, and round windows and painted murals.

Inside, the sensory overwhelm continued. After I passed through the glass atrium, I came to a standstill in the tiled rotunda.

To the right, a band of monitors rivaled those in any electronics department. Placards below each screen denoted the area of the facility the display featured: math department, music room, arts and crafts studio, computer lab, reading fort, basketball court, quiet room, parents lounge.

To the left, a cobblestone street marked the path to "Wonderland," an area that had been constructed to play on the nostalgic appeal of a small-town Main Street. Inviting storefronts beckoned: a farmer's market, a soda fountain, a barber shop, a community center, a clothing boutique. I half-wanted to spend my days here until I realized the look was almost identical to one I'd seen recently in a locked Alzheimer's unit.

Before I could venture down Main Street, a perky receptionist ushered me into the "Consultation Room," a parlor designed to emulate the feel of a friend's living room. Somehow, though, I sensed a trap. Standing, I thumbed through the *Learning Emporium Gazette*, a monthly tome written and designed by the children,

Two minutes later, Robert Hoppe, CEO, swept into the room.

"Would you like something to drink? Mocha, espresso, herbal tea, fruit smoothie, Perrier?"

I raised one eyebrow and cocked my head. "You have all those?"

"We have a complimentary beverage bar available to parents at their morning and evening visits." He gestured toward the outer room, waiting for my order.

Reluctantly, I said, "Nothing, thanks."

"Very well. Let me know if you change your mind, Mrs. Ashe."

"Ms.," I said staunchly. "Kristin."

He directed me to a seat next to him on the long leather couch. "May I ask, will your husband be joining us?"

"I'm not married."

I plopped down while he hitched up his trousers and sat carefully on the edge.

Robert Hoppe had tried to turn back the clock with a tan in the middle of winter, Botox, and a closely cropped dyed goatee, but his fifty-pound pot belly, liver spots, and vanishing hairline proved that time was relentless.

Robert reached toward a glass stand on the steel coffee table and extracted a full-color, glossy booklet. "I'd like to, if I may, point out the amenities the Learning Emporium has to offer."

Caressing the pages, he opened the promotional piece to the middle section. A pull-out listed at least forty features. Dry cleaning services, hair salon, all-you-can-eat snacks, parents lounge, they all blended together, and these were only the parent perks.

I could see the rest of the afternoon disappearing past the thirty minutes I'd planned for the visit.

"How much does it cost per month?"

"We offer different pricing tiers. Your son Devin is two, correct?"

"Bevin."

Robert cleared his throat. "We have an intern at the front desk. She must have jotted the name down incorrectly on our inquiry form."

"No problem," I said agreeably. "And he's a she who just turned three."

His cheeks reddened, and he made a big production of correcting notes in the folder. "My sincere apologies. We don't generally make mistakes."

"How much will it cost?" I repeated.

"The cost will be far less than the value, I assure you," he said, modulating his deep voice for maximum emphasis. "Why don't we take a walk around the campus before we talk specifics." He stood and pinched at the crease of his tailored pants.

I didn't move. "The price?"

"We like to think of it as an investment, something often hard to evaluate with mere numbers. In fact, most parents prefer—"

I cut him short. "Try."

His smile froze. "May I inquire as to where Bevin's interests lie?"

He must have seen my incredulity because before I could concoct passions for my made-up child, he continued, "We tailor our programs to the goals of the parents and the needs and interests of the child. Is Bevin presently in an early childhood development center?"

I improvised. "My sister watches her while I'm at work."

"In the company of other children?"

"Six others."

An eyebrow rose in judgment. Whoops, I'd overshot it.

"But she has help," I said quickly. "A teen-age girl comes over after school."

He stroked his chin with the tips of his fingers. "Adolescents rarely make the best caregivers. What's the age range of the other children?"

"Infant to twelve years old. Why?"

"At the Learning Emporium, we segregate children into age-appropriate groups and activities."

"You don't ever mix them?"

"At prescribed points in the day, with certain tasks. A controlled amount of mingling can be productive. For example, kindergartners can act as mentors for toddlers."

My blank stare didn't seem to throw him. He plowed forward, "What type of curriculum does Bevin undertake in her current setting?"

I couldn't understand the question enough to fabricate an answer.

He rephrased in simple English. "What does your daughter do all day?"

"Watch videos," I began, but hastened to edit when I saw his dismay, "educational ones, with classical music. Also, they go to the park a lot, to ride the swings and feed the ducks."

If the disgust crossing his face was a conscious part of the sales presentation, he was a pro. I felt like a lousy mother, abusive almost. Poor Bevin.

"They made chocolate chip cookies yesterday."

His silence hurt more than a scream.

"They were pretty tasty. I ate four," I added meekly.

"How long has your sister been entrusted with Bevin's care?"

"About a year."

"Have you noticed significant advances in Bevin's cognitive or motor skills?"

"No," I said truthfully. How could I spot them if I couldn't define them?

"I believe you'll find our services a bit more comprehensive than those your sister has to offer. No offense meant, of course."

"None taken."

"For example, we offer experiences to promote the children's physical, intellectual, social, and emotional growth. We believe happy children are productive children, ones who will excel in their futures. Wouldn't that give you the peace of mind to perform well in your own job?"

"I guess."

He took a step toward the door. "Why don't I show you the paradise we've created."

My butt was permanently attached to the seat as I persisted in my earlier quest. "Cash?"

"Certainly, we accept cash, check, and major credit cards."

"How much of it per week?"

Robert Hoppe emitted a sigh that alluded to his exasperation. "I'd be more comfortable outlining our suite of services after we've had a chance to take a stroll, or better yet, on your next visit. I'd love to meet Bevin and give you both a VIP tour."

I couldn't help but wonder how many parents had been lured into long-term contracts after their children threw fits at the thought of missing out on this daily circus.

Pleasantly, I said, "That's a shame. It's been a pleasure meeting you."

A look of alarm crossed his face, and I enjoyed watching his internal struggle as he debated whether to stick to his proven, artful marketing scheme or to cave in and utter a dollar amount out of sequence. "I typically don't do this, but for you, I'm willing to make an exception. I can see you're a mother who appreciates value and strives for the best for her lovely daughter."

"Nothing but the best," I said tersely. "How much, Robert?"

He leaned closer and said conspiratorially, "From the low one-hundreds."

"Per week?"

I couldn't have caused more harm if I'd kidnapped all the children in the Emporium. "Per day," he said, flashing a pained smile.

"Wow. That's a lot more than I pay now."

"Most people say 'wow' when they tour our facility. We pride ourselves on being the leader in the field. The caliber of what we offer certainly exceeds the benefits derived from an in-home setting."

I had tired of the bantering. "But the benefits are similar to those at the Children's Academy, correct?"

"I see you've done your homework," he said in a casual tone, but his face hardened. "Our facilities differ in significant ways. May I ask, have you visited the Academy?"

"Three times, and Bevin loved it. Everyone was so nice to her, especially the owner, Lori Parks."

"Yes, Dr. Parks has quite a reputation."

"Have you met her?"

"I know her quite well. For a time, we worked together. More recently, we've served on an industry board."

"You worked for her?"

He gave a slight nod. "For five years, before I was offered this position."

"How would you compare the liberal arts education offered at the Academy to the one provided here?"

"I wouldn't know where to begin."

"Do all your instructors have master's degrees?"

"No, but—"

"Bachelor's with certificates in teaching?"

"No, but—"

"Some higher education?"

"Our diversified faculty enjoy a wide scope of—"

I interrupted again. "Could Bevin learn five foreign languages here?"

"Two, but it's my understanding the Academy teaches only Spanish and French, as do we."

"They recently added Chinese, Japanese, and Russian. At no extra cost."

His breath became shallow, and in a clipped tone, he replied, "While language is certainly an important part of a child's development, no one can touch our physical fitness program. We have a rock-climbing wall, a trike raceway, a half-size basketball court. We also have a putt-putt golf course, a regulation putting green, and two tennis courts, complete with ball machine, umpire stand, and bleachers. I'm sure you noticed the ice skating rink as you came in. In the summer, it's a water park."

"Sounds a little dangerous."

"Not at all. Safety first is our motto, and I must say, over the years, we've welcomed students who have left the Children's Academy for various reasons."

I launched a more direct attack. "Wasn't the Children's Academy designated the top educational center in the United States?"

Robert Hoppe stifled a snort. "I'm not privy to inside information concerning other facilities. At the Learning Emporium, we compete only with ourselves. Every day, as individuals and as a team, we strive to live up to our mission statement: To honor every child's individuality and to promote his/her growth and enrichment. Believe me, Ms. Ashe, we are our own motivators."

"Does that mean the Learning Emporium has never been recognized nationally?"

I'd pushed him too far. His cheeks turned bright red, and he struggled to maintain composure. Sweat started to bead on his forehead. "Because you seem well-informed about the reputation of the Academy, I'm sure you've heard the rumors about Dr. Parks."

"Not really."

He proffered a patronizing smile. "About her lifestyle?"

I sat up straight. "No."

"And her questionable judgment?"

"Really?" I said, in a neutral tone. "Dr. Parks seemed like such a lovely person when we met."

"Oh, I wouldn't be so sure about that," he said, with a hint of menace. "Not everyone would feel comfortable turning a child over to her custody, but of course, that's your choice."

Before I could deliver a lecture on homophobia, he placed a final blow that had nothing to do with Lori Parks' sexuality.

"They say she killed a girl, you know."

Chapter 7

I could have killed Robert Hoppe when he refused to impart another scintilla of information.

Suddenly, he "wasn't at liberty to discuss unsubstantiated gossip." Probably, he feared a libel suit after the slip.

I tried everything to get him to cough it up, but he wouldn't budge.

I went on the obligatory tour and drooled over all aspects of his operation. I filled out an application and left a nonrefundable deposit. I praised his commitment to children when I saw the gold-letter mission statement in a gilded frame in the lobby. I lauded his dedication to children after we read the statement together, aloud.

As I departed, I told him I needed time to consider my decision, but Bevin was as good as his.

How low had I stooped, and even that hadn't worked.

In all, I'd stayed two hours past my allotted thirty minutes and felt drained when I left.

I arrived home at seven o'clock and carefully climbed the mansion's back staircase to our third-floor apartment.

With help from her parents, Destiny had bought the stately house on Gaylord Street twelve years earlier, at a low point in Denver's real estate market. Over the years, by trading construction services with various handywomen, she'd managed to convert seven dingy apartments into three stunning units, one on each floor. She'd also transformed the basement into laundry facilities, a workout room, and a wine cellar, which everyone in the house shared.

I loved everything about living on the top floor, especially the surrounding oak trees and the view of downtown skyscrapers, except the climb.

I treaded lightly, cautious on the wet steps. It had started snowing at dusk, a light mist, more drizzle than flakes. Once it froze, streets, sidewalks, and porches would become slippery with thin layers of "black ice."

I could have taken the front stairs, which cut through the interior of the house, but I didn't want to bump into Joelle or Frida who lived on the first floor. Destiny viewed them as excellent tenants because they paid rent on time and cleaned frequently, but I longed for less social housemates.

Stepping on the floorboards of the porch created a sound louder than most alarm systems, which invariably prompted one of the women to run to the door. Joelle never failed to hit me up for tips on how to start a business, and Frida had no shortage of causes, most of which involved pleas for cash. Half the time, I think that's how she scraped together her portion of the rent.

Tonight, I didn't have the energy for deflection. I wanted a quiet hour to myself before Destiny arrived at eight with dinner.

In the cold apartment, I cranked up the heat, closed the blinds, turned on the gas fireplace, and settled in to compile notes. At the end of every day, I summarized my thoughts in a brief report. The routine helped clarify what progress, if any, I'd made.

The Crumpler case: I ruled out Florence Bailey as a suspect and turned to the Pollards. Who would care to dismantle the Crumplers' display, at a slow rate, a few items over the course of years? In a sense, that cleared the Pollards, because according to Florence, they'd only arrived on the block three years ago.

Still, they might be able to provide insight into the current situation. Acknowledging the potential waste of time, I vowed, nevertheless, to pay a visit to the Pollards in the morning.

The Children's Academy case: This one, I contemplated as I sipped a Virgin Mary and gnawed on a celery stick. After two days on the job, I better understood Lori Parks' adamant need for discretion. What seemed like paranoia Monday morning made perfect sense now.

These learning institutions generated fortunes based on the assumption that children left in their care would remain happy and safe. The Children's Academy and Learning Emporium assuaged two strong parental emotions: guilt and fear. Bring those back into the picture, especially fear, and a company soon would declare bankruptcy.

Did Robert Hoppe, CEO, stand to gain professionally from the Academy's decline? Possibly. Parents removing their kids from the Children's Academy would likely make the Learning Emporium their next stop. What other choice did they have? While the two facilities weren't identical, in the eyes of a consumer, they were more similar than Lori Parks had led me to believe.

Personal gain, though, felt like a stronger motivator for Hoppe. I jotted down two reminders to myself: Ask Lori if she and Robert Hoppe had parted amicably; and find out if she knew what he meant by his comment that she'd killed a girl. The answer to that second question would certainly prove illuminating.

I had almost completed my notes when I heard Destiny coming through the front door. She removed her black blazer and red scarf, we hugged and kissed, and she rested her cold cheek against the warmth of mine.

"Mmm," she said, lingering. "I would have been here sooner, but Frida convinced me to write a check for orphan wolves. You look tired."

"I am, a little. What's for dinner?"

Destiny gestured at the brown paper sack she'd set on the entryway table. "Fish tacos from Surf City."

"Yum. How was your day?"

She released her ponytail and ran a hand through her hair, shaking out the water drops. "Productive. I met with representatives from the Stanton Foundation. They might provide funding for a program for lesbian teens. I have to submit a thirty-page proposal by Friday."

"Two days from now?" I said, dismayed. "Does that mean you'll have to work tomorrow night?"

"Unfortunately. Why?"

I made a face. "Gay Bingo with Fran."

Destiny burst out laughing. "Oh, no! You told her you'd go?"

"Yes, but I hoped you'd substitute for me," I said plaintively. "She misses seeing you."

"I can't, honey."

I sighed. "I was prepared to offer you anything you want."

"Such as?"

"Nightly back rubs for a month."

Destiny brightened. "Lovely."

"Plus an evening in Blackhawk." This represented an enormous bribe. Destiny loved to play slots in the gambling mecca west of Denver, but I could barely stand an hour of the smoke and noise.

"You are desperate!"

"You know I hate Bingo, plus Fran's wearing me out. She calls me all the time."

"You two always talk a lot."

"Not every hour."

"It's that bad?"

I rolled my eyes and nodded my head as I let out a deep sigh.

"Why don't you keep her busy? Can't she help with one of your cases?"

"Yeah, but—" I stopped mid-thought to search for the right words. "I don't want to become too attached. She's suffocating me."

"It'll subside. And you know you hate commitment."

"I do?"

"Yes," she said with good-humored exasperation. "Yet, you're the most committed person I know."

"I am?"

"How many jobs have you had in your life?"

"One. Waitressing in high school. Plus, my own businesses, Marketing Consultants and the detective work."

"All right, three total. But how often do you talk about getting rid of Marketing Consultants?"

"Every other month."

"How many cars have you owned?"

"Four."

"But how often do you read the want ads?"

"Every Sunday."

"How many serious relationships?"

"Only you," I assured her.

"And how many times did I have to ask you to live with me?"

"Less than twenty," I said, touchy.

She continued her inquisition. "How often do you visit your grandma?"

"I never miss a week."

"But are you going next week?"

"I have to see what my schedule looks like," I said, before adding quietly, "I get your point."

Destiny smiled broadly. "Kris, you are committed to Fran. More than you'll ever admit. You just don't want to think you have to be, or you rebel. Pretend like Bingo's your choice, and you'll look forward to it."

Destiny was right. While I didn't eagerly await the outing, at least I didn't lie awake worrying about it. In fact, I barely gave the game a thought the next day.

But then, I had a few distractions.

Overnight, the storm had broken up, leaving a messy early morning rush hour, according to radio reports, but no lingering effects by the time I drove to the Pollards' at ten. The skies were a dull gray, not atypical for December, but still disheartening.

I pulled up to the block where the Crumplers, Florence Bailey, and the Pollards lived. Of the three homes, the Pollards' was the smallest, a mini-mansion built in the style and architecture of the Tudor homes Denverites favored in the early 1920s.

The absence of nighttime lights did little to dim the luster of the Pollards' Christmas display.

Granted, the reindeer quartet was quiet, the multi-colored lights were extinguished, and the ice ball with exploding stars was on hold. But that left candyland, the North Pole, and hundreds of figurines.

Not to mention the fifteen-foot Ferris wheel with stuffed animals, two to a seat, and the carousel with Teddy Bears dressed in red and green. I could stretch my imagination to its breaking point and relate most of this to Christmas, but the dolls in full leather, riding miniature Harley Davidsons, defied all logic.

When Alison Pollard promptly answered my ring, in a peculiar way, she matched the look of her yard. I had never seen breasts so large on such a tiny frame, but they weren't what first caught my attention. In the middle of her black V-neck sweater, she wore a diamond the size of a small marble on a fishing-line necklace. The bauble blinded me, and I struggled to overcome the distraction long enough to utter a plausible reason for my presence.

She must have accepted my vague neighborhood mischief explanation, because she invited me in for hot chocolate and offered to help in any way possible.

Fortunately, for that day's outfit, I'd chosen a white turtleneck, because when Alison served Christmas cookies drenched in powdered sugar, most of the confection ended up on my chest. My hostess would have been within her rights to stare, but she was too polite. Far more fastidious than I, she never replicated my blunders. She held each cookie between her thumb and forefinger, never losing a flake of sugar, never letting a drop smudge her perfectly-painted burgundy-red lips. Maybe she'd had more practice.

"Do you have a display of your own?" she asked, after we'd downed a few goodies and exhausted opening remarks. As she spoke, she fiddled with long black hair pulled into a clip and gazed at me languidly through narrow eyes highlighted with thick mascara and eyeshadow.

"Er, no," I said, "I could never assemble anything like this. But I do look forward to the displays every year." I started choking, maybe from the lie, maybe from an ill-timed powdered sugar inhale.

She ignored my distress. "That makes me happy to hear. If you'd like a display of your own, I could provide you with endless advice. I've learned so much over the years, I feel I should write a book."

I took a gulp of hot chocolate. "Really?"

"I have wonderful tips. Start small and work your way up, that's what I tell the wives of Tony's associates who want to pursue this." Alison laughed, a hollow sound. "They all want their homes to look like ours, and of course that's not possible. Most women are too busy with careers. They want mystical lanterns, but do they care to make 500 by hand, with ketchup cups, light bulbs, and wire frames?"

I felt, as much as saw, the sneer, and she seemed to have forgotten I had expressed no interest, because she babbled on. "If you're going to have a display, you should decide in advance what you want. Some people favor the old-fashioned look, but I prefer a more contemporary one."

Las Vegas on steroids.

"Tony likes to make sure the lights are warm before he takes them outside. That way, the strings are easier to work with, and he always plugs them in before he hangs them. Otherwise, you run the risk that a string won't work. Get permanent hooks in place on the gutters and roof areas, that was my husband's idea. In fact, it forced us to have to leave our old neighborhood."

"Too ostentatious a display?" I said blandly.

"The homeowner's association threatened to sue us because we left our light clips mounted year-round. They claimed the clips detracted from the beauty of the neighborhood."

"They were that picky?"

"You have no idea. Tony offered to paint the plastic clips the same color as the house, but the head of the association said the shadows would mar the appearance of our home. My husband almost killed himself falling off the roof one year. That's when he came up with the idea of permanent hooks. Would they rather have had a death on their consciences?"

"Yes, they would have," she answered before I could.

"Did you lose the lawsuit?"

"It never went that far. The next season, someone put our reindeer in compromising positions, and that was the final straw."

"Not Rudolph?"

"Yes."

"Not with his red nose in . . ." I couldn't complete the treacherous thought.

"Yes. But at least he was on top," she said, seriously. "After that, we sold our house, and I'm glad we did. The people on this block are more supportive."

"Have you or Tony noticed any vandalism, anything missing?"

"Nothing."

"Does Tony ever go into the Crumplers' yard?"

Alison glanced at me sharply, her open, friendly expression giving way to suspicion. "Why do you ask? Is this about the sisters' display?"

I invented a little fiction. "Not necessarily, but Florence Bailey saw your husband rooting around their yard the other day."

"Oh that," she said absently. "Tony goes over once in awhile."

I couldn't believe I'd hit the bullseye. I waited for her to elaborate.

"He'd be angry if I told you . . ." she paused.

"But . . ." I prodded.

"He replaces missing bulbs. When he sees them go out, he sneaks over and replaces them."

"That's nice of him," I said, unsure whether to believe her.

"He doesn't do it to be nice," she retorted, as if the thought were moronic. "He can't stand to see anything out of place."

For a moment, deep lines in her forehead revealed the pain that must have come from living under her husband's control. However, as quickly as her guard dropped, it rose, and she added, "But I suppose he is charitable, which is more than I can say for their helper Leonard."

"What's wrong with Leonard?"

"I'm sure he charges those women for more hours than he puts in. Every time I look out the window, he's resting. I never see him working, except when he hires those dirty men to help. Then his job seems to consist of yelling at them, and that's not the worst of it."

I leaned forward eagerly.

Alison Pollard continued, "He's stealing from those poor women."

I sat back, folding myself into the couch, suddenly bored with this woman's arrogance and judgment. "In addition to the fraud of billing for hours when he's resting, not working?"

Her next words startled me out of my ennui.

"I've seen him take cut-outs and figurines. I'm sure he sells them at the flea markets. Last week, he put Mrs. Claus in the back of his truck— in broad daylight."

Chapter 8

Finally, a break in the Crumpler case!

Alison Pollard was more than happy to divulge specifics, demonstrating both heightened recall skills and a gift for spying. In no time, I had dates, times, and modes of transportation. I even learned when to approach Leonard. He came to work at the Crumplers' home every Saturday morning.

I left the Pollard house with a spring in my step. Too bad my elation didn't carry through the rest of the day.

"How was Bingo?" Destiny asked ten hours later, reaching up from her chair in front of the television.

I marched past outstretched arms and collapsed on the couch. "I'm not speaking to you, Destiny Greaves."

"You didn't win?" she said innocently.

"Who cares about winning. You have no idea what I had to endure."

"What did you expect?" she said, putting the volume on mute and yawning loudly. "You hate Gay Bingo."

"Well I didn't know Ruth would be there, on a walker, did I?"

"You're kidding!" she exclaimed mid-yawn.

"With another woman on oxygen."

Destiny couldn't seem to close her jaw. "No!"

"Yes!"

"What happened?" she asked softly.

"Ruth said she mixed up their nights, but she lied. She came to show off Janet." I stood and paced, gesturing wildly every time I passed Destiny's chair.

"Who's Janet?"

"I have no idea. Fran didn't recognize her. The one person in Denver she doesn't know," I said bitterly.

"That must have been awkward for you, watching Fran suffer," Destiny said, attempting a compassionate tone, but I could tell she was trying to abort a laugh.

"Suffer! Fran? Hardly! All her coping mechanisms were intact. She kicked into full gear putting the moves on me."

"On you?" Destiny's expression became a mixture of offense and flattery, that someone would use her girlfriend for revenge.

"It was mortifying," I moaned, lowering myself to the footstool in front of Destiny, grasping my head, as if that could erase the memory. "When Fran won a game, she made a show of hugging and kissing me. Then she tried to leave her arm around the back of my chair, as if she owned me. Finally, when she started squeezing my thigh, I told her to back off, that she wasn't respecting my relationship with you."

"Good for you, Kris," Destiny said, patting my knee. "Did she get it?"

"That slowed her down for about five minutes. She's lost it, Destiny. She's hanging out all over. Someone has to stop her."

"You should talk to her, tell her how you feel."

"Me?" My voice cracked. "What am I supposed to say?"

"Anything, Kris. Just be a friend to her. She's been a helper all her life, so she might not be good at accepting help, but you need to try."

"I do?" I said wearily.

"Yes," she said firmly, patting me on both shoulders. "You can do it!"

"Damn," I groaned.

•••

That night in bed, Destiny held me tight. As my body began to relax from the long evening of Fran Green's pawing and groping, she said, "Kris, if we split up—"

"God forbid!" I exclaimed, sitting upright.

"God forbid, but if we split up, let's not be spiteful. Let's not tear away at each other to convince ourselves we made the right decision."

"Done," I said, lying down.

"I mean it, Kris. Promise!"

"I promise," I said, but my tone sounded as empty as the pact. How could either of us know what the end would bring?

I suddenly felt fall-down tired. "Swear you'll never mention the embarrassment of this night again."

Destiny giggled and squeezed me. "Never."

Unfortunately, I knew I'd soon be reliving it all with Fran.

I shouldn't have fretted about how I would tackle the contentious subject, because the next day, when Fran stopped by my office at nine o'clock, she dove in, without compunction.

"You tell Destiny about our fiasco?" Fran said, eyes blazing.

"I did, and I wanted—" I began tentatively.

"That roaming Ruth. What a charlatan. Has no problem tracking eighteen Bingo cards but mixes up our weeks. Ha! And the walker, give me a break! Pulls out that rusty contraption every time she needs attention or close-in parking at a store sale. Said her hip acted up, please. Pulled that hip out of her ass."

"Fran!" I protested, as her rant gained steam and volume.

"What's with that Janet-jerk on oxygen. Didn't slow down Ruth's smoking one butt, I might add. Finds someone as decrepit as she can, then pushes her to an early grave. Should be ashamed of herself."

"Fran! Fran! Fran!" I shouted.

Finally, she looked at me, almost surprised by my presence. "Fran," I began more gently, "There's enough shame to go around."

"What're you driving at?"

I swallowed hard. "You were a little lively yourself last night."

"The flirting? Nothing meant by that, Kris. Hope you didn't take offense. Destiny neither. Love you both like—"

I couldn't resist interrupting with a little payback, "Granddaughters."

"Love you like sisters."

"Fran, you've got class—"

She cut me off. "You got a lecture prepared? 'Cause I'm in no mood."

"What about the thirty-three good years you had with Ruth? You don't want to trash those because of Helen Reddy records or Bingo weeks or some rival on oxygen."

"The hell I don't!"

"You don't, Fran. It's not you. It might be Ruth, but it's not you."

Fran turned red and wouldn't meet my gaze. "Don't know what came over me. Saw daggers when I spotted her with that other lady. Couldn't believe she could drive on like that after parking in one place for so long."

"If we were lovers, it'd take me years to get over you," I said earnestly.

Fran blinked back tears and said in a strained voice, "Appreciate you saying that."

"No, really. You're attractive and intelligent and kind. You have more enthusiasm and energy than people half your age, and you have a huge heart. I've never met anyone who cares as much as you do."

"Can be irritating sometimes."

"You have your quirks, who doesn't? Women would love to go on a date with you."

"Don't have to go on and on," she said, blushing.

"I mean it. And you shouldn't let Ruth ruin your life."

"What life? At sixty-six, been cast out on the street! What's left?"

"You have your health, and me and Destiny, and snowboarding. Don't forget, you want to hit that 360. Plus, you have these cases. I couldn't do this work without you. And if it makes you feel any better, Ruth's probably hiding her anguish."

"Could be," Fran said thoughtfully. "In any case, got to be more dignified."

"That's the spirit," I said encouragingly.

"Have to let go with honor."

"Exactly."

"Feel better already. Ask a favor of you?"

"Anything," I said, pleased my talk had made such an impression.

"Any chance of you following Ruth and that dame and letting me know what they're up to?"

That took the air out of my buoyancy.

Instead of following Ruth, I followed Destiny's advice and sent Fran off on an assignment in the Children's Academy case.

Tuesday evening, Lori Parks had left a message on my voice mail. Maybe someone did feel resentment toward her, she'd acknowledged, giving me the name of Sylvia Sewall and an outline of the circumstances that had led to her son Jason's dismissal from the Academy. After consulting my notes, I passed on the information to Fran, who headed to the back room to concoct a strategy.

I settled in to read the movie section of the Friday paper.

I had barely rustled the sheets when the phone rang, a return call from Lori Parks. She apologized for having been out of reach the day before, attributing her absence to an all-day retreat at Spring Forward, an expensive downtown spa.

"No problem," I said. "I just wanted to touch base. I got your message about the disgruntled mother and am following up on it. Did you get mine about the note I found in the mitten?"

"Yes. Someone's quite clever in these pranks."

"You're not worried?"

"Not particularly. Do you have anything else?"

"I toured the Cherry Creek Learning Emporium Wednesday afternoon."

"Where happy children become productive children," she said in a more relaxed voice.

"You've been reading their brochures," I said, recognizing her mockery of the company's slogan.

"I used to secretly send in friends to gather information, in order to keep up with the competition. Now, they post all their marketing materials on a website, which makes my job easier. I assume you met Robert Hoppe."

"I did. I spent several hours with him."

"He's an interesting man, isn't he?" she said, in a catty tone.

"Interesting good or bad?"

"Both. He's an excellent business manager, but his philosophy of child development seems to be based primarily on distraction."

"Wow!" I said, in my best imitation of Hoppe's signature exclamation.

Lori laughed easily. "I can see he subjected you to the usual overdose of his favorite word."

"He did, but I could get used to that snack bar."

"That's typical. He gears everything toward the perception of adults, which isn't entirely off-base. Image is everything in this business."

"When he left to open the Cherry Creek branch, did you part on good terms?"

"I thought we did, until I discovered he had taken our client list and was soliciting parents. I put a stop to that with one call to my lawyer."

"And you get along now?"

"We're civil. I see him once a month at a children's foundation we both chair."

"I'm wondering, have you had any serious injuries at the Children's Academy?"

"Did he accuse us of that?" she remarked airily.

"Not exactly," I said cautiously.

"Bumps, bruises, stitches—typical active child injuries. Certainly, nothing life-threatening. I've done everything in my power to prevent it. We have a rigorous safety program, emphasizing preparedness. Several times a year, we put the staff through CPR training, Red Cross certification, and fire drill enactments."

"And you haven't been responsible for anyone's death, at the Academy or outside it?"

"What an absurd question. Where did you come up with that?"

"Actually, Richard Hoppe implied it."

"I can't say that surprises me," she said offhandedly. "Perhaps he needs another call from my attorney."

"He might. He made a curious comment about you."

"Me personally? What was it?"

"He said he'd heard that you killed a girl."

Complete silence. For such a length of time, I finally said, "Lori, are you there?"

When she spoke, she sounded as if she were having trouble breathing. "How ludicrous! What basis does Robert Hoppe have for making that kind of remark?"

"I don't know. He wouldn't say anything else."

"He's mistaken."

"You have no idea what he's talking about?"

"People in this industry can be vicious."

"If you decide to call your lawyer, I'd be happy to recount what Robert Hoppe said."

"No, no," she said, sounding jittery. "It doesn't have to come to that. We'll pretend like it never happened."

Super, I thought, hours after Lori and I had concluded our phone call.

We'll act like it never happened, but what was "it," and how did it relate to the incidents at the Children's Academy?

They had to be connected, or I wouldn't have heard such distress in Lori Parks' voice.

Chapter 9

"Gotta tell you, Kris, we have a genuine loony on our hands." Fran said later that afternoon, apparently recovered from the Bingo episode. Color had returned to her cheeks, her hair looked more tame, and her hands were in motion again.

"Sylvia Sewall?" I confirmed, referring to the mother whose son, Jason, had been dismissed from the Children's Academy.

"One and the same. She's so far over the top, coming down the other side. Way she acted, you would've thought Parks gave her the boot, not the kid. Speaking of—you catch that story last spring about the moose in Estes Park, the one that rammed a tourist as he took a picture?"

"No."

"Tickled my funny bone. The moose chased the man and stomped him. What's the shutterbug expect in calving season? Mother protecting newborns. Pretty straightforward. Gave me a good belly laugh. Ruth didn't see the humor."

"I don't either. Could we get back to Sylvia Sewall?"

"Sure thing. Not one to force a chuckle." Fran pulled out a small spiral notebook, donned a pair of reading glasses and began a recital. "Left a message this morning at 9:13 a.m. Suspect returned call at 10:01 a.m. Agreed to be interviewed for upcoming issue of *Parent* magazine. Article on child prodigies. Met for ninety-one minutes this afternoon, commencing at 2:00 sharp. Consumed 2.75 cups of coffee and eleven hard candies, mostly lemon."

I looked at her sharply. "You ate that many?"

"Small ones. Sugarless. Carried out the wrappers."

I sighed.

"To continue, present for duration: Fran Green, detective; Sylvia Sewall, suspect; Barky Black, suspect's dog. Apparent flatulence disorder. Compensated by breathing through mouth most of the time. Me, not the pooch."

"Understood," I said, trying unsuccessfully to hide a smile.

"Interrupted briefly twice. Once by son, Jason, age eleven. Other time, daughter, Jasmine, age nine."

"You met Jason?"

"Just said I did."

"What's he like?"

"Quiet kid. Overweight. Big eyes. Solemn look. Arms too long for his body. Greasy hair. First stage acne. Doesn't look like the world leader his mother envisions someday."

"And the daughter?"

"Animated. Big ears, crooked nose. Skinny as a rail. Feet too small for her body. Came in playing a violin. Mother took no notice 'til I commented on the ruckus. Couldn't put two notes together without a squeal. Girl deserves a refund on those Academy music lessons."

"Too late for that," I commented mildly. "Jasmine doesn't attend the Academy anymore. Sylvia pulled her when Jason left."

"Figures. The mom's barely aware of the daughter. Can't see her investing much in her future."

"Did Sylvia mention why Jason was kicked out of the Academy?"

"Getting ahead of my notes," Fran scolded.

I rolled my eyes but held my tongue.

Fran smiled broadly at my surrender. "Made a meticulous record here. Appreciate your patience. Mother noticed Jason's gifts at an early age. Read newspaper headlines by four. Adult-level books by six. College art courses by eight. Mother loved the Academy. Impressed with curriculum and teachers. All smooth sailing until about a month ago."

"When they kicked out Jason for cheating?"

"Didn't put it quite like that. Coy phrase, something like, 'More parental participation than required.' Played it off as a misunderstanding, no hard feelings. But beneath that calm exterior, she's smoldering."

"Whose version do you believe—hers or Lori's?"

"Gotta side with Parks. No question Mumsie did a majority of the kid's schoolwork. Discussed a variety of projects they allegedly did together. Built a roller coaster out of Q-Tips, scale replica of a vintage ride at Lakeside Amusement Park. Botanical project, collected fifty kinds of leaves from around the neighborhood, dried 'em, glued 'em, catalogued 'em. Sewed a backpack from scratch, from an original pattern. Call me jaded, but can't see the boy twisting his interests in these directions."

"I agree."

"Kid acts more like a hacker. Built his own computer out of discarded parts. Set up a motion detector to keep his sister out of his room. Those plums, I believed. Went too far with the others."

"Why? Obviously, she has a talented son. Why not accept that? Why did she have to make him something different?"

"Good point. Especially when the plan backfired. Parks held a conference in early October. Accused the mother of cheating, but Sewall denied everything. Kid wouldn't say a word. Parks gave a warning only. Mid-November, without notice, she threw the kid out."

"Lori claims she sent two warning letters and called three times."

"No argument from me. Sylvia Sewall has the rare gift of selective amnesia. Odds on, she could tell you how many Rice Krispies kernels were in her son's bowl this morning, but hard-pressed to describe the color of her daughter's hair."

"She's that bad?"

"Worst I've seen. Gotta remember, yours truly spent twelve years teaching in Catholic schools. Which reminds me, is that Academy as fancy as Suspect Sewall claims?"

"Oh yeah, and it's austere compared to the Learning Emporium."

Fran shook her head in disgust. "What's the world of education coming to? Give me a blackboard, straight chairs, books, sack lunches. Could prep those kids as well as these modern day country clubs. Oh, and a ruler. Can't forget the ruler."

I raised an eyebrow. "The ruler would be for . . ."

"Sure never measured anything. Love taps, we used to call 'em. The good old days," Fran recalled fondly.

"You'd be closed down if you tried that today," I said sternly.

"Could be," Fran admitted easily. "But never turned out a serial killer. My students may not have pretty knuckles or nails, but they're upstanding citizens."

She caught my anxious look and chortled. "Kidding, Kris. Anyway, back to Mother Sewall. Seen the type. Give her time, the behavior escalates. Prepping kid for SATs. Forcing him to join debate club and run for class treasurer. Filling out essays for college applications. Classic example of mother morph."

I cocked my head to one side. "Okay, I'll bite: What's mother morph?"

"Invented the term myself. Mother lives her life through the child's. Won't find it in any psych journal . . . yet."

I scoffed at her sexism. "What about father morph?"

"Happens, but rare. Pops get self-esteem from other sources. Moms, though, watch out! Especially stay-at-home breeders. They make sacrifices, they expect compensation."

"And you, a childless woman, are an expert on this subject?" I said, grinning.

Fran returned my smile. "Darn near. And remember: Barren by choice, not lack of eggs."

"Okay, Freud, do you think Sylvia Sewall is behind these incidents at the Academy?"

Fran furrowed her brow. "Could be. Fits her style. Sneaky, subtle, clever."

"Hmm."

"Me, I'd take an entirely different approach. Firebomb Ruth's car. Direct, effective, spectacular."

I glanced at her in alarm.

"Don't worry. Love that car too much," Fran said, without a hint of humor.

She paused in her contemplation to pull an antique gold cigarette case from her jacket pocket. From it, she extracted a plastic toothpick and went to work on her molars. "Beg pardon. Ribs for lunch. Delicious first time around."

I tried to move my attention away from Fran's dental hygiene. "Let me get this straight. You would consider Sylvia Sewall a prime suspect?"

"Only 'cause we ain't got no others. One glitch with putting Sewall in the frame, though."

"Which is?"

"Can't believe she'd harm the Academy. Still loves the joint." Fran stopped excavating long enough to reference her notes again. "Stays in touch with some of the teachers. Recalls the time there fondly."

"What about Lori—would Sylvia go after her?"

"Now her, she despises."

"And would Sylvia be capable of revenge?"

"No doubt," Fran said, pausing in her retrieval only long enough to scratch her nose with the toothpick. "Think about that moose, my friend."

The next morning, at the house tour to benefit the Children's Academy, Lori's wish came true. No snow, temperature in the low fifties, and full sun. No excuses for a poor turnout of volunteers or visitors.

The Baker-Brown house was a jewel, well worth the ten-dollar price of admission. Built with gold rush money in the late 1800s, the home had been restored it to its period glory, with modern touches added.

A gay couple shared more than 10,000 square feet (not including the pool house or carriage house), yet their presence was nowhere to be seen in the building. I couldn't picture them coming home at the end of a work day and depositing themselves in the living room large enough for field hockey, the library the size of a small convention hall, or the kitchen fit for a catering operation. Maybe they lived in the basement or the third floor, both of which were off limits to the tour.

At eleven o'clock, I breezed through the house before a snippy middle-aged man, on loan from the Historical Society, put me in charge of the master bedroom and bathroom on the second floor.

He handed me a cheat sheet, told me to memorize it, and instructed me not to let anyone touch or take anything.

Easy enough, I thought, until I arrived at my quarters.

I could barely read the crib notes, much less stencil them on my brain.

"Designed to bring the neoclassical elements of the exterior architecture inside."

"A soft Wedgewood blue, with a warm, creamy ivory as a secondary hue, and a sumptuous mocha for subtle accents."

"A simple Matelasse coverlet and single pair of tailored bolsters elegantly dress the bed."

Talking about this stuff would have been hard enough, but keeping people from touching the cartload of items in the room, ranging from "stitched heirloom pillows displaying the family crest" to "monogrammed and engraved objects" seemed impossible.

I decided I would relax in a big, fat chair near the window, read salient facts to interested parties, and hope for time to pass quickly.

My plan worked to perfection, except for the part about time. Nearly two hours and a hundred people passed, but it seemed like a day and no one.

At one point, I caught myself daydreaming, imagining I had joined Fran and Lori's lover Donna, who at that very moment, according to their plans, were snowboarding at Loveland. Or I could have been tailing Leonard, the Crumplers' handyman. I had met him earlier that morning and managed to extract nothing useful.

Fortunately, during a lull in traffic, a young girl skipped in from the hall.

Dressed in a red and black plaid skirt and green turtleneck and sweater, she stopped in the middle of the floor to gaze at me.

"What's special about this room?" she said, pushing strands of long, wavy auburn hair from her face.

I started to read from the page, then wadded it up. "I have no idea, but there's a TV in the bathroom. Want to see it?"

"There is?"

"Come here." I led her into the master bathroom, otherwise known as the "spa-like haven," and showed her around.

"May I sit in the tub so I can see the TV better?"

I turned around and peeked out the door. "Just for a second."

I stood guard while she hopped in the cavernous claw-foot tub, lounged back, and stared at the TV. She didn't care about the "French Deco sconce," or the "grapevine motif tile." She wanted to know the location of the remote in order to change from CNN.

"I haven't found it yet. I think they hid it."

"Oh well," she said bouncing out of the tub. "I'm not supposed to watch TV during the day anyway."

"Your mom's pretty strict about that?"

"Yes," she said aggrieved.

"Mine was, too," I said. "One time, she went on vacation with my little brother and sister, and I watched TV the whole time my dad was at work. And ate snacks, which I wasn't supposed to do either."

"How old were you?"

"About fourteen."

"I'm eight."

"Guess how old I am now."

"Twenty-five?"

"Thanks," I said, beaming. "I'm thirty-six."

"That's old!" she exclaimed as we traipsed back to the bedroom.

"Yeah, but I get to watch TV whenever I want." I sat on the edge of the bed, and she sank into the chair. "My name's Kris. What's yours?"

"Erica."

"Parks?"

She looked at me, impressed. "How did you know?"

"I'm friends with your mom," I said, chastising myself for not having picked up on the family resemblance. She shared her mom's hair color, high cheekbones, and long neck. But her eyes sparkled with a vibrancy Lori's had lost, and she had the most engaging smile, one that demanded reciprocity.

"Mom or Mommy Donna?"

"Mom."

"How come I've never met you?"

"We've only been friends for a little while. I'm helping her with some things at the Academy."

"I've never seen you there."

"I do most of my work outside the school."

I prayed she wouldn't ask for more details. Fortunately, the oil painting above the bed distracted her.

"I can do that. Could I draw a picture so I can remember you?"

"Sure," I said, flattered.

Erica ran to retrieve her backpack. When she returned, she pulled out a pad of paper and a set of colored pencils.

"You come prepared."

"I like to draw."

"Do you erase much?"

"Not too much."

"Just in case, maybe we should sit in the window seat. That way if you have to erase, we can throw the shavings outside."

Her eyes grew big. "Are we allowed to do that?"

"I don't see why not, as long as we don't hit anybody." I glanced out the window. "There are just bushes down there. We should be okay."

The next hour passed like a minute, and very little erasing occurred.

I tried to hold still, even as I directed visitors to the cheat sheet, which I'd smoothed out and left on the bed. Many people commented on the likeness of my portrait-in-progress as they wandered through the room, but Erica refused to let me peek.

Midway through, she stared at me for a full minute, and said tentatively, "You know, you have a big line in your forehead. I should put it in, but I could leave it out if you want me to."

"You can put it in, but thanks for asking. I've had it since I was a baby. I frown a lot."

"How come?"

I scowled as hard as I could and lowered my voice in mock-secrecy. "I don't know."

Erica giggled and continued her work. When she had completed the last stroke, she started to hand me the masterpiece but pulled back. "Don't be mad."

This time, I frowned genuinely. "Why would I be?"

"You're pretty, but I'm not very good at drawing yet," she said in a tiny voice. "I've asked Mom if I could draw her, and she always says she doesn't have time. But I know it's because she thinks I won't make her pretty enough."

"Let me see, and I'll let you know if you have talent. I'm a good judge of art."

Reluctantly, she handed me the picture, face down. When I turned it over, I let out a sharp breath.

The portrait was stunning.

Erica Parks had better drawing skills than most professional illustrators, and she had instilled uncanny details in the image, down to the last freckle. She had captured the shape of my frameless glasses and blue eyes, the curve of my smile, the tip of my nose. My short brown hair looked a little flat—no sign of the mousse, gel, and blow drying I'd applied that morning—but the effort was magnificent.

I complimented Erica repeatedly, but the praise brushed past her.

"Do you think you're pretty?" she asked, eyes cast downward.

"You know what," I said after a moment's consideration, "I never really thought of myself as pretty, yet somehow, you made me look pretty."

Finally, the approval penetrated, and Erica's features stretched in happiness. She hugged me, a fleeting clutch of my shoulders.

"Have you taken drawing classes at the Academy?"

"Not yet. Mom wants me to study music. I play the piano. Want to hear something?"

"Sure," I said, and she sprinted down the hall to the drawing room.

I settled back and studied my own reflection. The reproduction really did look like me, or at least a caricature of me. She had made my mouth about half its actual size, and my nostrils were bigger than dimes, but there was something there. The young artist had captured a radiance, one I sometimes felt but rarely saw in mirrors or photographs. I'd always considered myself average—in looks, height, weight, build, even shoe size. But this portrait seemed to give me distinction.

I couldn't believe Erica had never taken a lesson.

Based on the aesthetic talent revealed so far, her piano playing shouldn't have surprised me, but it did. I had imagined her going to the keys and pounding out a facsimile of "Jingle Bells." Instead, I heard a beautiful, moving piece.

She returned to the room, out of breath. "Mom made me stop playing. She says people don't want to hear music on a house tour."

"Well, I liked it."

"I wish I could have played more," she said, pouting.

"It was beautiful, even if you did cut it short. What was it?"

She brightened. "I made it up, but I copied a lot from *Moonlight Sonata*. Beethoven is my favorite composer."

Right then, the alarm on her pink wristwatch tinkled.

"I have to go," she said loudly as she stuffed supplies in her backpack. "Miss Sally said she'd pick me up at two o'clock, and I can't be late."

Erica started to dart out, but stopped at the threshold. "Will I see you again?"

"I'm sure you will."

Hurriedly, she took off her backpack, unzipped it, and pulled out a sheet of paper. "Then I won't need this to remember you. You can have it."

She handed me the drawing of myself and rushed off, leaving me with a disquieting feeling.

I hadn't lied when I said we'd see each other again, had I?

Chapter 10

I'd begun to believe all the volunteers had forgotten about me when one finally came to spell me for lunch. A local restaurant had donated sandwiches and drinks, which were spread out in the servant's galley off the kitchen.

By the time I arrived, the buffet had been ransacked. I could barely assemble a turkey and cheese sandwich, forget about the lettuce, tomato, and sprouts earlier diners had enjoyed. I filled a plastic cup with lemonade, grabbed dessert, and ducked out the nearest door.

In the garden area, one other volunteer rested, a woman in her early twenties with brown hair streaked with blonde and a slight gap in her ever-present smile. A smoker, she used a Pepsi can as an ashtray.

"Can I join you?" I asked, balancing my plate, drink, and napkin-wrapped brownie.

She gestured toward a deck chair. "Be my guest."

I reached across the table to shake hands. "I'm Kris."

"Sarah."

"I had to get out of the house," I blurted. "All that history started to weigh on me."

"How did they rope you in?"

"I know Lori Parks."

"Which room?"

"The master bedroom and bath. You?"

"Library, right off the front door."

I took a small bite of the sandwich and washed it down with sour lemonade. "I had no idea being a guide was this dull."

She waved a hand. "You're too far away from the action."

"What do you mean?"

"After lunch, switch with someone and come to the main floor. There are plenty of fireworks going on."

"Like what?"

"We had a visit from Stacey Tobias, the music teacher Parks fired a month ago. That was interesting."

"What happened?"

"Oh, she moped around, trying to conjure up sympathy, but no one paid attention. I mean, the girl couldn't read music or play an instrument. Her resume was complete fiction. When she got caught, she thought they'd transfer her to her specialty, sculpture, but that didn't happen. At least she was fired for cause, which is more than I can say about Rebecca."

"A friend of yours?" I guessed from the emotion in her voice.

Sarah nodded. "Our reading specialist. One week, she was there, participating at a staff meeting. The next week, gone. Parks never gave a reason, and none of the staff had the guts to confront her about it. I talk to Rebecca every day, and she swears she did nothing wrong."

I deliberately kept my tone mild. "Is she angry about it?"

"More confused than anything. But talk about an anger waiting to happen, you could cut the tension when Robert Hoppe came by and Parks asked him to leave."

"The head of the Cherry Creek Learning Emporium? Did he make a scene?"

"He's too professional for that. But he did ask for a refund, because he'd only seen four rooms of the house before he bumped into Parks. You should have seen it when she threw a ten-dollar bill at him."

"Sounds pretty exciting," I said. "I'll have to move down."

"Hurry and you might see Mike Stanley, the ex-husband of our business manager. She has a restraining order out on him, so he can't come within a hundred yards of the school grounds, but if he's clever, he'll pay us a visit."

"You don't sound worried. Is he dangerous?"

"I've never met him, but from what the other teachers say, he's a harmless romantic. He'll come with flowers, not guns."

"I should hope so," I said nervously. "The master bedroom's looking better and better."

"You look like you could use a little adventure," she said, lighting another cigarette with the butt of her used one. "You're a lesbian friend of Parks, right?"

I frowned slightly. "Is it that obvious?"

She took a quick puff from her cigarette. "More a vibe. I spotted myself when I was nine, and I've been eyeing other women since."

"I didn't know until I was fourteen, and it took a few years to fine-tune my radar," I said, a tad uncomfortable.

She lowered her voice. "You should give lessons to our dyke-in-hiding director."

I smiled involuntarily. "You know?"

Sarah let loose an insane cackle. "The minute I met her, and if I hadn't felt it myself, I would have figured it out. She thinks no one knows, but most of the staff do. Some of the parents, too. Anyone who's met Erica hears about Donna in the first five minutes. And most women over thirty don't live together for financial reasons. It's pathetic. One time Parks actually started a rumor about herself, that she was dating the copier repairman."

"Does Lori know you're a lesbian?"

"Maybe now, but she didn't in the beginning. I'm sure if she had, she never would have hired me. I toned it down for the interview. You know, no dreadlocks, took out seven of my earrings, put on a little lipstick, borrowed a purse. She didn't have a clue."

"Was it worth the deceit?"

"Who can say, but the money's great. The job pays twice the starting salary of a Denver Public Schools teacher, and I have some expensive interests."

I looked doubtful. What could warrant soul-savaging? "Such as?"

"Jewelry-making, for one," she said fervently.

I pointedly looked at the four southwestern-style necklaces dangling at various angles on her chest and smiled. "I should have guessed."

She put her cigarette between her lips and extended her arms to their full reach. "Hang gliding."

"That one, I wouldn't have known."

She cupped her hands together, as if cradling an imaginary bird. "Rescuing animals." She listed a dozen other pastimes, the least expensive of which was scrapbooking.

"Do you like working at the Academy?"

Sarah nodded. "The days are always interesting, and you should hear my friends who teach at public schools complain about out-of-control kids. Here, if they violate conduct and behavior rules, they're gone. One chance, sometimes two, then we never see them again. Parks is good about that—she'll back up the teachers and take the wrath of parents."

"Do a lot of kids get kicked out?"

"I only know of one, Jason, a fifth-grader with pathological mood swings. We really questioned his mental health when he drew something for our Christmas card contest. Every year in September, we choose the best drawings for different age groups and have them printed on cards, which we sell as fundraisers."

"What did Jason's look like?"

"He'd drawn a gory picture of Christ on the cross, blood dripping from his body, a tortured look on his face."

I gasped. "Not exactly a light holiday greeting."

"That wasn't the worst of it. The kid had added sparkling ornaments hanging from Jesus' arms and dozens of gifts surrounding his feet. Needless to say, we didn't choose his drawing."

"Did that upset Jason?"

"Not noticeably, but in November, Parks expelled him, supposedly because his mom had completed most of his homework. I'm betting you'll see that kid on the news someday. He'll have hurt himself or someone else."

"When Lori expelled him, were his parents upset?" I asked, curious to hear if Sarah's version of Sylvia Sewall's reactions matched Fran Green's.

"His mother was, because she thinks he's an angel. But she's trying to kiss up to Parks and the director of admissions. I saw her downstairs earlier, talking to them about having her daughter rejoin us after the holidays."

"Would they allow that?"

"Why not? The whole family can't be crazy, right?"

The rest of the afternoon passed uneventfully. I returned to the master bedroom and didn't hear any screams or sirens, so I assumed everything went smoothly downstairs as well.

Shortly after five o'clock, the last group of visitors left. I tried to get a moment alone with Lori, but she had a crowd around her. I told her I'd call Monday, and she thanked me for coming.

As scheduled, I spent Sunday in bed with Destiny. Well, not all day. By late morning, after we'd exhausted our libidos and most positions, we moved to the living room to watch football.

Snuggling in front of the fire, with a light snow falling, a big bowl of popcorn, and a close game, felt almost as good as sex.

Or so I believed until we made love once more later that night. That time, I felt explosions, and before dropping into a deep slumber, I made Destiny admit setting aside time for sex was a splendid idea.

We agreed on a return engagement the following Sunday.

Monday, I began the day by placing a call to Lori Parks to follow up on the house tour. While waiting for a return call, I worked on Marketing Consultants tasks, unable to proceed with the Children's Academy case and uncertain how to move forward with the Crumpler case.

Mid-afternoon, Fran Green broke my concentration with a loud entrance. Wearing goggles and a knit cap with ear flaps, she looked comical.

Snow had been falling lightly all day and showed no signs of letting up, but the amount of moisture in no way warranted this extreme.

I started to rib her about the protective eyewear when she dropped a suitcase on the hardwood floor. A brown hardback version without wheels or collapsible handles, it had dozens of stickers attached, all touting snowboarding gear.

Fran ripped off her coat, slung it on the rack, and turned to me. Her shirt's sentiment, "Life's A Bitch Until You Divorce One," was mild compared to her glower.

Before I could say a word, she thundered, "Kicked out of the Gertrude Center this morning. New director, Mary, used the bylaws against me. Tarnation! I wrote every word of those charters myself."

My face fell. "What rule did you break?"

"Can't stay more than seven consecutive days. Put that in to prevent members from using it as a homeless shelter. Never enforced it before. Temporary home for plenty of ladies over the years, including scary Mary, who stayed a month last summer. We used to call it the Breakup Motel. Never thought I'd live to see the day, tossed from my own bed by my honey, thrown out on the street by my community. What's next?"

"Any chance of reconciling with Ruth?" I said timidly.

"Rather drink my own urine. Ten-to-one odds, that old coot's behind this. Mary apologized enough times to embarrass us both. Cheeky broad shed a tear for effect but wouldn't budge from her stance. Claimed she'd had a complaint from the membership. Now we both know that's a smokescreen for Ruth."

"I'm sorry. I know you've put a lot into the Gertrude Center." I led Fran into my office, and we sat down.

"May as well be called the Fran Center for all my sweat the building holds," she snapped. "Any idea what I've done to that place?"

Without waiting for a response, she began a rapid-fire list, punching her fist into the couch with each item. "Laid every vinyl tile in the kitchen. Fixed the downstairs toilet more times than I used it. Cleaned the downspouts every spring and fall. Mopped out three basement floods. Installed outdoor lights for security. Seeded and sodded half the yard on my hands and knees. Saved 'em tens of thousands in handyman bills. And they dare begrudge me a peaceful stay?"

My eyes glistened. "You deserve better."

"Flat out do," she said heatedly. "What kind of respect is this? Ashamed to show my face down there anymore. Nothing like those Friday night poker games. Wouldn't have missed one for a nuclear war. Now, wouldn't go if you staked me."

"Maybe you'll change your mind by Friday," I said soothingly. "That game's your part-time income."

Fran grinned sheepishly, but quickly frowned. "Don't be so sure."

"Why would Ruth act this vindictive?"

"Could be payback for me emptying a few joint accounts."

I looked at her in surprise. "When did you do that?"

"Last week, the day after she put her slipper up my crack, but it took her time to discover it. She's not good with money. I handle all the finances."

I grinned appreciatively. "You stole her money."

Fran grunted. "Get a grip, Kris. Took what was rightfully mine. Left the sums that belonged to her, plus fifty grand for good measure. More than generous settlement, but couldn't see leaving my mother's inheritance behind. Shared it with Ruth dollar for dollar while we were together. Ain't foolish enough to throw away cash now that we're apart. Like to see Ruth get by on her pension. The Catholic Church spends more on candles than they do retired nuns."

"Where will you go tonight?"

"Wherever the winds carry me," she said dramatically. "Or the Brown Palace, whichever's closest."

"Downtown?"

"You bet. Ruth and I slipped out of the convent and spent a few days honeymooning there. Always wanted to go back, but cheapo argued we shouldn't spend good money on a hotel in our hometown. Figure this'll give me closure. Bookend visits. Can't wait to experience the luxury. About froze a toe in that ramshackle Gertrude Center this week. Years ago, told the board we needed to buy a new furnace. Fell on deaf ears. Space heaters everywhere, and felt like I was sleeping in a meat locker. Deserve a little comfort in my time of turmoil."

"You could stay a few nights with me and Destiny. I'd have to check with her, but I'm sure she'd approve."

"Couldn't impose," Fran said stoically. "Good friends stay friends 'cause they know when to say no."

"It wouldn't be any trouble. We have a vacant unit in the house. We could set you up with a futon and some—"

She waved both hands in protest. "Say no more, kiddo. This weary traveler's heading to world-class pampering, the domain of kings and presidents. Hot bath, cold drink. Firm mattress, soft pillow. Could use a ride though, if you're leaving early and it's on your way somewhere."

She knew I rarely left the office before seven and that the Brown Palace wasn't on my way home, but for the sake of her pride, I pretended to clock out at four and drove her to the hotel.

On the way, we discussed both cases, and I asked her to reinterview Leonard, the Crumplers' handyman. I felt certain he held the key to solving the case of the dwindling Christmas display, but I couldn't begin to decipher the solution.

Fran agreed to take a run at him, and she also suggested we install a video camera, hidden somewhere among the lights and figurines. She'd already called her friend Mabel, an insurance agent, who had agreed to lend a system.

The prospect of performing these two tasks seemed to renew Fran's energy. As I pulled away from the circular drive of the Brown Palace, I couldn't help but smile at the sight of her chatting up the ornately adorned bellhop as he carried her tattered luggage.

I returned straight to the office and tried again to reach Lori Parks. An administrative assistant assured me she'd given Lori my first message and would do the same with the second, but the director had left for the day.

I promptly called Lori at home.

Erica answered the phone, which instantly improved my mood.

"Erica, hi. This is Kristin Ashe. We met at—"

She interrupted with a giggle. "I know who you are, silly."

"I need to talk to your mom, Lori. Is she around?"

"She's here, but first, may I do a puppet show for you?"

I rubbed my forehead. "Over the phone?"

"Please, I have everyone here."

"Okay, but not too long. How about five minutes?"

"That's not enough for three acts. Don't you know anything about theater?"

"Not much. Will ten do?"

"Yippee," she said triumphantly.

She wasted no time weaving a tale that would have flourished on most stages. However, the show came to an abrupt halt when she exclaimed, "Oh, no. Harry Houdini fell off the stage."

"He's not dead, is he?" I said, feigning alarm.

"No that would have been awful. He's my favorite."

"If he's not feeling well," I hastened to reassure her, "you can call in his understudy."

"What's that?"

"Understudies are actors who train for the role and prepare for the parts, but they only perform when something happens to the stars. They do the same amount of work, behind the scenes, but they never get credit."

"Sort of like mommy Donna?"

My heart sank. I had to change the subject. "Gee, look what time it is. We'd better wrap it up, Erica, so I can talk to your mom."

"Okay," she said easily. She soon brought the play to a satisfying conclusion and ran to hand the cordless phone to her mother.

Lori's voice came on the line as a highly agitated whisper. "Can you hear me, Kris?"

"Yes," I said loudly.

"Something else has happened. Someone placed another note in my purse."

"When? Where?" I asked swiftly.

She cleared her throat. "On Saturday, at the house tour."

"Why didn't you call?" I said hotly.

"I didn't find it until last night, and today I was preoccupied with an all-day board meeting," she hissed. "We'll talk tomorrow."

"I'll come by the Children's Academy in the morning."

"No, not there," she commanded. "I'll meet you at my house in the evening."

"Do you want to wait that long?"

"What choice do I have?" she said, aggrieved. "I have a business to run."

"Did anyone else—"

"I have to go, Kris," she interrupted gruffly. "I'll see you at six."

"At least tell me what the note said."

She lowered her voice to an almost unintelligible level. "You say good-bye never knowing . . ."

Chapter 11

Damn Lori Parks!

That's all I heard before the dial tone. Or at least I thought she spoke those words. Who could tell with such a soft utterance?

For the next hour, I obsessed about the new message.

"You do try to prepare." This had appeared five weeks ago, inside a mitten, left on the playground at the Children's Academy.

"Still, you believe no harm will ever come to your children." This one had arrived two weeks ago, taped to the door of the Children's Academy, on the back of a photograph of a young girl.

"You say good-bye, never knowing." This had materialized two days ago at the house tour, slipped into Lori's purse by a visitor, volunteer, or staff member.

I sat quietly, trying to unravel the messages, searching in my subconscious for a pattern.

I rose and paced madly, the length of the hall outside my office, muttering the three sentences and frantically asking "What do they mean?"

I lay on the couch and urged myself to be patient, to let the process unfold, to content myself with taking another step, and another, knowing the technique had often brought results.

I felt unnerved.

Somehow, this case was different. In part, because I didn't know who had sent the notes or why, but also because I felt a vague dread the situation would escalate.

Yet, I had to wait. And nothing felt worse than waiting for doom.

The notes were innocent enough. In fact, if Lori had agreed to go to the police, I felt certain they could have done nothing. Law enforcement isn't designed for prevention. Officers can't take action until something awful happens.

Little comfort for potential victims.

Fortunately, I wasn't bound by the rigidity of police procedure. I felt comfortable intervening at the first hint of trouble, no matter how nebulous, but I didn't possess even that.

Who could I chase, and what would I do?

How about Robert Hoppe, the CEO of the Learning Emporium in Cherry Creek, Lori's competitor and rival? Obviously, bad blood ran deeper than either would admit, as evidenced by the nasty exchange at the house tour. Hoppe had jumped at the opportunity to spread the rumor Lori had killed a girl but had refused to substantiate his claim. How could I push him further? Sooner before later, he'd want to meet Bevin, my imaginary daughter, and that would blow my cover.

However, someone else could verify his story with absolute accuracy: Lori Parks. Surely, she wouldn't have forgotten if she'd almost killed someone. Either she had brought about a death, or she hadn't. I could try to gain her trust, press harder for the truth.

I turned my attention to Sylvia Sewall, the disturbed parent of the unbalanced son. The method suited an angry mother, and Fran Green certainly had given Mrs. Sewall high marks for instability. Still, how duplicitous was she? The three quasi-threatening notes didn't fit with her goal to have her daughter reinstated at the Children's Academy. What next? Under some guise, maybe I could visit her and add my impressions to Fran's.

And what about Jason Sewall, her son? It seemed possible that a bright eleven-year-old could pull off the three stunts, until I factored in transportation. How could he have made his way to the Children's Academy before dawn, on two separate occasions? Also, no one had mentioned seeing him at the Baker-Brown house tour. I pegged him as a long shot.

I aimed my spotlight in a different direction. Sarah, my lunchtime companion at the house tour, had introduced three new suspects: Mike Stanley, the ex-husband of the business manager; Stacey Tobias, the fired sculptor who had posed as a music teacher; and Rebecca Ramirez, the reading specialist Lori had canned, ostensibly without cause.

I felt much better after my brainstorming, positively invigorated. I had two threads to probe more deeply and three new tangents to pursue. I decided to start with Rebecca, and after careful consideration, devised a way to approach her.

I called Sarah, who readily gave me Rebecca's number. I reached Rebecca on the first try and, with a few well-placed fibs, secured her agreement to meet the following morning.

Leaving the office around six, I felt uplifted, a euphoria that soon evaporated when I trudged through an inch of snow on the sidewalk and stepped into a deep pile of slush in the street.

In loafers, my feet soaked and half-frozen, I scrambled to brush all the snow from the car, a task Fran had handled two hours earlier when I drove her to the Brown Palace. Inside the vehicle, I wiped off my glasses.

As I waited for the engine and interior to warm, I listened to radio reports of multi-car pile-ups and felt thankful my commute didn't include any highways. On the drive with Fran, the roads had been snow-packed but not dangerous. However, the increased snowfall and surplus traffic had converted a challenging drive into a potentially deadly one.

I vowed to take my time on side streets. I stretched a ten-minute journey into thirty and arrived home safely. Before I entered the house, I used a shovel and broom to remove snow from the sidewalk, the front and rear steps, and the path through the side yard. Despite an aerobic pace of snow removal, I couldn't stop shivering.

Once inside, I dawdled in a scalding bath, trying to warm my body's core. When that didn't work, I changed into sweats and a pull-over I'd heated up in the dryer. I was sitting in front of the fireplace when Destiny arrived a few minutes later, dinner in hand.

She kissed me. "How was your day?"

"Draining," I said, reluctant to disentangle from our embrace. "These cases are consuming me, plus I have Fran to worry about."

"Come talk to me in the kitchen."

We chatted as she plated up soup and salad she'd picked up at Whole Foods. "Fran's T-shirt on Friday said, 'Barbie's a slut.'"

Destiny laughed.

"The one before that was 'Don't breed 'em if you can't feed 'em.'"

My lover's smile faded. "That doesn't sound like Fran."

"I know. She's unraveling. Today's was the worst: 'Life's a bitch until you divorce one.'"

"Ouch."

"This morning, she was kicked out of the Gertrude Center, and she thinks Ruth's behind it."

"That's awful! Where will she go?"

"I dropped her off at the Brown Palace this afternoon."

Destiny stopped slicing bread and stared at me, aghast. "She can't stay there, Kris. A room must cost $300 a night."

I shrugged. "She reserved the Presidential Suite."

"Where will she get the money?"

I reached across the counter, stole a crouton, and crunched it decisively. "Apparently, she already has it. Her mother left her a hefty sum, which she was sharing with Ruth but has pulled from their joint account."

Destiny's face crinkled in distress. "They're serious about this, aren't they? They're really going to break up."

"It seems like they already have. Ruth won't budge, and Fran's given up."

"I don't blame her, but the Brown Palace? A hotel's no place to go at a time like this."

"She looked happy when I pulled away from the curb."

"No, no, no! She needs to be surrounded by people who love her. What other friends does she have?"

"Not many who aren't connected to Ruth or the Gertrude Center. And she's so mad, she's planning to boycott the Friday night poker game."

Destiny's grimaced sympathetically. "Fran must really feel hurt."

"She seems fine," I said mildly.

"Let's ask her to move in here."

I shook my head with gusto. "We'd never get rid of her."

"She can stay in the second-floor apartment. It's vacant, and this is a terrible time of year to find tenants."

"You know Fran, she'd probably have her ear to the vent, listening to us having sex."

Destiny laughed easily. "We're not that loud. A casual scream here or there. Mostly moans."

"Loud enough. One peep, and her ear would catch it. Plus, I did invite her. Contingent upon checking with you, of course," I said hastily. "And she turned me down."

"How many times did you offer?"

"Once. Half-heartedly."

"Kristin Ashe!" Destiny abandoned her food preparation and came to take my hands into hers. "This has to be the worst time in Fran's life, but you know she's proud. You have to ask, then beg, then insist."

I arched an eyebrow. "I'm not good at begging."

Destiny drew me close and administered her best guilt-provoking stare. "Look how much Fran has done for you."

"All right," I said, shamed by the memory of Fran's prompt agreement to meet the cantankerous handyman and work in freezing conditions to install a video camera at the Crumpler estate.

Destiny beamed in victory. "Call and tell her you'll pick her up tonight. She can sleep in our guest bedroom. Tomorrow, we'll get the apartment ready."

I lowered my head in defeat. "I just came home and changed. I haven't even warmed up yet."

"Kris!"

"But Fran's paid for the room," I whined.

"That doesn't matter. She shouldn't be alone." Destiny flashed her most winning smile, her green eyes full of promise.

"But she couldn't wait to stay in the suite," I protested. "She and Ruth spent their honeymoon there, and—"

I stopped mid-sentence, unable to avoid Destiny's chastising glare or the admission of my own ignorance. I sighed. "I'll call her right now."

"Better yet, go get her. Don't give her a chance to say no."

I heard the wind whistling through the kitchen window, one of the single-panes Destiny hadn't replaced, and attempted another retreat. "It's snowing pretty heavily. I think an advisory went into effect."

"For the mountains, not Denver."

"We're not on accident alert?"

"No. And you drive in much worse all the time."

"Have the plows been out?"

"Kris, go!"

"What if she won't come?"

"Try harder."

I winced. "Let's hope she only stays a few nights."

"A month might be more realistic."

I scowled. "A week?"

Destiny smiled broadly. "Two weeks!"

"Okay," I conceded, "But you have to drive her around to find a place, or she'll never leave!"

When Fran answered my knock on the penthouse suite door, she looked terrible. Red eyes, sagging cheeks, stooped shoulders. For the first time since I'd met her, she looked her age, as if a decade had caught up to her in a single day. She'd changed shirts and now broadcast, "Just screw it."

She expressed no surprise at the sight of me and jumped into conversation as if I'd just returned from a walk down the hall for ice. "Kris, 'bout to call you. Watching the news. Big story. You catch it?"

"No, what?"

"Kid missing from a daycare."

I grabbed her arm as she turned to usher me into the room. "The Children's Academy?"

"Learning Emporium in Highlands Ranch. That the one you visited?"

My heartbeat slowed. "No. Cherry Creek."

"Uproar for nothing. Divorced parents, father picked up the kid on the mother's day. Mobilized half the uniforms in southeast Denver for a false alarm. On a night like this. Can't be good for business."

"No kidding!"

Fran shut the door, lowered the volume on the television, and gazed at me inquisitively. "Destiny send you?"

I nodded sheepishly. "She insisted I bring you back to the house."

Fran dismissed the idea with a wave. "Thoughtful of her, but shouldn't have come out on a night like this. You see many accidents?"

"Not too many."

"How were the roads?"

"Not bad," I lied again.

"I'm comfortable enough here."

"I can't go home without you." I pointedly eyed the king-size bed. "Either you come, or I stay."

Fran didn't hesitate. "Wouldn't be proper. Better pack up, but have to wait for room service. Ordered $18 chip and dip. Ought to be mouth-watering at that price. Care to join me?"

"I'd love to, but I'm parked illegally. Could we get it to go?"

"Can't see why not."

"We can eat in front of the fireplace."

"And share with Destiny," Fran said enthusiastically. "Hate to cut her out of this treat. Might cheer her up."

I scoffed. "Destiny doesn't need cheering up."

"Kris, 'course she does. Has to be feeling blue with this weather. Hates the cold."

"She does?"

"Talks about it all the time," Fran said firmly.

I shook my head in chagrin. "Okay, let's go cheer her up."

After Fran packed her suitcase and clamped it shut, she surveyed the posh surroundings one last time. "Made a mistake coming here. No matter what happens, gotta keep moving forward."

The next morning found me deeply engrossed in a job interview. Not for Marketing Consultants, the company I legitimately owned. Rather, I sat mired in lies as president of Traveling Tutors.

Rebecca Ramirez had arrived five minutes early for her interview at eleven, only seconds after me, because I'd spent thirty minutes digging out my car, scraping bubbled ice formations off the windows, and creeping along snow-packed streets. The glaring sun was doing its best to restore order to the city, but it would take days for the four inches to melt, longer if the thermometer kept hugging thirty degrees.

"The job would involve tutoring children, in their homes, between six and nine o'clock," I said to the reading specialist Lori Parks had fired from the Children's Academy.

"At night?" she confirmed, brushing back a strand of hair that had escaped from her black ponytail. She'd dressed conservatively for our appointment. Her pleated brown skirt, beige cable-knit sweater, and boots that reached to her knees added bulk to an otherwise cardboard cut-out figure. Her jewelry was understated—small diamond post earrings, a gold chain necklace, and an inexpensive watch that she glanced at incessantly. She had an unusually long neck, which gave her the appearance of perpetual, anxious craning.

I nodded. "Each session would last forty-five minutes, giving you fifteen minutes to get to the next one. We'll schedule your appointments in the same neighborhood, and we'll pay twenty-two dollars per session. We'd book you up to four nights per week, up to three students per night. Are you currently employed?"

"Not presently. But I have several interviews lined up for teaching positions."

I fidgeted as I studied her resume. She sat calmly, waiting for my next question. "The Children's Academy . . . you were there eighteen months. Why did you leave?"

Rebecca paused before she said, "The director fired me for personal reasons."

"Dr. Lori Parks?"

Rebecca nodded glumly.

"Would you care to reveal the circumstances?"

"I'd rather not."

"Could you describe your work at the Academy?"

"Certainly." She straightened up. "I was hired as the reading specialist."

"Did you create the program?"

"Not entirely. I based it on models from across the country and modified it with Dr. Parks' input."

"The two of you worked closely?"

"We met at least two hours every week. She was very generous with her time and knowledge."

"How would you describe Dr. Parks' managerial style?"

Rebecca reflected for a full minute. "Hands-on."

"Could you be more specific?"

"She keeps a tight hold on everything at the Academy. Which is good," she scrambled to add. "But sometimes, nothing could satisfy Dr. Parks. If something was done perfectly, she demanded the level above. It could be stressful."

I consulted notes I'd jotted down from a book on interviewing techniques. "Can you describe some of the strengths you would bring to Traveling Tutors?"

"I'm a team player. I work well with different personalities. I have a minor in psychology, as you can see from my resume."

"Yes," I said, after a glimpse.

"That serves me well, especially with parents."

I nodded slowly, debating how to take another run at her relationship with Lori, when she saved me the trouble. "Dr. Parks fired me because I ran into a friend of hers," Rebecca blurted out.

"Excuse me?" I said, unable to keep the shock from my voice.

"She fired me after I told her we had a mutual acquaintance, Deborah Kennedy. She and Dr. Parks skied together when they were teenagers. I'd recently met Deborah in a hiking club."

"Why would your employer do that?"

"I don't know, but it's the only explanation that makes sense. In my termination interview, she claimed she fired me for incomplete lesson plans and lack of self-motivation, but that wasn't true."

"How can you be sure?"

"Because Dr. Parks gave me four commendations last year. And when I filed for unemployment, the Academy didn't fight my claim. I know for certain they always try to deny unemployment benefits."

"How do you know that?"

"Sally Patterson, the concierge, told me one day on our way to work. She'd heard Dr. Parks boast about her unblemished record. She'd never had to lay off workers, and no one had successfully claimed they were fired without cause and collected benefits. I was the first."

"The termination must have been painful."

"I couldn't sleep for a week. I wish I knew what I could have done to prevent it."

"It sounds like you couldn't have."

"Maybe I shouldn't have mentioned her friend's name. That cost me the best job I've had."

"It shouldn't have," I said, regretting I couldn't offer her a tutoring job.

"When I brought up the subject of Deborah Kennedy, Dr. Parks' voice went hoarse, and she spilled coffee across the desk. She started to blot it up with her shirt sleeve. I ran to the kitchen for paper towels, and when I came back, she was shaking. I'd never seen her like that. She's always calm, in every situation."

"Did she remember Deborah Kennedy right away?"

"Instantly. She asked if Deborah had talked at all about their past. I said only that they'd enjoyed skiing together. I told Dr. Parks that Deborah and I had chatted about our favorite trails and wildlife and that she seemed nice."

"That was the end of it?"

"For that day. The next week, she called me into her office and fired me. Don't you think that's coincidental?"

"Hmm," I said, noncommittal.

"I probably have grounds to sue for wrongful termination. What do you think?"

I shot her a look. "Would that be wise?"

"I couldn't," she said softly, perhaps realizing this type discussion wouldn't lead to a job offer. "I respect her too much."

A few minutes later, I wrapped up the interview. As we shook hands in farewell, I couldn't help feeling a twinge of guilt at her parting words.

"If I don't get the job," Rebecca Ramirez said, "I appreciate you listening. It felt good to talk about what happened. Maybe it will help me let go."

Chapter 12

Time for me to talk to someone myself.

I couldn't wait to approach Lori Parks with this new information. Wouldn't she be startled, given that she'd kept the Rebecca Ramirez lead from me, conveniently forgetting to tell me about an employee she'd shafted?

I was eager for six o'clock to arrive, but I passed the time by surprising Destiny with lunch at her office and spending the balance of the afternoon at my grandma's, playing canasta and drinking hot cocoa.

Shortly after darkness had fallen, I found Lori Parks' home with ease. She lived in a two-story brick Denver Square in Congress Park, a diverse, family-friendly neighborhood in the heart of the city. Built in the early years of the twentieth century, the house looked identical to the ones around it, distinguished only by its orange brick, pale yellow trim, and dark brown shingles. I'd toured different versions of Denver Squares, and the layout rarely varied: living room, dining room, powder room, and kitchen on the first floor; an L-shaped staircase with handcarved rails leading to a second floor of three small bedrooms, a tiny bath, and a built-in linen closet; and a straight stairway or drop-down ladder servicing attic space on the third level.

In the double-track driveway on the side of the house, I didn't see Lori's Volvo, and the detached garage at the back of the lot appeared as if it hadn't sheltered cars in some time. I parked on the street and trudged up a narrow set of uneven flagstone steps, holding on to the railing tightly, trying to avoid patches of ice.

By the time I stood on Lori's doorstep, I was so focused on how to get my tight-lipped client to talk, that when her partner Donna answered the door, it threw me.

About the same age as Lori, Donna possessed no other outward similarities. Dressed in sweats and an oversized Melissa Etheridge T-shirt, she was barefoot. Her short, blonde hair was thick and wavy, with a pronounced cowlick on the left side. Probably as an aftereffect of the weekend's snowboarding with Fran, her nose and forehead showed signs of sunburn and peeling. She had an easy manner and warm brown eyes that betrayed intense curiosity.

I extended my hand in greeting. "I'm Kris Ashe. I'm here to see Lori. You must be Donna."

"Lori's not home. Does she know you're coming?"

"I'm helping with the incidents at the Academy. I'm a little early," I said apologetically.

"No problem." She gestured for me to come inside and led me to the living room. "I'm making myself a cup of tea. Can I get you something to drink?"

"No, thank you."

"I'll be right back," she said with a friendly smile.

She left for the kitchen, giving me a chance to study my surroundings, which resembled those in a model home. The room had been furnished and decorated to the nth degree. The walls were finished with customized paint, borders, murals, and faux finishes, all presumably meant to evoke images of a Tuscany farmhouse. With mirrors, impressionist landscapes, sconces, and display shelves with mementos, the effect was overwhelming.

The overkill didn't stop there. Elaborate window coverings (blinds, drapes, valances, and sashes) overshadowed every opening, darkening the space. On the dark green sectional sofa, at least a dozen throw pillows rested, in various sizes and autumn colors. Every coffee and end table had at least four layers of accessories, some combination of decorative lamps, centerpieces, candles, coasters, wooden boxes, and pottery. I was afraid to move, paralyzed by the ingrained notion that if I broke it, I'd have to buy it.

Carpet runners and rugs in mustards and reds separated the expanse of gleaming oak floors, and a glance into the dining room revealed a table set for six. Three sizes of plates, silverware, cloth napkins, and wine glasses implied guests were expected any minute, yet somehow, I sensed they rarely came.

Overall, the main floor gave off the impression it had been decorated in a week, under deadline, not over years, as a loving collection. It stood in stark contrast to the hodge-podge Destiny and I had accumulated. We had the Japanese-Quaker-California Contemporary look going on our third floor of the mansion, the unfortunate result of combining two households when neither of us had paid much attention to material surroundings.

"How's Erica?" I said conversationally after Donna returned with a mug of tea, which she clasped with both hands.

Donna looked at me sharply from her end of the couch. "You've met our daughter?"

"At the Baker-Brown house tour. She drew a picture of me."

"Ah!" Donna smiled, relaxing. "She mentioned meeting a new friend. I didn't make the connection."

"She's quite talented."

"Thank you."

After an awkward pause, I said, "So . . . you and Fran met snowboarding?"

She nodded. "She's one of my students at Loveland."

"How long have you been riding?"

"Eight years."

"Does Erica go, too?"

"She's shown interest, but Lori won't permit it."

"Well, Fran seems to be addicted. Is it hard to learn?"

Donna laughed ruefully. "Very painful. My first time out, I fell at least a hundred times."

"I'm surprised you didn't quit."

"I couldn't, not after I felt the sensation of gliding. It was better than sex. The next day I bought my own board."

I shifted in my seat. "Really!"

"There's an utter beauty to being on the mountain," she said, an enchanted look in her eyes. "The first run of the day on groomed corduroy. Or better yet, on fresh snow. Riding on six inches of powder feels like floating on clouds. And a run through the trees, what a magical combination of danger and stillness."

"Hmm."

Donna must have heard my doubt, because she leaned forward, her voice dropping seductively, "I hold on to the memory of certain days for months. I can picture the weather, the snow, the condition of the trails, the people on the lifts. Every detail in relief. Mostly what lingers, though, is the sense of peace I cradle in my body. Everything becomes quiet, and nothing else exists."

I felt tension in my shoulders, and my voice cracked as I said, "Lori doesn't snowboard?"

Donna shook her head briskly. "I begged her to come when I first started. That's when I needed her, but she refused. Her parents own a cabin in Winter Glades, and she hasn't been there in twenty years. She doesn't like to go into the mountains. Plus, she'd never understand snowboarding."

"The sport?" I said, confused.

"The culture. I wear my jacket into the grocery store, and it brands me. I run into snowboarders in all areas of my life, and we're linked by this passion. Most of the world wonders why we snowboard, and we wonder why anyone does anything but," she said, animated. "Lori mocks it, saying my role models are teenagers. So what? Maybe they're ten or twenty years younger, but in my mind, I haven't grown up or grown old."

"That sounds appealing."

Donna looked at me intently. "I can see why Erica bonded with you at the house tour. When she came home, she said she liked you because you really listen."

"I try," I said, deflecting the compliment.

"Her comment made Lori jealous, but I see what she meant. You have a quality that's engaging. Would you consider snowboarding?"

I felt perspiration coat my eyebrows. "Fran's been hounding me, but I don't know."

"I'll bet you'd be good at it," she said with an air of quiet amusement. "There's an honesty to it. And a fluidity, like making love. You should try it. I'd be happy to—"

I'll never know what Donna intended to offer, because at that precise moment, Lori burst into the room, breathless. At the sight of me, she looked flustered and faintly alarmed.

"I'm not late, am I?" she asked, knowing the answer perfectly well, as the clock in the hallway chimed six times. "What did I miss?"

"Nothing," I mumbled. "I arrived a few minutes ago."

I moved uncomfortably in my seat as Lori crossed the room and took her time removing her shimmering burgundy chenille jacket and smoothing out her matching moleskin pants and ribbed ivory turtleneck. She leaned down to give Donna a kiss, one that almost turned into foreplay.

Donna, who didn't blush over the interruption in our conversation or the intimate exchange, broke away. "Where's Erica?"

"She ran upstairs. I told her she could see Kris when we're done. I didn't know you'd be home this early," Lori said, looking at her steadily. She sat next to Donna on the couch, almost on her. With both arms, she pulled her close.

"They canceled our meeting. Why, did you want to meet with Kris in private?" Donna asked coyly, as her body stiffened.

Lori ignored the double meaning. "That might be better."

"Actually, Donna might be able to offer insight," I broke in. "The more I look into this, the more I believe it's personal, that it has nothing to do with the Children's Academy."

"How could embezzling not involve the Academy?" Donna asked.

Lori's eyes warned me off, as she said, "We need to talk about this in private."

"What embezzling?" I exclaimed. "Someone's threatening you *and* stealing money? Why didn't you tell me about the theft?"

"What threats?" Donna said, her tone steely.

Lori stared at the floor and said quietly, "There is no embezzlement, Donna. I hired Kris for another reason, but it doesn't concern you."

"Swell. You decide what concerns me and what doesn't, exactly as you decide everything else in our lives," Donna said, lips quivering.

"Donna, please," Lori said scornfully. "Can we not go into this right now?"

"Into what? God forbid, someone should see our true relationship, the way you dismiss me, the way you shut out your daughter."

"Not now, Donna!" Lori shouted.

"When then? When will you look at the dysfunction?"

Yes, I was still in the room, and no, they didn't seem to care.

They hardly missed a scream when I rose and said nervously, "I think I'll go say 'hi' to Erica."

I found their daughter in her third-floor hideaway, a playroom in the attic.

The room felt a world away from the formality and excess of the downstairs, except for the rising sounds of ugliness. Every wall was painted pink, scraps of pastel carpet covered most of the wooden floor, and neon mobiles hung from the ceiling. The room was filled with toys and stuffed animals and games, scattered across the floor and bulging out of storage containers.

In the center, the little girl sat, her back to the door.

I traversed the room, and in stealth surprise tapped Erica on the shoulder. She squealed in delight, ripped off her headset, and jumped to hug me tightly. After much debate, we decided to play with dolls.

Erica dropped back into a cross-legged pose, and I lowered myself to my stomach.

"Do you have a husband?" she asked, after we'd divided the stash: five for her, two for me.

"No, but I am very close with another woman, Destiny," I said earnestly.

"Like Mom and Mommy Donna?"

I could still hear the rancor below. "Something like that."

"Do you fight?"

"Sometimes."

"I want my Barbie to have a husband," Erica announced determinedly.

"Okay."

"Yours can't have a husband, because I only have one Ken doll."

I tried to look suitably disappointed.

Erica rushed to add, "Sometimes, though, I pretend this one's a boy. I put a hat on her and push her hair up in it."

She demonstrated by grabbing a brunette and stuffing her locks under a baseball cap. The doll still possessed the 36D chest and death-defying heels, but the alterations did give her a slightly boyish appearance.

"That looks perfect," I said after a moment's review.

"Or, you could borrow Ken after a little while. We could share."

"That'd be nice."

"Do you have two moms, too?"

"No, I have a mom and a dad."

"Most of my friends have dads."

"Mine, too. Do you wish you had one?"

"Sometimes."

I looked at her closely. "Why?"

"Then I could be like everyone else."

"There's nothing wrong with being different," I said, but the sadness in my tone implied the opposite.

"I get tired of explaining everything over and over and over and over again," she said with a heavy sigh.

"I do, too."

When she seemed perplexed, I added, "You know, about me and Destiny and no husband."

Erica shook her head knowingly. "Do your mom and dad love each other?"

"Not anymore. They're divorced."

"Did they fight a lot when you were little?"

"They did," I said, trying my best to block out the sounds of Lori and Donna's ongoing battle.

"Mommy Donna's my favorite because she fixed my hair this morning."

"It looks very pretty," I said, touching Erica's pigtails.

She grinned shyly. "Thanks."

"Is she always your favorite?"

"No, I change a lot."

With that, Erica and I set about dressing the dolls. After an hour of fashion shows, I told her I needed to go check on her moms.

The eerie silence below disturbed me almost as much as the previous blasts.

We hugged good-bye, and when I stood, she looked at me and said resolutely, "Mommy Donna will probably be crying. She cries a lot when they fight, after she's done yelling."

"What about Mom Lori?"

"She never cries."

"How do you know?"

"Because she didn't cry after our dog Cuddles died. She told me the last time she cried was when her friend died. They were in college."

I felt a chill. "How did her friend die?"

Erica wrinkled her nose. "Mom didn't say."

My hand was on the doorknob when Erica came running to hug me again. Mid-squeeze, she said, "What did you do when your mom and dad used to fight?"

"I tried to pretend I didn't hear," I said truthfully, suppressing a shudder.

"It makes my stomach feel funny."

"I know what you mean." I brushed the top of her hair.

She bent back and looked at me desperately. "Will you stay for dinner?"

I rubbed my eyes. "I'm not sure that's such a good idea."

"Mommy Donna said I could invite a guest whenever I want, but I never do," Erica said gloomily.

"I don't know."

"Please, please, please! I know they'll let you stay if I ask."

I took a deep breath. "Sure, why not?"

The little girl burst into a face-widening smile, and she clenched me again. When I tried to detach, she held on more tightly and whimpered, "Sometimes, I feel like I have a hole in my heart."

There was nothing I could say to that.

I could only kiss the top of her head, next to where my tears had fallen.

Chapter 13

I slinked down the stairs and peered around the corner. Lori was on one end of the couch, staring straight ahead, emotionless. Donna sat on the far end, hunched over, crying softly.

I cleared my throat, and they both looked up.

"Is it safe for me to come back in?" I asked, forcing a faint smile.

"Sure," Donna said wearily. Lori shrugged.

I remained standing, leaning against the doorway. "I need to level with you, Lori. The threats seem personal, and Donna needs to be involved. Have you two talked about them?"

"In minute detail," Lori said nastily.

I stayed calm. "Good. Obviously they're coming from someone who has access to the Academy. If the threats are directed at you, they could be aimed at your family, too. It wouldn't hurt to take precautions."

"Such as?" Lori asked.

"Calling the police, for one."

"I agree," Donna chimed in, coming out of her slump.

"Absolutely not," Lori retorted.

"You're so stubborn."

Lori responded to Donna's remark by glaring at me. "I told you from the beginning, I won't do it."

"You value that damn business over me and Erica, don't you?"

"Of course not. But the police would laugh if we tried to bring them in."

"They might be aware of a pattern," Donna said pleadingly. "Something that hasn't been disclosed to the public. Remember the Capitol Hill rapist—he assaulted five women before the media released information. What if other learning centers have received threats?"

"She just said she thinks it's personal."

"Why do you think that, Kris?" Donna asked, wringing a tissue in her hands.

"Every time I interview someone, it comes back to a relationship with you." I directed my attention toward Lori, who avoided eye contact. "For example, why did Robert Hoppe accuse you of killing someone?"

"The man's deranged."

"He didn't say anything negative about the Academy," I pointed out. "Only you."

"You can't go by what he said alone."

"I'm not," I said, my throat constricting. "I also interviewed your ex-employee, Rebecca Ramirez, and she told me—"

Donna interrupted with, "Rebecca quit?"

"I let her go two months ago. Didn't I mention it?"

"No."

"What did Rebecca have to say? She probably hates my guts," Lori said.

I looked at her in surprise. "She has enormous respect for you."

Donna slid across the couch and nudged Lori on the arm. "Why did you fire her? She was your favorite teacher."

Lori didn't divert her stare from the wall. "Sloppy lesson plans and lack of self-motivation," she said dully.

"She always had those weaknesses," Donna objected. "You spent extra time mentoring her because you said she had a gift for breaking through learning barriers."

Lori threw up her arms and raised her voice. "Whatever talent Rebecca had couldn't compensate for her pathological disorganization. I had to let her go. I had no choice."

I moved into Lori's line of sight and said, my voice steady, "Did Deborah Kennedy influence your decision to fire Rebecca?"

Lori's eyes exploded in panic. "I have no idea what you're talking about."

"Who is Deborah Kennedy?" I pressed.

"I've never heard the name."

Donna, furious, said, "Your friend Deb from high school, Lori. You have her photo next to your computer upstairs. Why are you lying?"

Lori stabbed her with a stare. "I did go to high school with a Deborah Kennedy, but we're no longer in touch, and I can't fathom how this relates."

"Rebecca claims you fired her the week after she told you she knew Deborah. Is that true?"

"Yes," Lori said testily.

"Why?" I asked quietly.

"Because I won't tolerate blackmail."

I couldn't extract anything more from Lori Parks that night.

After she stormed out of the room, I pursued her down the hall. She would agree only to come by my office the next day. She swore she'd see me at noon and we'd clear up the matter. She claimed she didn't feel well and wanted to go straight to bed.

Predictably, the dinner without her was awkward.

Donna tried to act the part of gracious hostess, but she'd left the room, too. Physically, she was present, removing the three extra place settings from the table, retrieving polished chopsticks from the sideboard, exchanging light banter with Erica, asking questions about my business. But the light had gone from her eyes.

Donna had ordered take-out from a new Chinese restaurant, and we all struggled through an abysmal meal. A teaspoon of grease leaked from every wonton, I had to hide three half-chewed pieces of lemon chicken under a mound of rice on my plate, and the eggrolls tasted as if they'd been flavored with bleach.

Still, no one said anything about the culinary abomination until Erica innocently raised a question that made me laugh all the way home: "My goodness, when did Chinese food start tasting this bad?"

I chuckled some more when I discovered the horror of Destiny's day had eclipsed mine.

Shortly before ten, she staggered in the door, threw her keys on the table, and still wearing coat and boots, dove onto the couch. "I have such a headache!"

"How did it go?" I said pleasantly. "Did you find a place for Fran?"

"I have two words for you, Kristin Ashe," Destiny said, holding up two fingers to accent her point. "Goldilocks Green."

I laughed until my sides hurt.

"This is not funny. Let me tell you about our afternoon and evening. Too big, too small. Too hot, too cold. Too close to the park, too far from the bus line. Too trashy, too tidy. Too expensive, too cheap. Too gay, too straight. Too quiet, too loud. Too many dogs next door, too many cats in the alley."

Destiny momentarily fell silent before crying, "Jesus, Kris, she'll never move out, will she?"

"Destiny, she'll hear you."

"I wish," she said, exhausted. "She's out shoveling because she needs to clear her head."

"In the dark? She already did the walks."

"She has one of those snake lights she wears around her neck. Maybe she's doing the streets. Who cares? We have bigger concerns, like whether she'll live in our second-floor apartment the rest of our lives. She will, won't she?"

I gave my lover a huge smile and shrugged. Destiny looked so down-trodden, I joined her on the couch, helped her peel off her clothes, and rubbed her temples until she stopped moaning.

In that dark moment, it wouldn't have been proper to tell Destiny, "I told you so."

•••

The next day, Lori Parks showed up at my office ninety minutes late, smelling of alcohol. She hadn't bothered to conceal the bags under her eyes or the rash-like colors of her complexion, and she'd barely managed to comb her ragged hair. She was dressed casually in gray corduroy trousers, a black squareneck tank, and a duster jacket with large roses imposed over a black geometric pattern.

She didn't bother with niceties. "When I was nineteen, I went on a hut ski trip with three friends. One of them died."

My eyes bulged. "This is what Robert Hoppe hinted at?"

"I suppose."

"How could he have known?"

"I can't imagine," she said numbly.

"Was it in the newspapers?"

"Yes, but thirty people died that season in the Colorado backcountry and fifteen more at resorts. We represented one insignificant group."

"And Deborah Kennedy, the one Rebecca Ramirez befriended, she was on this trip?"

"Yes. She and another friend from high school, along with a girl I knew from college."

"And when you heard Rebecca had recently become acquainted with Deborah, you fired her?"

"Yes," Lori said uneasily. "The day after she told me about Deborah, she asked for a raise. It felt like blackmail, and I reacted accordingly."

"Were you hurt on the trip?"

"No."

"What is a hut trip?"

"You ski in and stay overnight in a public or private hut. We were in the Winter Glades area, trekking to a national forest service hut four miles from the Hunter Creek parking lot."

"Is a hut similar to a lodge?"

"Most are simple structures, with hot plates and bunks, no running water. You bring in all your own supplies and pack out trash."

"Did you have a guide?"

Her eyes flickered. "We didn't need one for such an easy route."

"Were you experienced skiers?"

"We were all capable," she said, after a split-second hesitation.

"What went wrong?"

"In a snowstorm, we lost the trail. We made camp and tried to wait out the conditions. We had to sleep outdoors three nights. On the fourth day, rescuers found us and brought us out on snowmobiles."

"Which friend died?"

"Jodi Wilde," Lori said faintly. "My friend from college."

"How?"

"She froze to death the night before we were rescued. Her circumstances, and those of Liz, the other girl, were aggravated by a fall into a small creek."

"Were you and Jodi close friends?"

"Intimate," Lori Parks said flatly.

"Liz or Deborah, do you think either is capable of revenge?"

"Against me? Why? They survived, and why would they have waited this long?"

"What about Jodi's family?"

"I assume they've put the incident to rest. I know I did, long ago."

"Are you in touch with any of them?"

"No. I never met Jodi's family, Deb and I drifted apart in our early twenties, and Liz and I were never close. We were both friends with Deb, but we weren't friends." Lori drew in a sharp breath. "I'm not trying to micro-manage, but this path of inquiry seems pointless."

"Could I please have the three women's full names and any contact information you might have?"

Her eyes darkened with anger. "Did you hear me?"

"Yes," I said neutrally.

She stared at me, and I returned the favor.

After a long silence, she said tensely, "Jodi Wilde. She grew up in Hartford, Connecticut. I have no idea if her parents still live there. Deborah Kennedy obviously lives around here, if she hikes with Rebecca. And Elizabeth Decker. She may or may not be in the area. I doubt she married."

"Have you talked to Donna about any of this?"

"No, and I don't intend to."

"How does she feel about that?"

"Not that it's any of your business," Lori said bitingly, "but she slept in the spare room last night. She claims she'll stay there until I open up."

"Why don't you?" I asked calmly.

"I can't," she muttered between clenched teeth. "This doesn't concern her. My past has nothing to do with her or any part of my life today. I don't need to share every detail of my life with Donna, or anyone else."

"I get the message, and I quit."

"What?"

"I quit," I repeated loudly.

Lori Parks shook her head and showered me with disgust. "You can't be serious. I didn't pay you to do half a job."

"I haven't invoiced you, therefore you haven't paid me at all," I said, my voice growing more quiet as hers rose. "Don't bother. Effective immediately, I don't work for you anymore." I rose, but she remained stubbornly seated.

She glared. "You can't do this. What am I supposed to do?"

"Call the police. Hire someone else and lie to her. Or bury your head for another twenty years and do nothing."

"You believe what's going on at the Academy is related to the ski trip?"

"How can it not be?" I cried.

"And you won't help me?" she said, her voice breaking slightly.

I sat again. "Not if you refuse to level with me. I've learned a lot about you in the past two weeks, and none of it has come from you."

Lori cast a sideways glance at me. "Such as?"

"I know you're driven, loyal, and hard-working. Bright, caring, and fastidious. I also know you're close-mouthed, bitter, and ruthless. I think you set something in motion on that ski trip that lay dormant for a long time but has come to life. I have no clue about what, or why, or where this will head. But if you can't be truthful, I can't continue."

"You really take this seriously?"

"I do," I said adamantly. "And it's time you started."

Lori Parks didn't speak for a full minute. When she did, she'd adopted a more placid tone. "If I make an attempt to reveal more, as it's relevant, would you stay on the case? Would you see it through to the end?"

"Maybe," I said, faltering. "But you need to understand the gravity of the situation."

"I believe I do."

I sighed. "No, Lori, you don't. You still view this as a public relations snafu which will go away, no big deal."

"How would you prefer I see it?" she asked tartly.

"As the threat it is."

She let loose a grimacing smile. "Don't you think you're being a little melodramatic?"

"There's no doubt in my mind," I said, leaning forward and slowing down my words. "You are in danger. Absolute. Real. Tangible. Danger."

Chapter 14

I know Lori Parks didn't believe my ominous prediction, but she played along, and we crafted a prevention plan.

She would carry her cell phone at all times and return my calls within an hour. No more hiding behind her administrative assistant at the Children's Academy.

She would remain in a state of hyper-vigilance, on the lookout for anything out of the ordinary at work and at home.

If I requested, she would call a staff meeting and alert others at the Academy. I held this as a last resort because I agreed that spreading such incendiary news would cause irreparable damage and probably net nothing.

She would keep Donna in the loop. I had to remind her several times Donna was her partner, not her enemy.

Most importantly, she would never let Erica out of her sight unsupervised. Her daughter would be handed off from one trustworthy adult to another, never left alone. Not for one minute!

Meanwhile, I faced the daunting task of uprooting memories from an ill-fated ski trip twenty years earlier.

I'd start with the Colorado connections and track down Deborah Kennedy. Easy enough to do through Rebecca Ramirez, and I hoped she could lead me to Liz Decker. After that, I'd focus my energies on the East Coast, in search of the family of Jodi Wilde, the girl who had died.

Before I could begin, however, I had to attend to an urgent household matter when Destiny phoned, irked.

"Frida called to say someone tore up our yard and put snow on one side and wood on the other. Is this some kind of joke?"

I had a feeling I knew what was going on. I shared my hunch, then immediately dialed Fran's cell phone.

"Fran, this is Kris."

"Hey, kiddo. Just came in from outside. Gimme a second to shed these wet clothes," she said, out of breath. In a few minutes, she spoke again. "What's up?"

"Frida told Destiny someone messed up the backyard. Are you home now?"

"Sure thing. Let me explain."

My patience had worn thin. "What's going on, Fran?"

"Took some old lumber from the garage and attached it to the stoop. Packed snow on it. Boning up on tricks."

"You're snowboarding in our backyard, which is completely flat?"

"Wouldn't call it ridin' yet, but another foot of the white glory, and sit back and behold."

"There's hardly any snow."

"Had to act fast. It was melting like crazy. Moved it from all over the yard." Fran lowered her voice and added, "Filled in with a skosh from the neighbor's, too. Mite skinny, though. First run, most of the flakes slid down faster than me. 'Bout broke my neck. Spent another hour with a rollin' pin, mashing it down real good. Not a problem, is it? You told me to make myself at home."

"No." I exhaled deeply. "I'll call Destiny and tell her to explain it to Frida."

"Could use it herself. Wouldn't take offense. Took me three hours to sculpt, but happy to share with you gals. Gotta be careful, though. Zip off the stoop, little jump, fast turn before hitting the garage. Takes concentration. Might be a stretch for civilians, but no problem for an experienced rider."

I couldn't tell which irritated me more: Fran's takeover of our space or her cockiness. "You've snowboarded four times."

"Five. Pick up this sport quick, though. Learn it or die." She chuckled. "Born to do it. Haven't had this much fun since I gave up the chopper. Ruth nagged for years about the dangers of motorcycle riding, but I never listened. One day, saved my own life twice on the way home from work. Packed up the leathers and never looked back."

I was about to launch into a full-bore lecture about the courtesies of sharing a house and yard when she added, "Lovin' staying here. Couldn't have had a morning like this in the apartment with Ruth. Blue sky, fresh air, sun warming my head. Good to have my feet on the ground again."

I swallowed hard and made closing remarks. If something this minor gave Fran pleasure, who was I to dampen it?

However, her last comments tested the limits of my generosity. "Might consider takin' out the garage. Never park cars in it anyway. We'd need the room for a top-of-the-line terrain park. Saw a snow-making machine in a catalog. Wouldn't mind springing for the four-grand investment, if you and Destiny are short on cash."

Fortunately, Fran hung up before I could muster a reply.

An hour later, I found myself face-to-face with Fran's ex, Ruth.

I'd stopped by her apartment with the best of intentions. The sooner I smoothed over this domestic misunderstanding, the sooner Destiny and I could share our house with a less irritating tenant.

In the six days since I'd seen Ruth at Gay Bingo, it seemed as if her hair had thinned, her bulk had grown, and her eyes had crossed behind thick frames she'd mended with Scotch tape. The stained housecoat she wore, despite my phoning ahead, did little to enhance her appearance.

Maybe I hadn't gotten a good look in the dim light of the church basement. More likely, I'd been distracted by Janet, her companion on oxygen, and hadn't noticed the decline in Ruth.

"How have you been?" I asked loudly, fighting to override the sound of the television, leaning from my lounger toward hers.

Ruth took a long drag from her cigarette and stared at the newscaster. "Not well. I'm not feeling good at all. I don't drive anymore after dark or on the freeways."

"I'm sorry to hear that." I fumbled for a positive remark. "Your Christmas tree looks nice."

Ruth didn't bother to glance at it. "This is the last time. I won't be able to put it up next year. I'm having trouble with all kinds of things. One of the areas that's come to my attention is the medicine I take for depression. I'm on a new one, and it has a number of side effects. I'll read them to you."

I didn't have to strain to hear. She'd always possessed what Fran politely categorized as an "outdoor voice." However, before I could protest, she'd reached for the container. "I'll just list the ones that affect me. Muscle spasms. Light-headedness. Nervousness. Fatigue. Dry mouth. I know that's a side effect of several medicines, but it's gotten much worse. I can barely get my lips apart."

Reflexively, I pursed my lips.

"Vision changes," Ruth continued. "I'm fighting to see both close and far. I have an appointment with the eye doctor on Friday, and I'm going to get to the bottom of this. I told the internist I want to stop taking this medicine, and she didn't like that."

"Huh." My eyes had started to burn from the thickness of the cigarette smoke, and my nose itched from the stale odor I'd smelled as soon as I stepped off the elevator. Having passed three doors to arrive at Ruth's corner unit, I questioned how her neighbors could tolerate the pollution.

"Tuesday's the dermatologist. I have a rash on the back of my neck again. He gave me an ointment, and I used it up. I'm hoping he'll write another prescription." Ruth slowed down only long enough to stretch out another puff. "Thursday's my hair appointment with Bob, and Monday, I see the GP. Blessedly, I have a doctor who doesn't think my health problems are my fault."

Before I could interrupt, she changed topics. "Which is more than I can say for Frances. She wanted me to get out more and smoke less. She never did understand me. She pressured me to have sex, at our age, in our condition!"

I looked at Ruth in surprise. We should all be so fortunate! If Destiny still craved my body when I reached the other side of seventy, someone needed to put me out of my misery if I bitched.

"My friend Janet understands what I'm going through. She has health problems of her own—a knee and hip that need replacing. She's on oxygen, too, you know, but you never hear her complain."

"I know. I met her at Bingo."

"God help Frances when she takes ill. She's a terrible patient. All eleven of my doctors tell me I'm a very good patient."

I smiled sweetly. "Practice makes perfect."

My words didn't register. "Frances panics at the slightest ailment, and you can't tell her anything. I told her she shouldn't snowboard, but would she listen? No! She wants to barrel down icy slopes, just to make me worry. What about that gondola crash in Italy?"

"Loveland doesn't have a gondola," I said mildly.

"She has no consideration for other people's feelings. If I had a teen-age son, I wouldn't let him near such danger. They classify it as an extreme sport. I saw that on the news the other day. Some ski areas won't allow it," she said smugly, blowing smoke toward me.

I turned my head and coughed. "Don't you think Fran's careful?"

Ruth showed no sign of hearing. "Frances has lost her senses. She has a whole new language: freshies, ollies, big air, schwag. I can't keep up. Nor do I care to. One day, she called me 'dude' and told me she wanted to introduce me to her 'posse.' That was the final straw as far as I was concerned. The things I've put up with over the years. She never did share my taste in fashion. I used to buy all her clothes. Frances once said she'd shop only when they opened a black slacks store. Look at her now. She won't wear a pair of slacks. She goes around in sweat pants and bawdy T-shirts. Everything is baggy. She claims that's the 'in thing,' but what sort of image does that portray?"

I studiously avoided looking at Ruth's rabbit-head slippers. Instead, I fiddled with a bottle of medicine on the table between us and noticed with alarm that the prescription was in Janet Howard's name. Damn, had Ruth and Janet moved in together already?

Ruth didn't notice my distraction or concern, such was her single-minded focus on using the remote to flip between four news broadcasts as she continued her diatribe. "How much was I expected to tolerate? Her hollering at the television set in football season. Watching games Saturday, Sunday, Monday, and Thursday. Her playing golf with younger women. Tee times at dawn and dusk. Her assignments with you. Taking unnecessary risks and staying out all hours. Her caring about every stray soul who crossed her path, as if we were still in the convent. We retired a long time ago, or so I thought, but Frances won't quit."

"Maybe she's—"

"I decided I'd had enough when she told me she fell off the ski lift. She laughed it off, but it could have been serious. Some kids sat down too soon, and by the time the chair came to her, there was no room. She tried to hold on with her arms, but a woman her age doesn't have the strength. The people at the ski area gave her a coupon for a cup of hot chocolate, and she thought that was fair."

"She wasn't injured, was she?" I asked innocently.

"No, but she very well could have been." Ruth shook her cigarette at me. "And if it doesn't happen this season, it will soon, mark my words. Her goal is to go heli-boarding before she turns seventy. Ride in a helicopter to the top of a mountain and come down 'virgin tracks.' Whatever in heaven's name those are. She's told me, but I don't try to understand."

Not knowing how much more tirade I could swallow, I opted for accelerated bluntness. "Did you have Fran kicked out of the Gertrude Center?"

"That sour puss! I did nothing of the sort. Other members thought she had taken advantage of her former position. Being founder of the club doesn't mean you can rewrite the rules to suit yourself. The bylaws clearly state members are supposed to use the guest suite for no more than seven days."

"Haven't other women bent that rule? Haven't some stayed for months?"

She stared at the television. "Frances always was selfish. I might need the room myself next week when I have the apartment painted. I may have mentioned that desire to one or two people, but I didn't conspire against her. She certainly has an overactive imagination."

Without preamble, I rose to leave, but couldn't resist one last question. "Don't you miss Fran at all?"

Ruth bellowed over the increased volume of a commercial, "We had as much relationship as I cared to have. It had a beginning, a middle, and an end. I'm satisfied I've done the right thing, for my own physical and mental health."

On that downer, I exited with more haste than grace.

Chapter 15

"I'm distraught. I'm beside myself with worry. Why would someone do this?"

My head felt as if it had split in two from a combination of little sleep the night before and a dream about me and Ruth sharing a bed in a nursing home.

This, the first call of the day, further frayed my nerves. Nonetheless, I mustered a soothing voice and said, "Calm down. Tell me what happened."

"Someone took baby Jesus from the south manger," Clarice Crumpler replied in a quivering voice.

"We'll get him back," I said, silently giving thanks for the surveillance system Fran had installed. "All we have to do is check the tape."

"No, dear, that won't work. Eunice unplugged the camera last night. She blamed it on the cat, but I know she did it."

"Why?" I practically shouted, exasperated.

"My sister wanted to watch her favorite show," Clarice said meekly.

I blinked furiously. "But aren't there other televisions in the house?"

"Three, but she insists the one in the living room has the best reception. I told her she should be ashamed of herself, after all the time you and Fran put into helping us. And now, this, the son of God, stolen!"

"What did Eunice say?"

"She said I was the one who should be ashamed. You can't reason with her when she gets like this. There's no sense trying."

"You're sure the tape recorded nothing?"

"I'm afraid so. I'm not very good with technology. I can barely use the portable phone I'm on. You can hear me, can't you?" she asked loudly.

"Yes," I muttered.

"Very well then. I watched the tape this morning, and all I saw were black and white squiggles. You may look for yourself, if you'd like."

"No," I said, completely discouraged. "That means nothing recorded."

"Oh, my," Clarice Crumpler said, near tears. "We'll never see baby Jesus again, will we?"

"We'll find him," I promised, a vow I made more in the interest of getting off the phone than from certainty.

Several hours later, as I drove to LoDo, the trendy area at the western edge of downtown, I congratulated myself for delegating the Crumpler case. Fran had accepted the assignment with gumption, assuring me she'd wrap it up quickly and completely.

Her confidence had eased my mind, allowing me to concentrate on my interview with Deborah Kennedy. Using the connection of Rebecca Ramirez, the teacher Lori Parks had fired, I'd tracked down Lori's high school friend and secured a lunchtime appointment at her loft on Larimer Street.

It took three trips around the block before I found an open meter a hundred yards from the entrance to the Sugar Lofts, a turn-of-the-century brick warehouse that had been converted into residences.

As I passed through the lobby, wiping slop from snowmelt on the industrial carpet runner, I admired the designer's taste. Gleaming hardwood floors, miniature track lighting, potted plants, and original oil paintings all conveyed understated elegance.

I took a freight elevator to the top floor of the four-story building and knocked on Deborah Kennedy's door.

When she showed me in, I was torn between staring out west windows that provided an unobstructed view of the snow-capped Rockies and gaping at her. I hadn't come with a preconceived notion of what one of Lori Parks' childhood friends would look like, yet this one surprised me.

For starters, she was tall, well over six feet, and she rose to the full extent of her spine proudly. She wore black silk pants, a short-sleeve knit sweater, and a tapestry vest that accentuated her slender waist. She had prematurely white kinky hair that swept past her long forehead and well beyond her shoulders. Everything about her seemed long—long hair, long teeth, long fingers, long nails, long nose. She favored heavy make-up, but it couldn't completely mask pock-marked skin.

She welcomed me into her home and seated me on a short couch, low to the floor. From the adjoining dining room, she dragged a captain's chair and pulled next to me. Although a large coffee table separated us, I couldn't escape the feeling that she loomed over me. The light coming in the windows, conveniently at her back, almost blinded me.

She offered me a stick of gum, which I refused, and lustily began to chew a piece herself.

"Deb—" I began.

"Call me Deborah," she said with a broad smile.

"Fair enough. Deborah—"

She interrupted again as she adjusted the five gold rings on her fingers. "How's Lori?"

"A little worried about these threats," I said briefly. Over the phone, in the interest of securing cooperation, I'd given Deborah a bare outline of what had happened at the Children's Academy.

She gazed at me with acute fascination. "Is she happy?"

"She's a successful businesswoman," I said with trepidation.

"Is she in a relationship?"

"Yes."

"With a woman?"

"Donna. They have an eight-year-old daughter, Erica."

"You're kidding!" she said, her astonishment mixed with jealousy.

"She's a sweetheart, Erica that is. Extremely bright and likable."

"Does Lori still have that mischievous look, the half-wink when she smiles?"

"I hadn't noticed," I said truthfully.

"Is her hair still red?"

"Sort of." Artificially.

"I miss her," she said wistfully, studying the clear polish on her manicured nails.

"You could call her."

"Did she ask me to?"

"No, but you—"

"I couldn't," Deborah said, clipped. "After the ski trip, I tried to stay in touch but eventually gave up. We couldn't talk about the weekend. Or Jodi. Or Liz's injuries. It was futile."

"Liz was your close friend?"

Deborah nodded. "Still is. She and I have been best friends since elementary school."

"What injuries did Liz suffer?"

"She lost part of her leg, from about mid-calf."

Another Lori Parks omission. All at once, I felt hot enough to faint. I discreetly searched under my armpits for moisture and shuddered when the radiator hissed out another round. "Does Liz live around here?"

"A few miles away, in northwest Denver."

"And you survived the ordeal without any injuries?"

"No major physical ones. I had frostbite on my hands, but doctors treated it. The tissue is still sensitive, but when it acts up, I take a two or three Advil."

I leaned back on the couch and studied her closely. "How did the trip affect you emotionally?"

Deborah took a shallow breath and crossed her legs. "In a lot of ways, actually. I started drinking heavily, living fast, like every day could be my last. I couldn't keep up that pace for long. After the winter break, I returned to college in Boulder but dropped out after a week."

"Why?"

She blinked slowly and massaged her forehead. "Mostly because I wanted to support Liz in what she was going through. I couldn't keep up with the classes and studying and commuting back and forth to the hospital in Denver. I moved back home, thinking Liz and I would skip a semester and go back in the fall."

"You didn't?"

"No, Liz wasn't ready, and my heart wasn't in it. When I'd gone back for that week in January, everything seemed trivial. The girls around me worried about their hair or which weekend party they'd attend. I couldn't tolerate that bullshit. I'd faced down death, but I couldn't deal with life. Contrary to what other people with near-death experiences have reported, life isn't precious. It's small and meaningless, or at least it was from my perspective."

"Did you ever get your degree?"

"No, and only about five years ago did I stop regretting that. I wanted to be a journalist, and instead, I went back to work in my family's restaurant. Food's in my blood, I guess."

"What kind of work do you do?"

"I'm district manager for Surf City. I work out of an office in the back of the loft," she said gesturing toward a room off the kitchen.

"I love your fish tacos. I eat take-out from the restaurant on Colorado Boulevard at least once a week."

"Next time you're in, tell Charlotte to give you the Deborah Deluxe, on the house. It's a special concoction she makes for me. You'll love it."

"Thanks, I will. Back to the ski trip, for a moment, if you don't mind—"

"Not at all."

"How did it come about?"

"Lori planned it. She wrote to me in October to tell me she was coming home for Christmas and would be bringing a friend from Middlebury."

"Jodi Wilde?"

Deborah nodded.

"They were lovers then?"

"Probably, but Lori neglected to mention that in her letter."

"Would it have made a difference?"

Deborah pondered. "It might have. I think it made Liz uncomfortable, but I found it amusing watching Lori try to prove something."

"Such as?"

"She was a lesbian and proud of it, even if I wasn't."

"You were straight?"

Deborah smiled wryly. "I don't have a straight impulse in my body. Lori made a pass at me in high school and misunderstood my rejection. Her ego wouldn't allow her to see I chased after women, practically every woman back then, but not her."

"When Lori wrote and suggested the trip, you and Liz agreed to go?"

"Liz took some persuading. She'd only been downhill skiing, never cross-country, but I convinced her we'd have a good time."

"Had you cross-country skied much?"

"Maybe ten times. Day trips, mostly with Lori."

"The overnight aspect didn't concern you?"

"Not at all. I thought we'd have a ball, out in the middle of nowhere, playing cards, drinking schnapps. I figured it would be similar to two short day trips, except we'd lug in food and sleeping gear. Really, it should have been easier. We had to ski four miles to Heartbreak Hut, over mostly flat terrain. That's nothing."

"Heartbreak Hut?"

"Ironic, but true." Deborah Kennedy laughed, a booming sound that scared me a little. "Named after a miner who died in a camp nearby, after a hard life of never striking gold. A little Colorado history lesson."

I smiled. "You had no apprehension about the rigors of the trip?"

"None. I knew I could hold my own, and I love adventure."

"Didn't the winter weather make you nervous?" I prodded.

"Just the opposite. The night before the trip, we stayed in Winter Glades, in the cabin Lori's parents owned. It snowed heavily from about dusk on, and we were ecstatic. Like little kids, we jumped up to look out the window, measured the snowfall on the sill, predicted how deep it would be by morning. We couldn't get enough. There's nothing better than skiing through fresh powder, gliding without sound. No squeak, no crunch, no grating, just silence. I hoped for a foot of snow."

"How much fell?"

"About nine inches. We couldn't complain."

"So you had fun that first night, in the cabin?"

"We did. I loved meeting Jodi. She was a cute, mellow girl. And it was good to catch up with Lori."

"How about Liz, did she enjoy herself?"

"Not entirely. Lori's displays of affection made Liz uncomfortable. Lori couldn't keep her hands off Jodi, and Liz wasn't used to anyone being that demonstrative. She comes from a conservative family. A hug's a big deal for her. I took it in stride, but it was inconsiderate. The morning after, they looked like they'd gotten an hour's worth of sleep between the two of them. Lucky girls," she said enviously.

"Was it still snowing in the morning?"

"Heavily."

"Did you consider canceling the trip?"

"Jodi expressed apprehension, but we talked her out of it. I told her skiing was easy, and Lori told her she wouldn't have to break trail, that we'd do the hard work. Honestly, even with the snow and weather, we planned on a two-hour trek to the hut, three at the most. Getting off to a late start didn't help, but we had plenty of cushion."

"How late?"

"We wanted to leave by nine, to be at the trailhead thirty minutes later. That timeline went out the window when Lori and Jodi didn't come out of their room until close to ten. By the time we packed and organized everything, it was almost noon."

"What time did you arrive at the trail?"

"Close to one o'clock. We were so far behind schedule, we decided to eat in the car. We had a cozy picnic, steamed up the windows, and dropped crumbs everywhere. Lori got mad because it was her mom's station wagon, but we told her we'd clean it up when we got back. We were finishing our lunch when some guy banged on the window and asked what we thought we were doing."

"Who was he?"

"A local. He told us we'd never make it to Heartbreak Hut in those conditions, not that day. Lori laughed and rolled up the window in his face."

"He tried to warn you?" I said, incredulous.

"I suppose he did," Deborah said casually. "At the time, we dismissed him as a male chauvinist know-it-all, but obviously, he knew the area better than we did. I later heard he was on the rescue team that brought us out, so I guess we should have listened."

I shook my head in amazement. After all these years, Deborah Kennedy still couldn't absorb the full impact of that understatement.

She spoke up, her voice rising an octave. "But we didn't. We piled out of the car, threw on our backpacks, and skied straight into the blizzard."

That night, I tossed and turned for more than an hour, sometimes reliving the horror of the three nights the four women had spent in an unforgiving wilderness, more often recalling the damning fact Lori Parks had conveniently excluded.

At the end of our meeting, as Deborah had walked me to the door, she'd mentioned, almost in passing, that Liz could never forgive Lori.

"Liz always felt Lori should have used her experience and judgment to call it off. She'd been in those mountains hundreds of times."

I'd looked at Deborah Kennedy, disbelieving. "That many?"

"Every winter weekend. Lori didn't tell you?"

I'd struggled to keep hold of my temper. "What?"

"About her nordic achievements?"

I'd drawn in a sharp breath and let it out slowly. "No."

"Lori skied competitively in junior high and high school."

Before I could absorb this stunner, Deborah had added, "She was ranked nationally, one of the top ten junior women in the country."

Chapter 16

"If I want your opinion, I'll give it to you."

In the early morning hours the next day, it took my foggy mind a few beats to comprehend Fran Green's T-shirt. She didn't wait for me to catch up. She threw her coat, cap, and gloves on the couch and began to pace, in an excited state. "Cross the Crumpler handyman off the list of suspects."

I diverted my attention away from the notes I'd been studying on Lori Parks, Deborah Kennedy, Liz Decker, and Jodi Wilde. "Leonard's innocent?"

"A saint. Saw him taking away one of the skinny snowmen. Confronted him. Told me he takes 'em away for refinishing. Doesn't want to charge the ladies. Enjoys doing it."

"Why didn't he tell me that?" I said, annoyed. I'd spent an hour with Leonard Maynard the morning of the Baker-Brown house tour and had discovered nothing useful.

"No need to bristle, kiddo. Couldn't trust you."

"Why?"

"You talk too fast."

"I do not. When I do, it's only because I'm nervous or my thoughts are coming too quickly, and I don't want to lose one," I said rapidly. "Plus, since when is that criteria for whether you like someone?"

"Better notch it down, girl. Ain't just your speech pattern."

"He must be homophobic."

"Didn't object to this birdie-loving-birdie. 'Course, probably helped I brought a few afternoon delights."

"So did I. Morning ones. Coffee and biscotti."

"Doesn't drink coffee."

"Neither do I, but I thought he might like some."

"Never heard of biscotti."

"I gathered that," I said, my voice dripping with scorn.

"Me, took him the refreshment any man can appreciate, a six-pack of Miller."

"How generous of you."

"Of you," Fran corrected with relish. "Be submitting it on my expense report."

"Great."

"No need for huffy, Kris. Takes teamwork sometimes. Case solved, thanks to Leonard."

I peered at Fran. "He told you who's taking parts of the Crumplers' display?"

"Good as," she boasted. "Give me one more visit to verify, and I'll hand you the thief."

"Who is?"

"Can't say?"

"Why?"

"Promised Leonard. He doesn't trust you."

"You already told me that," I said crossly. "Funny how you two managed to become fast friends."

"Sure is," she said, highly pleased with herself.

My voice rose. "With someone who has a gun rack on his F-350 truck?"

"Man's got to eat."

"Who stares at women's chests?" I said disdainfully.

Fran glanced down. "Not much to look at here. Speaking of racks, though," she made a point of leering at my chest and guffawed.

I was not amused. "This is my case, Fran."

"Thought it belonged to both of us. Informal partnership."

"Not anymore," I said coldly. "Not when you're trying to exclude me."

"Doing nothing of the sort," she said evenly. "You know me better than that."

"Then give me the name of the suspect."

Fran crossed her arms across her chest and stopped pacing. "Can't. Gave my word."

I looked at her speculatively. "It's not Tony and Alison, across the street."

Her face didn't change expression. "Didn't say it was."

"They want the neighborhood award, but it wouldn't mean anything if they won by destroying the Crumplers' display."

"Funny you should say that. Same observation Leonard made. Man doesn't miss much."

"And Florence Bailey can't lift anything."

"Couldn't agree more. Had to help her get the newspaper off the porch."

"He thinks it's kids in the neighborhood, doesn't he?" I said excitedly. "Someone who lives nearby?"

Fran shrugged her shoulders. "Interesting question, that one."

"Someone who objects to the display?"

"Getting warm, Kris, darn near toasty. But can't say. Have to wait a few days."

"All right," I said, pushing my chair away from the desk and rising. "I'll go visit your friend Leonard myself."

"Wouldn't do that if I were you," Fran said, shrewd eyes sizing me up. "Waste of time and gas."

"Then I'll solve it without him," I said hotly.

"Wouldn't try that either. Got your plate full with the Parks case. Threats. Children involved. Let me wrap this baby up."

"But it was *my* case," I said, dropping back into my seat.

"Honor to share it with you," Fran said heartily, coming around to pat me on the shoulder.

"You're not better at this than I am," I said darkly.

"Never claimed to be."

"We have different approaches."

"That's it," she said kindly.

"Sometimes my way works better."

"Couldn't agree more."

I shook my head, still in disbelief. "How did you do it—other than the liquor?"

"We compared ink stains. Man loved my rose."

My eyes widened. "You have a tattoo?"

"Small one, top right breast. Heck, with the sag, might be middle now. Could be long-stemmed."

I cracked a thin smile. "Too much information."

"My little bud nothing compared to his artwork. Entire story on his arms, continued on the back. Lost the train of thought there, too much hair."

"You bonded over tattoos?"

"That and my do," she said pointing to the top of her head. "Wants his wife to wear it like this. Short, gray, no fuss."

"He has a wife?"

"Six. Consecutive, not concurrent. Told him about me and Ruth. Same thing happened to him with wife four. For the best, too. Led him to wife five."

"Which must not have been a happy leap, if six came along," I said, with a smirk.

"Curb that cynicism, Kris. Five died of breast cancer."

"Sorry."

"Make fun if you will, but it gave me hope talking to him. Made me believe my number two's around the corner. Can't wait to see Leonard tomorrow."

"What's tomorrow?"

"Private time. Nothing to do with the case."

"What are you up to?"

"No good," she said with a maniacal giggle.

I tried to imagine what Fran Green and Leonard Maynard could do together. "Gambling?"

"Too much smoke."

"Strip club?"

"Too much grease."

"C'mon, tell me!"

"More fun to torment, but I'll spill. He's teaching me to drive."

"What happened to your AAA lessons? Safety geared toward mature drivers?"

"Auto club teaches automatic only. Need to learn clutch. Three on the tree, four on the floor. Don't worry, though, won't distract me from the Crumpler case."

I looked at her sideways. "And you don't need my help?"

"No, siree. Just be in the way."

"Okay," I said innocently. "Thanks for taking care of it."

"No problem." She returned my smile and added a wink. "Never let you down."

As soon as Fran left, my smile imploded.

Screw Leonard Maynard.

I refused to be shown up by a handyman. Or by Fran Green.

I'd go out and lie on the cold ground under the Crumpler hedges if that's what it took. I'd spend all day and all night until I got to the bottom of this. Nothing more would be stolen on my watch—nothing!

Maybe I didn't sport a tattoo or drink beer, but I had a hell of a lot of brain cells.

And I'd use every one of them if I had to.

I'd show them!

An hour later, I'd calmed down enough to find Liz Decker's house in the Highlands neighborhood. The enclave, up the hill from downtown, had experienced an increase in property values, but not much appreciation had reached the block where I parked. While Liz's small bungalow had all of its siding intact, the same couldn't be said for neighboring homes, and too many residents had used the previous summer's watering restrictions as an excuse for neglect. In contrast to Liz's manicured lawn, most others had deteriorated to dirt and weeds, which poked out among patches of brown snow.

I passed through a short, white picket gate and followed three signs that directed me to the side entrance for "White Feather Massage Studio." Careful not to ruffle the string of Tibetan prayer flags hanging from the railing, I picked my way down narrow cellar stairs.

I knocked on the ajar door, and let myself in, calling out, "Hello."

"Be right there," came the reply. It took my eyes a minute to adjust to the darkness. A table-top lamp with a low-watt bulb served as the only electrical source of illumination. Dozens of lavender candles burned, but the flames added more atmosphere than light, and heavy cloth covered the two book-sized windows. On first impression—other than the smell of mildew—I felt as if I'd entered a temple. In compliance with the directive on the door, I removed my shoes and tried to get my bearings among the dozens of crystals hanging from the ceiling.

From the shadows of an adjoining room, Liz Decker crossed to greet me. She shook my hand with a light touch and gestured for me to make myself comfortable on pillows on the floor.

In the dim light, I surmised she had gray hair, streaked with remnants of her original blonde. She'd pulled it back into a complex braid and pasted a brightly-colored faux stone to the middle of her forehead. Beaded bracelets extended halfway up both arms, and her purple tent-like smock hid substantial paunch, which tightened into rolls when she sat.

She offered me tea to drink, which I declined but should have accepted as a handwarmer. The lone space heater in the corner had done little to make the room warmer than the fifty-five degrees outside.

Oblivious to the cold, Liz lounged comfortably among three pillows. After about ten minutes, I had grown accustomed to the darkness, to her soft-spoken voice, and to her prosthetic limb, which she made no attempt to conceal.

Liz zeroed in on the reason for my visit before I could. "Deb hinted Lori Parks might be in some kind of trouble."

I said sparingly, "Lori's received threats at her school."

"The Children's Academy?"

"You know about it?"

"Only from the news. I haven't seen Lori since they put me in the ambulance in Winter Glades."

My mouth opened in dismay, and I had to blink hard before continuing. "We can't tie the threats into anything in her life today—"

"And you want to delve into her murky past?" Liz interrupted sarcastically.

"Something like that."

"And because of our ill-fated adventure, you have a host of suspects who may hate Lori, including me, right?"

"I didn't mean to imply—"

"It's all right," she said, unabashed. "I should despise her, but I don't. Mostly, I feel sorry for her."

"Why? She walked away without a scratch," I said, instantly regretting my choice of words.

"And I came away without a foot," Liz said, reacting calmly to my slip. "But I never felt guilty. If Lori Parks has a conscience, she'll never forgive herself."

"For surviving without injury?"

"For the way she treated Jodi Wilde the last seventy-two hours of her life."

I frowned in confusion. "I thought she adored her, was madly in love, couldn't keep her hands off her?"

Liz surveyed me keenly. "Is that what Lori told you?"

I shifted on the pillows, scrambling for support for my aching lower back. "Partially. Deborah filled me in, too."

"Well, the feeling apparently wasn't as mutual as they might have led you to believe."

"How do you know?"

"Jodi broke up with Lori," Liz said coolly. "The night before we started skiing."

Chapter 17

I stared at Liz Decker. She returned my confused gaze, never blinking. Questions raced through my mind, but I couldn't clutch one long enough to express it.

Liz broke the silence. "Jodi told me Sunday, when we were looking for wood, right before we fell in the stream. Lori had made her swear she wouldn't say anything to Deb or me on the trip, but she couldn't keep it in."

My head began to throb. "Why did Jodi break up with Lori?"

"Because she didn't want to be gay."

"Jodi said that?"

"Those were her exact words. I've considered them often over the years, as I've struggled with my own sexuality."

"Are you gay?" I asked gingerly.

"I suppose," she said, her face turning red. "I probably don't have sex often enough to qualify as a lesbian, but that's the label I'd choose."

"I don't think we have a quota," I said mildly.

"I like that." Her shoulders relaxed, but both hands remained clenched in fists.

"Why didn't Jodi want to be gay?"

"Because of her mother."

I looked at Liz doubtfully. "Most parents aren't thrilled when they hear the news, but they get over it, or we get over them . . ." My voice trailed off.

"Her mother was more extreme than most. When Jodi was sixteen, she told her mother she was in love with her best friend. Her mother walked into the kitchen, grabbed a steak knife, and stabbed herself in the stomach."

My eyes widened in shock. "She committed suicide?"

"She lived and made her point."

I couldn't keep the surprise out of my voice. "How do you know all this?"

"Jodi confided in me on the ski trip. It was something she hadn't told anyone."

"She must have trusted you, to have told you about her mother and the break-up with Lori."

Liz's features softened. "She did."

"When Jodi broke up with Lori, did you hear them fighting?"

"No. Deb and I were in a separate wing of the cabin."

"And you didn't notice anything in the morning?"

"Not at first. At the cabin, we were focused on dressing and packing. But I did pick up on something when we unloaded our skis at the trailhead. Jodi suggested kiddingly we should go back to the cabin and drink hot chocolate and play cards. Lori snapped at her that she'd had reservations for this trip for months and wasn't going to miss it. That was awkward, but it got worse when Jodi fell."

"What happened?"

"We'd been skiing for about an hour when she went down a slight pitch. One of her skis slipped out of the track, causing her to topple over. Nothing major, but it scared her, and she started to cry. She couldn't get up right away, not because of injury, just the clumsiness of skis, poles, and bindings when you're not used to them."

"What did Lori do?"

"Nothing. She was right behind her, and she stood there, watching. I had to ski around her to get to Jodi. That's when I said we should turn back. At the time, I had no idea what was going on, but I knew I wasn't having fun. We couldn't see three feet in front of us, we were freezing, and I couldn't imagine the situation improving."

"So you turned back?"

Liz prolonged a deep sigh. "No. Deb didn't care what we did, Jodi wouldn't speak up, and Lori insisted on pushing forward, with or without us. We had no choice but to follow her. Less than an hour later, we lost the trail at a section where avalanche debris had covered the tracks."

"You turned around then?"

Liz shook her head. "It was too late. The weather was worse—snow blowing horizontally—and Jodi wouldn't have made it back. She was so tired, she was falling every few feet or so."

Suddenly, the room felt chillier than when I'd arrived. Instinctively, I blew on my hands.

Liz, noticing my discomfort, said, "Are you cold?"

"A little."

"I could get you a blanket," she said, rolling over and starting to rise with a grunt.

"No, don't bother," I said hastily, not wanting to lose the thread of conversation. "That's when you decided to spend the night?"

Liz settled back in and nodded somberly. "It was almost dark, what with the clouds and the low light. We worked as fast as we could to clear a space under a pine tree, away from the wind, and to cover it with boughs so we wouldn't have to lie directly on the ground. We found branches to reinforce the sides, and we broke off lower-hanging dead limbs and twigs for firewood. We treated it as an adventure. We had plenty to eat, lots of water, sleeping bags. And we were still warm from moving around."

"It sounds like you have almost fond memories of that first night."

"I do. For one thing, I could still feel my foot. And I remember this intense feeling of being in the moment. My mind was empty, and I felt completely calm. No future or past existed. Time didn't stand still exactly, but it no longer pushed from both sides."

"You didn't feel scared?"

"Not particularly. I fully expected to ski out early in the morning."

"Did you try skiing at daybreak?"

"We couldn't," Liz said, a despair underlying her words. "If I hadn't looked at my watch, I wouldn't have known it was dawn. By morning, the snow was falling so heavily, it created this white shroud. And the texture of it had changed. Friday, it fell in soft, dry flakes. Saturday, it pelted us with hard, wet crystals. We made it through the day and night, but when I woke up Sunday, I felt horrible. That first moment of waking, when I realized where I was, that's when I knew we might die."

"Did the others feel the same?"

"We didn't talk about it. We just coped."

"Were Lori and Jodi still fighting?"

"Subtly. Lori avoided looking at Jodi or addressing her. Jodi overcompensated with perkiness, most of which Lori ignored."

"What was the plan when you woke up Sunday?"

"To wait out the storm. We couldn't do anything else."

"No one wanted to leave?"

"Only Lori. About noon, she announced she was tired of sitting around like a victim. She wanted to head back in the direction we'd come, toward the car—just a little ways, she promised—to see what the trail was like. Deb agreed to go with her, and they said they'd be back in ten minutes. Two hours later, when they hadn't returned, I told Jodi we needed to find more firewood. The amount we had wouldn't have lasted the rest of the afternoon, much less the night."

Liz gazed off, took a huge breath, and said, almost in a whisper, "Jodi agreed. She thought it was a good idea."

"I'm sure it was," I said gently.

"We had no idea we were near a stream. There was no sound of running water, no warning. We thought we were in a meadow when we heard the crack. We were within sight of the camp, no more than a hundred yards away when Jodi fell through the ice. She was in the lead and turned to warn me when I saw her sink to her waist. I tried to backtrack, but my right foot broke through before I could get to solid ground. Soaked, we both started shivering violently. A few minutes later, Lori and Deb reappeared."

"Where had they been?"

"They never said." Liz absentmindedly stroked her artificial leg. "Lori started screaming at me and Jodi for our stupidity and weakness, and Deb ran around trying to gather more firewood."

"I take it you don't have fond memories of that night, your third on the mountain?"

"No," Liz said, jerking involuntarily. "I couldn't focus on anything but my foot. I had an extra pair of dry socks in my backpack, but no other boots."

"What about Jodi?"

"She was in agony. Deb helped her change out of her wet clothes and into dry sweat pants, but she never warmed up."

"She died Sunday night, correct?"

"Technically, early Monday. Sometime after midnight, I could still hear her whimpering. I reached out and held her hand, which was shaking. In an eerie way, it was one of the most beautiful moments of my life. The storm had moved out, and we had spectacular moonlight, almost blinding, stars everywhere. Jodi said it felt like we were lying in the sky."

Liz became still and paused before a heavy exhale. "That's all I remember until Deb woke up screaming Jodi was dead. She'd felt the stiffness when she rolled over in the morning."

I blinked back tears. "She was on the other side of Jodi?"

Liz nodded. "The three of us had to share two sleeping bags, because the night before, Deb's had gotten wet and was ruined."

I tried to stifle my bewilderment. "What about Lori?"

Liz's face hardened. "She had her own bag, and she wasn't speaking to any of us. After her rant about our stupidity ended, the silent treatment began. Deb tried a few times to ask what was wrong, but she wouldn't answer. Lori had given up."

"On surviving?"

"On us! She was damn sure going to get out alive, but she didn't credit any of us with the strength to join her."

"How did Lori react to Jodi's death?" I said bleakly.

"Knowing Lori, you'd think she would have gone into a rage, but she didn't. Calm as could be, she began to undress Jodi."

I groaned aloud. "Why?"

"She said we needed her clothes to survive. Deb protested and tried to stop her, but I was too shocked to move. I did tell her I didn't need them. I'm proud of that. I wanted to leave Jodi with some dignity, even if it cost me my health. To leave her lying there, completely naked . . ."

Liz checked herself, then added in a controlled tone, "Lori didn't have to take her bra and underwear. No one needed those to survive."

I could see my distaste mirrored in her eyes, but I said nothing.

Liz swallowed hard. "Deb and I covered Jodi, as best we could, with tree branches, but I still remember how she looked. Her skin was all different colors from frostbite—no one should have to die like that. When the rescue team arrived a few hours later, you could see the horror on those guys' faces. I'll never forget the way they looked at me, and I was barely alive myself. Doctors told me my body temperature had dropped to eighty-eight degrees, and I'd started hallucinating. I imagined myself taking a warm shower, and when they first covered me with a coat, I threw it off. I was out of it. Still, I explicitly remember the shame."

"The rescuers blamed you for Jodi's death?"

"I'm not sure they were attached to our outcome one way or the other, but they resented what had happened to Paul Switzer. I heard them discussing his condition as they prepared us for transport."

"Paul Switzer?"

"One of the rescuers. He crashed his snowmobile on Flagler Pass while he was searching for us Sunday afternoon."

Every muscle in my neck begin to spasm. "Did he die?"

"No, but he broke his back," Liz said casually, "and is paralyzed."

Chapter 18

Maybe having a disability makes it easier to shrug off someone else's.

I spent the better part of Friday night contemplating this as I huddled in the Crumplers' garden. If I plugged my ears tightly, I could almost block out the cacophony of Christmas carols, which allowed me to analyze events of the past few days.

Deborah Kennedy. She didn't strike me as vengeful. A happy-go-lucky sort, she seemed to view the ski trip as a bump in the road, one that may have caused a detour, but certainly not a derailment. In fact, the most striking comment she'd made during our interview came after she mentioned she went into the backcountry almost every weekend. When I expressed surprise that she felt comfortable in the wilderness, she answered with a serene look on her face, "The only time my heart is at rest is when I'm in the mountains."

Liz Decker. The ski trip had been more catastrophic for her. She'd entered the woods wary of Lori Parks and exited permanently disabled. I couldn't rule her out as a suspect because I couldn't shake the feeling that despite claims she had no reason to feel culpable, she had indeed been the group's lightening rod for guilt. Liz could erect altars, adopt Buddhist traditions, and feng-shui every inch of her White Feather Massage Studio, but none of it would erase the anguish of those four days. Yet, she seemed to realize Lori had extinguished her grief long before rescuers had arrived. I couldn't envision Liz Decker using notes or pranks to reignite it twenty years later.

This led me to two questions at the core of the case: Who suffered the most as a result of the ski trip? And who was ignorant enough to believe Lori Parks could be made to suffer?

The next natural path of inquiry lead to Paul Switzer, the man who had lost his livelihood and nearly his life. I'd track him down in the morning. I'd also do my best to locate Jodi Wilde's family. Given the mother's mental health history—knife to the gut when her daughter had told her she was gay—the stunts someone had pulled at the Children's Academy seemed within the realm of possibility.

At the stroke of nine that night, the Crumpler sisters extinguished the Christmas lights and music, and I strained to keep my eyes open.

By midnight, after spending three hours in complete darkness with nary a rustle on the estate, boredom overcame stubbornness, and I headed home to the warmth of Destiny.

Saturday morning brought Fran Green to the doorstep of my office. Upon seeing her, I felt a pang of guilt and hoped she wouldn't ask about my previous night's activities.

As soon as she came close, I couldn't corral my shock. "Is that makeup?

"Don't know what you mean," Fran said, all innocent.

I squinted. "You have blush on your cheeks."

"Must be the poor lighting. Need to replace two bulbs," she said gruffly, pointing to the track of lights overhead.

"You look good." I nodded my approval. "Mary Kay?"

"How'd you know?"

"You told me you met a rep at your women's networking group."

"Couldn't say no."

"Did you try?"

Fran chuckled softly. "Not too hard. Gal gave me a free makeover. Looked like a tramp when she finished, but bought $200 worth of product. Don't even know what I got."

"She must have been cute."

Fran snapped her fingers. "Put it this way, I'll need to reorder soon."

"So, you thought you'd try some enhancements?"

Fran shrugged. "Had to see how the other half lives. Can't see the appeal. Takes too long. Smears off. Stinks. Hides wrinkles. Gives off the wrong color."

"Still, you're wearing it. What's the occasion?"

Fran looked chagrined. "Nothing special. Casual night out."

"Oh, really?" I raised one eyebrow, lowered it, and raised the other.

"Nothing that would interest a prude like you. Checking out a night-club, Dorothy's. Women's bar on Federal Boulevard."

I wrestled to keep judgment out of my voice. "Have you been there before?"

"Nope. Haven't stepped foot in that type establishment in decades. High time I started."

"How will you get there?"

"Bus. Take a cab home. Better yet, get an escort, if you catch my drift."

"Are you sure you're ready for this?"

"Can't wait. Speaking of, don't you and Destiny leave a light on. May not be catching much shut-eye tonight."

I eyed her with concern. "Seriously? Are you meeting someone there?"

"Hope so, but no one I know yet."

I frowned. "Be careful, Fran. You're vulnerable now. It might not be a good idea to—"

"Horse puckey. Put the men and children away, heh, heh. Fran Green's comin' to town."

"I don't know—"

"Fill you in on the details in the A-M," Fran said, firmly ending the discussion with her tone and look.

•••

"I met Jodi Wilde the first day I arrived on campus at Middlebury," Lori Parks said, a hint of color returning to her cheeks. "As I unloaded my car, she offered to help. From then on, we were inseparable."

That afternoon, I'd left a message for Lori, and as agreed, she'd returned my call immediately and agreed to meet within the hour.

We'd chosen a coffeehouse in Cherry Creek, and she'd arrived on time. I was halfway through a mug of hot chocolate. Lori was on her fifth cup of coffee.

I hadn't seen Lori Parks since Tuesday, and she looked as if she hadn't slept or eaten in that period. Her gaunt appearance highlighted deep grooves in her forehead and around her mouth, but she'd taken her customary care in dressing. She wore tight-fitting blue jeans, an ivory cashmere sweater with a collar that resembled a neck brace, and a wool tweed jacket with leather buttons. Her dark brown boots with two-inch heels looked brand new.

Earlier in our conversation, I'd told her I'd met with Deborah Kennedy and Liz Decker and that they'd separately recounted memories of the ski trip. Lori had nodded curtly at this information but made no attempt to inquire about her former friends. I'd told her neither had received threats or been subjected to odd incidents, but as her wishful thinking mounted, I'd added that I still felt the Academy incidents shared a connection with the ski trip.

"When did you and Jodi become lovers?"

"About a month after we met."

"Were you her first?"

"She'd had a girlfriend in high school. She came home from school one day and announced she wanted to be a lesbian. Her mother had a fit. Jodi never told me exactly what happened, but it must have traumatized her because she broke it off with the girl."

"Was Jodi your first lover?"

"Yes. I'd had intense crushes on girls but nothing physical."

"Was she excited about the trip to Colorado?"

"We both were. I couldn't wait to introduce her to my friends and share my favorite places with her. She'd never been west of Chicago, and coming to Colorado gave her an out. Her sister, Jill, had become engaged recently, and Jodi wanted to skip the wedding planning and congratulations. Mostly, though, we didn't want to be apart for a month."

"Jodi had never skied before?"

"No, but she was athletic."

"You arranged the trip and invited Deborah and Liz?"

Lori nodded. "I thought it would be a fun way to spend time with them."

"When they met Jodi, did they get along?"

"Famously. We had a blast together."

"There was no tension?"

"None whatsoever."

"How about between you and Jodi?"

"What do you mean?" Lori said cautiously.

"Liz indicated you and Jodi had a fight in the cabin, the night before you started skiing."

"What does she know?" she said, aggravated. "Did Liz hear us?"

"No, but—"

"Then she ought to mind her own business."

My temper flared. "Lori, we don't have time for lying. Could you please—"

She matched my frostiness. "Are you implying that I—"

"Jodi told Liz she broke up with you."

Lori winced, and her face lost color. She didn't utter a sound until I started to speak. Then, she interrupted with, "When?"

"On Sunday, when you and Deborah went looking for the trail, before Liz and Jodi fell in the stream."

"Why?"

"Because she needed to talk to someone."

"No, why did Jodi do that to me?" she said in a tiny voice.

"Betray your confidence?"

"Rip out my heart."

I couldn't answer that.

Lori lowered her head and covered it with her hands. Eventually, she raised up and spoke, but she had trouble catching her breath, and I had to strain to understand her words. "All anyone could talk about after the ski trip were the death and injuries and how fortunate I was to have escaped unharmed. No one noticed I'd been hurt. I stopped talking about it, all of it, right then. I moved on with my life and tried to make the best of the rest of it. What choice did I have?"

I looked at her peculiarly. "Do you still have feelings for Jodi Wilde?"

"Incessantly. I wake up with her and go to sleep with her. Everything I've accomplished since I was nineteen, every single achievement, I wish I could have shared with her. My business, the awards, Erica, everything. Sometimes, I have to stop myself, consciously limit how many times a day I fantasize about her."

I tried to disguise my shock by vigorously stirring my hot chocolate. "Did you see Jodi's family after the ski trip?"

"Only a glance at the trailhead. The rescue team moved us from snowmobiles right into ambulances. Most of that day's a blur."

"Did you try to contact the Wildes after they returned to Connecticut?"

Lori hesitated. "No."

"What reason did Jodi give for breaking up with you?"

"Her mother. She was terrified of her instability."

"Why did she come to Colorado if she'd decided to end the relationship?"

"She hadn't," Lori retorted, pain etched on her forehead. "Jodi was fine the first few days of the trip, until her mother phoned. That same day, she tried to break up with me. Whatever was said on that call drove her to the decision."

"You and Jodi stayed up most of the night in the cabin?"

Lori nodded slightly. "We didn't sleep at all. After she told me she'd always love me but couldn't lead a gay lifestyle, I cried for six hours. Jodi held me the entire night."

"You couldn't persuade her to change her mind?"

"I would have if—"

She hadn't died, I mentally added before Lori completed the sentence with an entirely different meaning. "If she hadn't started flirting with Liz."

"Jodi flirted with Liz?" I said, dubious.

"Blatantly."

"Given all these factors, you didn't consider canceling the trip?"

"How could I? If we hadn't gone skiing, we would have returned to Denver, and Jodi would have flown home for Christmas. I couldn't bear that."

"The weather forecasts didn't change your mind?"

"Weather was never a factor," Lori said belligerently. "I'd been out in conditions like that countless times."

"One of the most extreme blizzards in recorded history?" I said softly.

"At the time, we didn't have that information. We knew it was big, but not that big."

"And the warning from the man at the trailhead didn't slow you down?"

"That jackass treated us like little girls."

"Once you saw Jodi couldn't keep up, you didn't—"

"She kept up," Lori said purposefully. "She never fell behind."

"But she struggled—"

"We all struggled at different junctures."

I rubbed the back of my neck. "You didn't think to turn around?"

"Once I set a focus, I follow it to the end."

"No matter what?"

"Essentially," she said coldly. "It's made me successful at everything I've attempted."

"You *never* believed you were in jeopardy?"

"Not for a moment. Not at the trailhead. Not on the trail. Not through the first two nights. Not even after Jodi and Liz fell in the stream. I was never concerned."

"And after Jodi died?" I said tersely.

Lori laughed bitterly. "Especially not then. The worst that could happen already had, which left nothing to fear."

"What about your own death?"

Lori Parks let out a derisive grunt. "I would have welcomed that."

Chapter 19

Long after Lori Parks and I parted ways at the coffeehouse, the hollow look in her eyes disturbed me.

It didn't help that I had way too much time on my hands. Saturday night—date night for the rest of the world—meant a return to the Crumpler lawn for me.

Traffic had picked up, probably because of the weekend. Only five more days until the wretched holiday. Pretty soon, I'd resort to stealing parts of the display myself, just for amusement.

I called it quits around ten o'clock because I had an appointment the next day with Paul Switzer, the man who had crashed his snowmobile while trying to rescue Lori Parks' ski group. We'd agreed to meet at eleven in Winter Glades, a seventy-mile trek from Denver, which meant I'd have to leave the house at nine to allow for traffic and weather.

Before heading home, I dropped by Dorothy's on Federal Boulevard.

After pressing through the crowd of gyrating women at the lesbian bar, I found Fran Green outside on the back steps.

At the sound of the door opening, she turned, startled. "Kris, you following me?"

"I thought you might like company."

She shooed me away. "Pair-scene chases away girls."

"No girls are out here," I said reasonably, gesturing at the dimly lit alley. "Why aren't you inside?"

"Smoke burning my eyes."

"Tonight's smoke-free, at least according to the sign on the door."

"Lingers."

"I didn't smell anything." I could see my breath, something I hadn't been able to do an hour earlier. I zipped my jacket and thrust my hands deep in the pockets.

"Music too loud."

"They're playing oldies."

"Too old for the oldies," Fran said, glumly. "Promised myself I'd stay two hours. Couldn't last that long, but can't leave. Can't quit."

I had never seen my friend this defeated. I scrutinized her face and saw that she had wiped off all the make-up. "Can I sit?"

"Public stoop."

I lowered myself to the concrete next to her. "You should have called. I could play pool with you, or dance, or whatever they do at these places."

"Didn't want to be a bother."

"Are you okay?"

"Can't do it. Can't break up with Ruth," Fran said, her eyes dry and determined. "Thought I could, but can't. Won't."

"What choice do you have?"

"Plenty," she said dully. "Give up snowboarding, fantasy football, criticizing her doctors. Ruth's top three peeves. Ought to satisfy her enough to take me back."

"You can't negotiate away parts of your life."

"Can't go back in there," she said, her head inclined toward the door. "Gotta win back Ruth."

"It's not a game, Fran. You can't win."

"Point being?"

"Ruth won't take you back. I went to see her—" I said cautiously.

Fran's reply was immediate and heated. "Told me she wasn't home."

"Ruth was there," I said, suddenly overcome with weariness. "I lied because I didn't know how to tell you she's moved on."

"That quick?"

"A long time ago. You must have known on some level."

"Maybe I did," Fran admitted, almost in a whisper.

"And you need to move on, too."

"Tried tonight."

"Why here?"

"Thought at least all the broads would be gay. Can't tell in everyday life anymore. Straights look gay, gays look straight. Code of ethics gone. Butch introduces you to her husband and three kids. Femme makes a pass. Sometimes, attraction changes mid-date. Read that in a magazine. Part-time sexuality. Can't keep up with the rules."

"There aren't rules, Fran. And nice women, proud, full-time lesbians, are everywhere, not just in bars. We'll find you one."

"Soon?" she clambered up, eagerly.

I gulped. "Sure."

She leaned against a stack of wooden pallets and said, "Better locate myself before I go looking for a squeeze. Can't believe Ruth transferred her loyalties in warp speed. Hasn't told her family about our breakup, but keeping warm with a new gal. Ruth claims Janet's more her style, more refined. They spend their days watching the news and playing chess."

"You're not spying on them, are you?"

"I keep in touch."

"How often do you call or go by?"

"No more than five times a day. That's my limit."

I looked at her carefully but could detect no humor. "Maybe you should start dating. It might make you feel better."

"Not interested after this fiasco. Rather pass the time with you and Destiny. Couldn't ask for two better friends."

After such a compliment, why did my stomach hurt? I ignored the ache. "You deserve better than Ruth."

"Careful. That's my girl you're insulting."

I cocked my head.

"Ex-girl," Fran corrected before I could.

"By the way, I like your new shirt," I said, referring to the slogan "Ride 'til you die."

She glanced down and zipped her jacket. "Bought it yesterday. Hoped it might attract ladies with the same interests."

I pointed at the graphic of a snowboarder mid-flip. "Can you do that?"

"Not on purpose."

We both laughed, and I looked at her with open admiration. "You should give yourself a lot of credit for coming tonight."

"No success."

"At least you're trying to reach out. You didn't give in to bitterness and quit. Lots of people your age, or my age, would have shunned closeness."

"Can't let what happened change my outlook, even if it did hurt like a hemorrhoid. Some days worse than others, but all of 'em have something good. Little spray of light somewhere between dawn and dusk."

"I hope so."

"Today's was you comin' here."

I shrugged. "I needed a drink."

"Haven't downed three alcoholic beverages in your life," Fran countered. "Means a lot to me, your support."

She hugged me, and as she let go, I teased, "It's good to see your wrinkles again, without all that make-up getting in the way."

Fran punched me in the arm, but not hard.

In bed that night, after three apologies to Destiny for having to cancel the next day's planned sex-a-thon, I broached a delicate subject.

"What would you think about permanently offering the apartment to Fran?"

Destiny, who was teasing me with light caresses, stopped mid-stroke. "You want to listen to Judy Collins music all day?"

"We could ask her to lower the volume."

"And the jumping jacks every evening. You said they gave you a headache the other day."

"I had a slight one before I came home. They just aggravated it."

"What about the garlic? You bitched your clothes smelled like it last week."

"We could put an exhaust fan in her kitchen. She'd probably install it."

Destiny kissed me, a soft, open-mouthed wonder. "You won't like a cold shower after she's taken a nice, long, hot one."

"We could arrange a schedule," I said, breathless. "But it sounds like you don't want to do this."

"Nooooo," Destiny drew out her response. "I'm not saying that."

"Fran *is* gone a lot, and when she's here, she fixes everything before we know it's broken. She's done a nice job cleaning up the graffiti in the alley."

"I was doing that," Destiny said, moving away, a touch offended.

I drew her close, spreading the full length of her nakedness over mine. "Not on twice-a-day patrols, and you know she'd pay the rent on time."

"Early, but what about your reservations?" Destiny ran her fingers through my hair. "What about us having sex? I don't want Fran Green to cramp our style."

"We could scream all we want while she's shoveling snow. She'd never hear us over the noise of that blower she bought."

"And she does do the whole block," Destiny mused while nuzzling my ear, "which takes a while."

"Plus, she scrapes off our cars every morning," I said, between groans. "I've gotten used to that."

"I'm sure she wouldn't have loud parties."

"I do like those chocolates she keeps leaving at the door."

"And the homemade root beer. You love that." Destiny took a deep breath. "I think we have our answer. We're going to be living in the same house as Fran Green."

"Shit!" I said, as we stared at each other, eyes wide open.

After we stopped giggling, we closed our eyes and applied our full concentration to making love.

Chapter 20

"Every mountain group needs a leader. You don't wait for a crisis. You designate someone before you buy supplies or study a map. Problem is, almost no one abides by this basic rule of survival."

I was thirty minutes into the magazine interview I'd concocted as a means of setting up a meeting with Paul Switzer, and he showed no sign of losing steam. I couldn't write half as fast as he talked, and it took me fifteen minutes to remember the freelance project didn't exist and I could stop documenting every word.

Our beginning had been equally rugged, refreshing in a peculiar way.

On the drive to Winter Glades, I had enjoyed dry roads through Denver and the first hour of mountain driving. However, at the summit of Kennison Pass, as I crossed the Continental Divide, I had to steer and brake carefully on snowpacked roads.

Around eleven, I passed through the town of Winter Glades and pulled off US 25 at the first log cabin I spotted on the right. Expecting signage designating the North County Search and Rescue, I stepped out of the car into a few inches of powder and looked around, uncertain.

I vaulted over a snowbank to reach the porch. Holding on to the rails, I picked my way across the wooden planks, praying none of the giant icicles hanging from the roof would break free, when I heard a shout. "Should have taken the path around the side."

Paul Switzer must have witnessed my approach from one of the frosted windows that covered half the side of the tiny cabin. As he bellowed, "Get in here, I won't bite," he opened the door, maneuvering his wheelchair to the side.

Before I could introduce myself, he'd spun back to his desk and said stoutly, "I gave you detailed directions. If they confused you, you'd better stay out of the backcountry and stick to writing."

"I was looking for a sign," I stammered.

"For reassurance that what you thought was right was really right?"

"Something like that," I said as I studied him. Dressed in blue jeans, a black turtleneck, a fleece-lined flannel shirt, and work boots, he could have graced the cover of a ski magazine. No hair protruded from his denim baseball cap, but bushy eyebrows made up for the lack. Ruddy cheeks and a mesmerizing twinkle gave him a look of vigor that countered deep lines in his face. I guessed him to be in his late fifties, with most of his time spent in the elements.

Oblivious to my staring, he commented mildly, "It never works that way. One of the first rescues I did was near Crested Butte. We pulled out an experienced mountaineer. Know how he got in trouble?"

I shook my head and glanced around the one-room cabin. One side functioned as a museum. Attached to the walls and spread out in glass display cases, relics traced the history of the area. Railroad ties and ore samples, metal bindings and antique skis, vintage photos and trip diaries told the tale of the past hundred years. Initially a mecca for silver mining, in the most recent fifty years, the Winter Glades area had drawn income from the "white gold" of snow. More than a million visitors passed through the county each winter, drawn to skiing, snowboarding, snowshoeing, and snowmobiling.

In the center of the room, plastic stands held forest service topographical maps that probably made sense to someone with geography skills but looked like meaningless shades of green to me.

The near side of the cabin, next to two large windows by the front door, served as home base for Paul Switzer and Frenchie Breslin, who was at the hardware store, according to Paul. The two men couldn't have had more discordant organizational approaches. Paul's desk showed no clutter. Even the memo pad that covered most of the top of it didn't contain a scribble. Frenchie, on the other hand, would have had to perform significant filing duties before he could sit on his metal chair. By the looks of the wooden filing cabinet whose drawers wouldn't close, he had nowhere to put the assorted magazines, maps, and folders.

Paul's booming voice forced me to focus. "This guy was on a back-country ski trip in an area he knew like the back of his hand. When a blizzard moved in, he couldn't see ten feet in front of him. In a whiteout, above treeline, everything looks the same. He had a map and compass, and he consulted them. But they kept telling him the wrong thing. He swore he recognized a ridge, and he headed in that direction, opposite the way the compass steered him. He was less than a mile from his car, but he headed thirty miles the wrong way before we caught up to him and plucked him out of there. Goes to show, you can't always trust your intuition. Know what saves a man, young lady?"

I shrugged.

"Smarts. Physically strong men die every year when weaker ones with brains walk out."

"Hmm," I said, wondering how he would have categorized himself.

"Know what's the best thing you can bring on a backcountry trip?"

"Wits," he answered, before I could venture a guess. "When you get in trouble, know what's the best thing you can do?"

"Stay put," he replied, making me speculate as to how long he'd carry on both sides of the conversation. "Last season, we tracked a snowmobiler for close to fifty miles, all in circles. Those tracks took us through creeks and over cliffs. The only reason the fool stopped was because he trapped himself in a narrow gulch. If he hadn't gotten stuck, he'd be dead. Know what we call tourists with $7,000 snowmobiles?"

"Potential clients?"

"Backcountry Popsicles," Paul said, lacing the words with an insider's chuckle.

I tried but couldn't muster a smile.

"Know what kills people in the backcountry?"

This one, I thought I could get. "Weather and avalanches?"

"Mistakes. Know why ordinary people take risks?"

Again, he didn't pause. "They're addicted to powder. Used to be after a good storm, you could ski for two weeks at the ski area and never hit tracks. Now, you're lucky to get thirty minutes to yourself before the Front Range traffic hits the slopes. Every year I've done this, I see people go to greater lengths to reach secret stashes. Skiers and snowboarders hike into death chutes, and snowmobilers plow through avalanche zones."

Paul nodded toward the light snow falling outside. "We're in a touchy period right now. Everything is alive back there. We have advances in avalanche forecasting, not to mention better safety and rescue techniques. But what good does it do? People can study risk forecasts on websites, use an inclinometer, take collapsible shovels and a snow saw with them. Hell, throw in probe poles, a beacon so you can find the victim, and why not the AvaLung, a tube that provides oxygen while you're buried. Spring for a global positioning satellite receiver, and what do you have?"

I raised both eyebrows and turned up my hands.

"A false sense of security. I'm crossing my fingers no one gets any knucklehead ideas this weekend."

"Is this weekend worse than most?"

"With the conditions we've had recently, yes, ma'am. Low snowpack, all that crusty junk lying on the ground for a long time, exposed to the sun. It creates a condition similar to ball-bearings. The new snow falls on the old snow, and until the new stuff gets a chance to set up, it slides easily. Stay in this business long enough, and you'll see the same accidents repeat themselves. People think about what they want to do, not what the mountains will allow. Know how to tell if a slope is prone to a slide?"

"I have no idea."

"You ask yourself 'Would a cow be comfortable standing on that pitch?' If the answer is no, you'd better steer clear of the area," he said, laughing at his quip.

I did my best to join in his merriment.

"Know how to spot an avalanche zone?"

Defeated, I resumed the head shaking.

"Look for knocked over small trees or trees with broken limbs. Flag trees are a sure sign of trouble—they've been stripped of branches on all but one side, the downhill side. Past avalanches took out the rest. Know what to do if you're caught in a slide?"

I made a stab at this one, only because my neck was getting sore from all the negative movement. "Run?"

Paul Switzer cringed. "You can't outrun an avalanche. The only chance you have for survival is to move left or right, out of its path. Then you swim and try to punch your way out of the death-trap that's forming around you. If you can create an air pocket, you'll buy yourself thirty minutes, tops." He paused, before adding loudly, "Keep your mouth shut."

Because I'd barely eked out a few sentences, I resented the directive.

"Keep your mouth shut, or the snow will suffocate you," he clarified, nodding at his own wisdom. "About eighty percent of avalanche victims die from asphyxiation or suffocation."

Fearing I'd lost control of the interview (after all, I hadn't posed one question for every ten of his), I blurted out, "Do you ever wonder about what you do?"

Paul Switzer shook his head. "Never, but a few girlfriends have lodged protests. Rescuers, me included, are adrenaline junkies. We have to be. There's no money in it. Most are volunteers who buy their own equipment. Some guys lose their paying jobs because they'll choose a rescue over going to work. Don't let anyone kid you, we like going where there's risk. The taxpayers, they're not always happy footing the bill. Sometimes, we'll risk fifty lives to go in and save two idiots. In Breckenridge, we had to go after a suicidal man who kept dodging us. We sued for reimbursement, but a lot of good that did."

"He never paid?"

"He claimed he never asked to be searched for or rescued. He was a crazy son-of-a-gun, but the mountains can do that. Some men, the wilderness breaks; others, it saves."

"Obviously, you fall into the latter category."

"Damn right," he said, and for the first time since I arrived, his right hand quit tapping his thigh, and he became still, almost in a trance. "I spent a night on Flagler Pass one time . . ."

I fidgeted nervously as we came close to the truth I'd come to hear. "If there's something you don't want me to include in the article, I can respect that."

He glanced at me, narrowed his eyes, then widened them. For a moment, his arrogance vanished. "Better leave it off the record. The guys would never let me live it down." He stopped and stared out the window, as if documenting each falling snowflake.

I waited, listening to the deafening sound of the ticking wall clock.

He cleared his throat. "I felt close to God the night of my accident."

"Pardon?" I said, startled.

"The worst day of my life, when I was walking in the morning and couldn't move a muscle below my waist twelve hours later." He took a gulp of coffee. "I've never been able to explain it right, but I felt the presence of something. I'd go back there in a second and shiver all night if I could experience it again," he said, his voice dropping.

Goose bumps covered my forearms. My voice quivered, and when I spoke, I used carefully-chosen words. "How did you get hurt?"

"On a rescue."

"What happened?"

"Back on the record?"

"Either way," I said mildly.

Paul weighed the options, then said matter-of-factly, "May as well let some other hotshot learn from my mistake. I was part of a team that went in after four missing skiers. I drove my snowmobile off a cliff on Flagler Pass."

My eyebrows shot toward the ceiling. "A big drop?"

"They tell me I tumbled about a thousand feet. We shouldn't have been there in whiteout conditions, but we still had a chance of finding those girls alive. Every hour mattered, and we couldn't wait out the storm. That's what no one understood later. Hell, we didn't know up from down and had to pick our way through, like flying in the clouds. I was in the lead, cutting trail, when I came to a steep area, basically a controlled slide. As soon as the weight of my machine hit, a piece broke off, and I took the ride of my life."

"How did they get you out?"

"Another guy on the team, Dale, saw me go over. He came down in snowshoes and dragged me out of danger. He spent the night with me, fifteen hours in a snow pit. In the morning, it took a crew of sixty to rescue me. Sixteen at a time, eight using ropes to pull the bucket up the rocks across the knoll and eight moving alongside the carrier. You'd never know it, but I was a big guy. Six feet, two-fifty. It took four hours to get me to the top, then they took me down the trail by snowmobile, and airlifted me to Denver. I remember every bit of the days and minutes leading up to the accident, and I remember the night with Dale, but I can't remember much about the rescue or the next two weeks. Heavy-duty painkillers erased those memories."

"How did you and Dale survive the night?"

"At 12,000 feet with deadly-cold temps, no problem," Paul said sardonically. "To keep the blood flowing, we beat on each other's limbs. To stay awake, we kept talking. About midnight, the storm broke, the winds died, and we could see every star in the sky."

"That night . . ." I hesitated.

"Ask it!"

"Did you know you were paralyzed?"

"Hell yes, but I didn't tell the guys. They had enough to worry about with four girls still out there."

I'd come so close to the truth I sought I shook inside, but I willed calm into the tone and tempo of my next questions. "How long had the girls been missing?"

"Three days, and believe it, that's a lifetime in the backcountry in a blizzard. Even for grizzled mountain men."

"I take it they weren't too experienced?"

He let out a snort. "If they had been, they never would have left the comfort of their home. They planned a hut trip—ski in Friday, stay the night, ski out early Saturday. They must not have bothered to check the forecasts. Every other group that had a hut trip reservation in the Flagler area canceled that weekend. Not those girls, though."

"What happened?"

"The worst storm in a decade trapped them in a canyon, and they got disoriented. They didn't have any mountaineering tools or skills."

"Who called in Search and Rescue?"

"One of the parents called late Saturday afternoon when the girls hadn't shown. We mobilized but couldn't send a team that night. Too risky. The storm wouldn't give us a break. Hundred-mile-per hour winds. Snowing a couple inches an hour and freezing cold. By Sunday morning, we'd given them a zero to ten percent chance of having survived two nights outdoors."

"Couldn't they have been in the hut, unharmed?"

"Not a chance. Another group of skiers had used a hut in the area Thursday and Friday night and managed to pick their way out early Saturday. They said they hadn't seen the girls. Matter of fact, they told us they'd seen tracks leading into an avalanche that had sloughed off and no tracks leading out. Our rescue commander spent Saturday night creating physical and psychological work-ups of everyone in the party, trying to predict how each would react in an emergency."

"And it didn't look good?"

"Couldn't have looked worse. One experienced cross-country skier, one so-so, and two never-nevers, as we call them in the trade. They had the wrong gear for spending the night outdoors. No formal survival training. More than four hundred slides were reported to the Colorado Avalanche Bureau in the previous three-day period, hundreds in the Flagler area. I'll tell you how grim it was. Our chief asked for pictures of the four, so we could positively ID the bodies when we found them."

"Why did rescuers go out Sunday morning if the odds and weather were so bad?"

"The storm let up for a few hours, and it's what we do," Paul Switzer said grimly. "We see the faces of family and friends gathered at a trail-head, holding vigil, counting on us. We never want to use live rescuers to hunt for corpses, but lots of guys, me as much as anyone, held out hope. We chose to push forward. We were big boys."

"Did they ever find the girls?"

"Sure did, Monday morning, a couple hours after they pulled me off the cliff. It was some kind of miracle, one dead, but three alive. One of the choppers spotted them and directed a team on snowmobiles. They tell me the day was beautiful, blue sky and warm weather, but it's a good thing the guys got to those girls when they did. It's never good when someone in your party dies. When we're on a rescue, we try not to share that information with the people we're rescuing, if they don't know already. When they find out, their spirits crash. I've seen people make it to the ambulance, then keel over when they hear bad news."

I held my breath for a second before asking, "Given how it turned out, do you regret assisting on that particular rescue?"

"No," he said emphatically. "It's what we do every day."

"What about the consequences," I pushed. "No bitterness at all?"

"Sure, at first. Maybe for a year or two. But when I gave up booze, I gave up anger. Those girls didn't cause the whiteout or steer my sled over a cliff. They were in the wrong place at the wrong time, and so was I. We all make mistakes."

I searched his features for any contradiction but found none.

"I have to accept it," he added. "I broke my back but was given twenty extra years, and counting, to live. That's a better deal than Jodi Wilde got."

"The girl who died?"

"Yeah," he said in a low voice. "And lots of days, I've felt like the lucky one. Sure, I lost something, but others hurt worse. One of the girls had a foot amputated, and the guys on the team told me they didn't think the dead girl's mom would recover from the loss."

The hair on the back of my neck bristled. "How could they tell?"

"The copter couldn't land near the girls, so they brought all four out on snowmobiles, three as riders and the victim bundled in a bucket. You can bet they'd told the mother about her daughter, but when she saw the body, towed on a toboggan behind the lead snowmobile, she let out a scream that lasted five minutes. Some construction guys, who were a mile away shoveling snow off a roof, swore they heard the echo. When they've had a few too many at the bar, lots of guys in this town will tell you it's the worst sound they ever heard."

"The scream?"

Paul Switzer rubbed his eyes. "The words. The mother kept shouting, 'What will fill this hole in my heart?'"

"We'll continue to take calculated risks on behalf of people with bad judgment."

On the drive back to Denver, I couldn't get that particular Paul Switzer philosophy out of my head. He had delivered these final words almost proudly as he closed the cabin door behind me.

After I stopped ruminating about the notion of brave men and women traipsing after foolish ones, I used the time to consider Paul Switzer. He'd spent a career rescuing people, many of whom exhibited less sense than Lori Parks and her companions. No matter how far I stretched my suspicion, I couldn't put him in the frame for targeting a teenage skier, even if she had set in motion the events that had led to his paralysis.

I catalogued my thoughts as I drove, mostly in my head, but sometimes in a notebook on the occasions when it seemed safe to simultaneously steer and write. Fortunately, the snow had stopped falling shortly after I'd left the headquarters of North County Search and Rescue, which made my journey home blissfully uninteresting.

Only later that night, as I lay in the bushes on the Crumpler estate, watching happy families hold hands in the glow of Christmas lights, did I allow myself to think about my new prime suspect: Jodi Wilde's mother.

The woman who had waited by the trailhead, only to be greeted by the sight of her daughter on a toboggan, covered in a tarp, dragged behind a snowmobile—that visual tormented me without reprieve.

How did *she* feel about Lori Parks?

I'd have to track her down and find out if her grief still ran as deep as the scream she'd let out in the Colorado mountains.

I spent the better part of Monday morning tracing Wilde families who lived in Connecticut. Using Internet phone lists in major cities, I came up with a list of prospects. Fifty calls later, I had developed compassion for telemarketers. Didn't anyone answer the phone anymore?

On every voice mail, I left a succinct message stating I was a high school friend of Jodi Wilde's and wanted to renew ties with her. A morbid ploy given I knew she was dead, but what other choice did I have? Lori Parks couldn't recall the names of Jodi's parents, and the sister must have moved or changed her name when she married, because I found no Jill Wilde.

My tacky strategy paid off around eleven when a woman returned my call and informed me, without emotion, that her cousin Jodi Wilde had died some time ago. I asked for contact information for Jodi's parents and sister, in order to pass along my sympathies. The cousin brought me up to speed: the dad was dead, the mom had left the state, and Jill lived in Hartford with three kids but no husband. The relative readily provided Jill's phone number, which I dialed immediately.

My heart raced with every ring, but I experienced an awful anticlimax when an answering machine kicked in belatedly with a standard greeting. I used my same spiel and crossed my fingers the sister would call back soon.

By noon, exhaustion had overtaken me, partially because of the drudgery of the morning's task but also at the prospect of another night on the Crumpler estate.

Monitoring my fatigue pulse, I vowed this would be my last. Regardless of whether I caught the thief, I had to stop spending evenings on the frozen ground.

After lunch, to clear my head, I rode fifteen miles on my mountain bike, most of it on the paved path next to the Platte river. Despite blue sky and mild temperatures, few runners, inline skaters, or cyclists joined me. Maybe they were all out shopping, making the most of the final three days before Christmas.

At dusk, I renewed my vigil in the Crumplers' yard, and around six, the weather took a dramatic turn for the worse when a northern wind blew in and the air turned humid. How many years had I lived in Colorado? My whole life. How many times had I heard the tired expression, "If you don't like the weather, wait a few hours." More than I could count. How much longer could I endure under the scant protection of a windbreaker? Maybe an hour, probably less.

I debated knocking on the Crumplers' door and asking for a blanket, coat, or gloves. Any scrap of cloth would have helped, but pride prevented me from appearing before my elderly clients.

I had begun to fantasize about snatching the next fur that went by, for practical and political reasons, when a thought came into my head from nowhere.

Suddenly in one clear vision, I knew who had pilfered from the Crumpler display, and as soon as the realization hit, I berated myself for having overlooked the obvious.

I'd wasted dozens of hours searching for a solution that lay right before my eyes, and the thought depressed me. My misery grew with the certainty that the revelation would break Clarice Crumpler's heart.

Teeth chattering, I shivered violently.

I couldn't feel most of my fingers or any toes, and I felt like crying when the cell phone in my pocket began to vibrate.

Holding the plastic away from my numb ear, I whispered, "Hello."

The response came in a chilling wail, "Kris, she's gone!"

Chapter 21

"Lori?"

"She's gone."

"Who's gone?" For a sick instant, I prayed Donna had dumped Lori Parks.

"Erica. She's missing. This can't be happening to me."

I felt one of my lungs collapse. Somehow, I mustered enough oxygen to speak. "Where are you?"

"At home."

"Is Donna with you?"

"Yes."

"Stay put. I'll be there in ten minutes."

To hell with the Christmas kitsch.

I scrambled out from under the bush, much to the amazement of two families admiring the lights, and ran as fast as I could to my car.

By the time I reached my Honda, parked two blocks away, I felt physically ill. My throat hurt from the cold, my chest heaved in protest against the speed I'd achieved, and I couldn't stop crying.

I tried to catch my breath as I dialed Fran's number.

Thankfully, she answered on the first ring.

"It's me," I blurted.

"What's wrong?"

"Erica's missing. Meet me at Lori and Donna's house."

"Catch a cab. Be there in a flash."

"Hurry," I pleaded. "I can't do this alone."

A million thoughts screamed through my head. They fused together and exploded. They made no sense alone or grouped, like parts of a dream only half-realized when awake. The searing confusion left me befuddled and incensed.

Then, in a moment of clarity, the vortex stopped swirling, and two lucid thoughts crystallized into an excruciating epiphany.

The kidnapper was Jodi Wilde's mother, and Erica had met her.

The notes left at the Children's Academy telegraphed a mother's anguish, if the pronoun "you" was changed to "I," and the present tense converted to past.

The first note: "I did try to prepare." A message left inside a mitten on a playground.

The second note: "Still, I believed no harm would ever come to my children." Written on the back of a photograph of a young girl, in all likelihood Jodi Wilde.

The third note: "I said good-bye, never knowing . . ." What ending to this incomplete dispatch could exist, other than, "she'd die in the Colorado mountains."

And the kidnapper must have been someone Erica had met, or what else could explain Erica's adoption of the woman's language of grief?

In describing how she'd felt about her two moms fighting, Erica told me she had "a hole in her heart." Why hadn't I immediately connected that when Paul Switzer described the mother's cries at the sight of her daughter's dead body, "What will fill this hole in my heart?"

Why hadn't I realized it sooner? One day earlier?

How could I have been so stupid, so thoughtless, so slow?

One mistake, one slip, one oversight, and now this . . . such godless consequences.

Dread seized me.

As I drove with tears streaming down my cheeks, I shrieked, "No!" That simple word of denial, over and over, as I pounded my fists on the steering wheel, the sides of my head, the tops of my thighs.

By the digital clock in my car, I reached my destination in eight minutes, the longest span of my life.

Outside the house, I hurriedly wiped my face, and chanted softly, "Don't panic."

Donna answered the doorbell and practically shoved me into the dining room. All the place settings had been pushed to one end of the table in a jumble, and Lori sat at the head. She acknowledged my presence but didn't interrupt her call.

Seconds later, she put down the phone. "She's not there. They haven't seen her since she went to Heather's birthday party last weekend."

"We're calling the parents of Erica's friends," Donna explained.

"It's a waste of time," Lori said dully.

"Do you have any better ideas?" Donna asked loudly.

Hoping to avoid a repeat of my last visit, when two sentences had burgeoned into a full-blown skirmish, I gestured for them to calm down. I squinted to read the wall clock in the kitchen. "It's 6:30 now. When did you last see her?"

"At 4:30 at the Academy. Sally offered to give her a ride home."

"Sally Patterson, your concierge?"

Lori nodded bleakly.

"Is she trustworthy?"

"Completely."

"Has she driven Erica home before?"

"Many times."

"How long has she worked for you?"

"About six months."

"How did you find her?"

"She sent in a resume."

I tried to keep any hint of fright away from my next words. "In response to an ad?"

"Unsolicited. We weren't hiring at the time, but I filed her information. When an opening came up, I called. She has an impeccable resume. Degree from Smith, active in arts organizations back East. Her mother's family traces back to the Mayflower."

"Did you do a background check?"

"Of course. My business manager conducted the usual employment, criminal, and credit histories. Sally's background must have been clean, or we wouldn't have hired her."

"Is Sally usually reliable?"

"Always."

"Would she call if something came up?"

"In an instant. She phones when she's going to be five minutes late for work. If she could be here right now, she would. Something awful must have happened to both of them."

Or just one, I thought grimly. "When Sally brings Erica home, does she walk her to the door?"

Donna answered. "She stays in the car, but she honks and waits until Erica gets inside the house and waves from the window."

"They should have been here by 5:00?" I verified.

"At the latest."

"Did you hear Sally honk today, Donna?"

"No, but I didn't get home until 5:30."

Lori pounced on that. "Today's Monday. You're supposed to be here by 4:00."

"I had to stay for a meeting. I called and left a message with Sally. Didn't she give it to you?"

"No, or I never would have sent Erica home with her. I care about my daughter," she said defensively.

Donna glared at her. "Are you implying I don't?"

"This was your day to be here."

"I'm here four out of five days. You expect me to put my career on hold while yours soars. And Erica's not my real daughter. You make that clear every chance you get."

"I've never said anything to that effect."

"Yes, Lori, you have. You're just too drunk to remember. You hurl insults at me all the time from your alcoholic fog. The next morning, you forget, and I forgive."

Lori leaned toward Donna menacingly. "You made a mistake today, Donna, and you're blaming me."

"Ladies, please. This isn't—" I tried to intervene.

"Mistake! You, Miss Perfect, you're one to talk. Why don't you tell Kris about the mistake you made nine years ago."

"Donna, stop," Lori implored more than commanded.

"I really don't need to know—" I interjected.

"Ask her how Erica was conceived."

"Don't!" Lori whispered in anguish.

"In a moment of joy between us?" Donna's hysteria spilled out. "Artificial insemination with both of us selecting the father? No. Lori Parks, *the* Lori Parks, took off one night in the middle of a fight. When the phone rang six hours later, at 4:05 a.m. to be precise, a man told me Lori was in the emergency room at St. Anthony's. Alcohol poisoning. She was so drunk, doctors had put her on a suicide watch. The gentleman who phoned was a real winner. Lori had picked him up at a bar. A month later, she tells me she's pregnant. A lesbian, pregnant by mistake. That's rich irony, don't you think?"

Donna finally stopped screaming, not because she'd run out of emotion, but because her voice had gone hoarse.

While I could barely stomach Donna's tirade, I had never witnessed anything as disturbing as the look of hatred Lori directed at her.

As I tried to regain control of the situation, the doorbell rang, and we all jumped.

Before anyone could respond, Fran Green had let herself in and appeared before us.

She was a vision of peace, a serene air about her.

As soon as I saw her, I felt guilty about my foray back to the Crumplers' house and hoped she wouldn't notice the mud on my pants.

Fran breezed by me and hugged Donna, holding her for several minutes as she sobbed. Gently, she lowered Donna back into a chair and introduced herself to Lori. Me, she saluted.

"What'd I miss?"

"Not much," I said, my voice a bit unsteady. "Erica left the Academy at about 4:30. Sally Patterson, the concierge, was supposed to drive her home. We're not sure if she did."

"Anyone call the police?"

"No," Lori said quickly. "I won't involve them."

"The hospitals?"

"No."

"Friends?"

"A few. I just started."

"You believe this Sally's involved?"

"No," Lori said adamantly. Out of her line of sight, I shrugged my shoulders. Donna remained mute.

"You tried to contact her?"

"I've left messages on her home phone and her cell," Lori said.

"Two missing then, not one."

"Possibly," I conceded.

"You sure Erica didn't get here then go out again?"

Donna spoke up. "She never would. When someone drops her off, she knows she's supposed to ring the doorbell and wait until Lori or I answer."

"Any keys hidden?"

"One under the flowerpot on the porch," Lori said.

"Still there?"

"I'll look," Lori offered, hurrying out of the room.

"Anyone searched Erica's bedroom for clues?"

Donna answered. "I glanced in when I came home, but when I didn't see Erica, I assumed she and Lori were coming later. When Lori arrived alone, we panicked and called Kris, then her friends. That's all we've done."

"Better get up to the bedroom," Fran directed.

"I'll see if her backpack and homework are on her desk. That's always the first thing she does." Donna scurried away.

Fran and I looked at each other with the same sickening worry. Before we could whisper confidences, Lori burst into the room, "The key's missing."

Donna came in moments later, holding a note, and carrying Erica's pink backpack. She trembled as she said, "I found this on the bed."

Only one sentence was printed on the piece of paper. "You'll never see your daughter again alive."

Chapter 22

While Fran Green comforted Donna, I drew up a plan.

Lori Parks would go to her office and retrieve Sally Patterson's resume and application. From the Academy, she'd call to give us the concierge's home address. Fran and I would drive there to see if Sally had been home and whether Erica had been seen with her.

Donna would continue calling friends of Erica, hoping for good news.

Lori called twenty minutes later: 2249 Vine Street.

Fran and I ran for the car as soon as we had the information.

"Thank God you came when you did," I said, as I started the engine.

"I miss something?"

"Donna and Lori attacking each other. It was ugly."

"Physically?"

"Emotionally."

"To be expected."

"You'd think they'd pull together."

"Rarely happens. Folks can't focus on grief, have to distract themselves. Seen it more times than not."

"What do you do?"

"Keep 'em calm. Stop the free-for-all before it escalates."

"I tried."

"Don't feel bad. How do you reckon I came by all these gray hairs?"

"You're good. They calmed down as soon as you walked in, before you spoke."

"Have the gift," Fran said, without her usual bravado. "Enough about me. Give me your take on what's pressing down."

"It has to be Sally, and I think she's Jodi Wilde's mother."

"The girl who died on the ski trip? How'd you come up with that?"

I explained the notes, and Fran concurred that this fourth correspondence fit my theory perfectly. Change the pronoun and tense, and the words read less as a threat than a summary of what had happened to Mrs. Wilde years ago. The last two notes completed the recall: "I said goodbye, never knowing I'd never see my daughter again alive."

The precision phrasing matched the scenario. The mother had seen her daughter again, wrapped in a tarp, but she'd never seen her again *alive*.

Fran and I argued whether the notes told a story of the past or warned of a future threat. She thought both, while I tried to convince her Erica Parks wasn't in danger. She wouldn't change her mind, and her stubbornness contributed to my rising apprehension.

We both agreed the "hole in the heart" statement indicated Erica must have met her kidnapper, but it was too soon to tell, beyond doubt, that Sally Patterson was Jodi Wilde's mother. She could be an innocent victim, snatched because of her association with Erica, or she could be the perpetrator.

"You met this Sally?"

"Once, at the Academy. She gave me a tour when Lori had to leave for a meeting. We spent about an hour together."

"Give me your impression."

I struggled to remember back to that day, which now seemed as if it belonged in another lifetime. "She could be the right age for Jodi's mother, mid-sixties. Slight build. Frizzy brown hair."

"Psych profile?"

"Sort of timid. Judgmental. A deep unhappiness, which came across even when she smiled, as if she made the effort out of habit."

"She capable of this?"

I shrugged. "Who knows?"

"She in the right place for all four notes?"

"Yes," I said uneasily. "The first two she could have placed at the Academy, one on the playground, the other on the door. The third, we found in Lori's purse at the house tour, and I know Sally was there, because she gave Erica a ride home. And the fourth . . ." My voice trailed off helplessly.

Undaunted, Fran continued, "Go with what we got. Assume she is the perp, not the vic. Why Erica?"

"To get back at Lori."

"All goes back to that ski trip?"

I nodded. "It must. Unless Lori's pulled another stunt she hasn't told us about."

"Didn't share this one right away."

"True," I said, thoroughly disheartened.

"Wouldn't put it past her. Lady has serious issues. Confusing myself, though. Too many trains of thought, running out of track."

By then, I had turned onto the twenty-two hundred block of Vine Street. No such address as 2249.

I leaned my head on the steering wheel.

Fran said quietly, "Not surprised. Can't trust women with permed hair. Chemicals do something to their noggins."

I cocked my head and looked at her sideways. "Doesn't Ruth perm her hair?"

"My point exactly."

We returned to the house and bumped into Lori as she exited her car. I asked to speak with her in private before we went inside. She agreed, and we sat in her Volvo with the heat blasting.

In the dim glow of dashboard lights, I could see her eyes were red and puffy. Strands of hair shot in every direction, and she looked as if she'd slept in her clothes. Her white shirt with ruffles was wrinkled and untucked, and her gray silk pants with paisley swirls had lost their sharp creases. She had a full-length black down coat with raccoon fur hood draped around her shoulders at a sideways angle, and her silver suede boots were caked with mud.

I took a deep breath before I spoke. "I'm pretty sure Sally's taken Erica."

"No," Lori said, her voice husky. "She's a good employee. Reliable and punctual. Something's happened to them."

"I also believe Sally Patterson is Jodi Wilde's mother."

"No," she whispered. "That can't be."

I explained my theory about the notes and the "hole in the heart" expression, and she listened without emotion.

When I finished, she looked away. "This isn't related to the ski trip. I'm sure we'll receive a call from Sally, saying she was detained and they're all right. Or Erica will come home after playing this practical joke. She's paying us back, you know, for fighting so much."

"Lori!"

"You've met Erica. She's bright. She could have staged this," Lori said, her voice never rising or falling.

"You're not thinking rationally."

She turned her body to face me. "Under the circumstances, what qualifies as rational?"

I reached out to touch her arm, but she flinched and pulled it back toward her chest. A sob started to escape her throat, but she suppressed it with a raw shudder. "I will not cry about this," she said, every feature in her face fighting the emotion. "Tears are pointless. She's not coming back. I won't ever see her again."

"Sure you will. She's only been missing a few hours. There could be any number of explanations."

Lori Parks stared at me as if I were an imbecile. "Not Erica, Jodi."

I returned the incredulity. "Lori, you need to concentrate on what's happening today. Your daughter's life could be at stake. When we find Sally, you'll need to apologize to her."

"I did nothing wrong—"

My patience evaporated. "What do you call taking her daughter on a ski trip in conditions you knew she couldn't handle? Or stripping her, literally, of her dignity after she broke up with you? Why not beg Sally's forgiveness for having a healthy, vibrant daughter while hers lies in a cemetery in Connecticut?"

Lori looked at me with disgust. "If you had let me finish my sentence, I meant I did nothing wrong to make Jodi stop loving me. And it's not the same woman. Sally Patterson is not Jodi's mother."

"How can you be certain?"

"The voice isn't the same."

My eyes widened. "You've spoken to her?"

A hostile veneer enveloped Lori's face. "I've heard her speak. Once, after the ski trip when I phoned to offer my condolences."

"What did she say?"

"Jodi's sister answered, and in the background, I heard her mother yell, 'Don't let that pervert ever call here again.'"

A few minutes before midnight, the phone rang. The sound we'd anticipated for hours startled us nonetheless. Lori and Donna raced to pick up the receiver, and Donna's spryness won out.

"Hello," she said breathlessly and then fell silent immediately. As seconds passed, the blood drained from her face, and a vein in her forehead began to throb.

Donna didn't utter a word; she simply listened and then deliberately returned the phone to its cradle.

Fran rose to help Donna back to her seat, holding most of her weight to prevent a complete collapse. We all waited expectantly for her to speak. When she did, she took the air out of the room.

"All she said was, 'You have three days to wait for your daughter to die. That's how many I had. If you call the police, you'll have less than three minutes.' Then she hung up."

Chapter 23

If doubt had lingered in anyone's mind that Jodi Wilde's mother had kidnapped Erica Parks, none remained after the phone call. The time-frame fit perfectly with the days her daughter had been missing before rescuers found her.

If there had been support for bringing in the police, that, too had vanished.

Fran took control, ordering Lori and Donna to bed with the blunt observation, "Nothing we can do in the middle of the night. No good to anybody if we can't think straight." She kicked me out of the house with the promise she'd stay the night with the two women and call my cell phone if anything developed.

Well aware of my insomnia that surfaced in the best of times, Fran knew I wouldn't have slept a wink under the roof of virtual strangers. She didn't have to push me out the door, I practically sprinted as she walked me to my car.

After I started the engine and promised to return at dawn, Fran said. "Sleep fast, kiddo." Giving me the bent eye, she added, "And not in the Crumplers' yard."

She needn't have worried.

I drove straight home, but not only did I not sleep fast, I didn't doze at all. After talking with Destiny for an hour, I spent the rest of the night pacing in the living room and periodically trying to nap on the couch. The harder I fought to slip into unconsciousness, the more agitated I became.

Around four, I gave up the battle and spent the remainder of the dark hours crafting questions I could pose to Jodi Wilde's sister, if I could get her to return my call.

As the minutes faded toward dawn, my anxiety rose. The closer morning came, the more desperate I became to reach into the darkness and rip out the sun.

Right as I felt on the verge of hopelessness, the morning arrived in unforgiving tones of gray. Starting at six (eight o'clock Connecticut time), I dialed the number Jodi's cousin had provided, the one that supposedly would reach Jill Wilde.

I hit auto redial what felt like hundreds of times before a woman answered the phone, clearly perturbed.

I hastened to introduce myself, confessing I'd left a misleading message the day before, the one about my attempts to renew my childhood friendship with her dead sister.

At the first sign of Jill's hesitation, I also assured her if she cut me off, I'd redial another hundred times, a thousand if necessary. That caught her attention, along with my rapid summation of the truth about the notes, the incidents, and the kidnapping. I swiftly shifted from current events to the ski trip that had cost her sister her life.

When I finished, Jill said, "You suspect someone from my family?"

I kept my tone neutral. "Possibly."

"Well, I'll narrow the list. I'm Jodi's only sibling, and my father died two years ago."

"What about your mother?"

"I can't help you there. I haven't spoken to her in almost a year."

"If you don't mind sharing, why?"

"She always was unstable, but after Jodi died, she lost it completely. She and my father divorced years ago because he couldn't stand to be around her sorrow. I lasted longer, until last December."

"What happened?"

"I told her I wouldn't go to Jodi's grave with her. I wanted to get on with my life, without constant reminders. We'd gone every year on the anniversary of her death, all those cold, miserable days. I wanted to skip one measly year, but my mother came unglued."

"That's not fair," I said sympathetically.

"I lived in the same neighborhood as my parents in order for them to participate in my children's lives. I nursed my father in his illness. I went to church with my mother every Sunday, long after I'd stopped believing. I held my tongue every time she praised Jodi and, in her insidious way, reminded me of my failings. I lived this life, her life, without complaint."

"Until a year ago," I clarified.

"My mother crossed a line, and I crossed it back. I told her the perfect Jodi had faults, big faults."

"Such as?" I asked tersely.

"Jodi was a homosexual. She never would have married. She never would have had children. And she certainly never would have gone to church every week."

"How did you know your sister was a lesbian? Did she confide in you?"

"Jodi announced it to the family when she was a sophomore in high school. My mother became hysterical, because she could see all her plans being destroyed. Ballet, summer camps, piano and voice lessons, private schools. They were supposed to lead to a respectable college, a good sorority, a fruitful marriage, and a life devoted to family and philanthropy. That's the course my mother had set for herself and her daughters. When Jodi declared her intentions, my mother deliberately injured herself."

I had become accustomed to Jill's squeaky little girl voice but couldn't adapt to her odd cadence. She spoke as if she had to let out words between breaths on a ventilator. The pauses never corresponded with expected moments of contemplation, and I had to control the impulse to unconsciously mimic them. I sped up my words. "For attention?"

"For release from the pain, she claimed. After my mother's hospitalization, Jodi stopped seeing girls. My mom fooled herself into thinking Jodi was cured, but I knew better. When she phoned from college and said she wouldn't be home for Christmas, I felt relieved. I knew she and her friend Lori were girlfriends. I could tell by the letters Jodi wrote. She never revealed anything specific, but I knew she was in love. I didn't want her bringing some girl home to spoil everything," Jill said sourly.

"When did—"

"It was bad enough to hear comparisons when Jodi was alive. She was smarter, kinder, more athletic, more social. She looked like my mother. She didn't smoke, drink, or do drugs. She graduated from high school with the highest honors. She gave part of her babysitting money to charity. She excelled at everything she did and made any challenge look easy. That's what I had to contend with when she was alive. And then she died, and my mother compared me to memories. As the memories grew larger, I became smaller. One day, I realized she would never love me as much as she loved Jodi. All my life, I'd tried to pretend my mother's love wasn't important, but as my husband pointed out last year, it's all that matters. He made that quite clear when told me he wanted a divorce."

"I'm sorry. When was that?"

"Last year, the week before I told my mother she'd have to visit Jodi's grave without me."

"Did you and your husband separate?"

"Six months ago, and it's a miracle we lasted as long as we did. We had to postpone our wedding three times because my mother didn't feel like celebrating. It took two years before Larry and I found the courage to elope. One day, on our lunch hour, we drove downtown and stood before a justice of the peace. That's how we began, without a ceremony or the chance to have family and friends share in our happiness. No flowers or gifts. No acknowledgment that the most cherished day of our lives had passed. Only a piece of paper and a hamburger at Woolworth's afterward. That marked the official beginning of our life together, thanks to the ghost of my sister and the grief of my mother."

I tried to steer the conversation in a different direction. "Do you remember when your family found out Jodi was missing?"

"Saturday night. Mrs. Parks called my mother. Sunday morning, my parents caught the first flight out of Hartford."

"When did they arrive at Winter Glades?"

"Early Sunday evening, when Jodi was still missing."

"And Monday morning, your parents found out Jodi had died?"

"Yes. My father called me at Clothes Bar, the department store where I worked during school breaks. My supervisor took me into the break-room and told me, then she helped make travel arrangements."

"You flew to Colorado?"

"Someone had to. My father was beside himself trying to take care of my broken-down mother and deal with all the details. He asked me to come, and I obeyed."

"Did you go into the mountains?"

"By the time I arrived, my parents were at a hotel in Denver. We stayed for a few days until arrangements could be made with the authorities and a funeral home. On Thursday of that week, we flew home with Jodi's body. I always thought that was strange, my parents and I sitting on the airplane, with Jodi in a casket below, next to the luggage."

Jill took a deep breath before continuing. "My mother collapsed when we got back to Connecticut. She wasn't fit to attend the funeral on Saturday. My father and I and half of Hartford buried my little sister."

I winced at the sarcasm, more of which soon followed. "The next week, I had the privilege of cleaning out Jodi's dorm room at Middle-bury. What a treat that was, being exposed to pornographic perversion."

"Porn?"

"Love letters from Lori Parks. Stacks of them, filthy garbage."

"They were sexually explicit?"

"Thank goodness, no. More like poetry, but about love between two women. Lines such as this: 'Our love is a never-ending ascent, one with no limits or bounds, a love of forever.'"

"Huh," I said, astounded Lori Parks, albeit as a younger woman, had expressed and exposed herself.

"Or this is a good example: 'We can find truths evil will never touch. We can be alone in a place others will never know. This is our beginning, a lifetime of happiness.'"

"You remember this after twenty years?"

"I kept the letters."

I struggled to keep fury from my voice. "And you periodically re-read them?" Evidently, often enough to have memorized them.

"A year ago, I did, when my mother wouldn't believe Jodi was a homosexual. When she had the audacity to call me a liar, I read them to her over the phone."

"Your mother listened?" I couldn't refrain from exclaiming.

"Not in person. I left snippets on her answering machine every day. My favorite was 'A moment apart tears at my heart like a lifetime of separation.' That was a good one."

"How did your mother react?"

"She didn't, at first. After about a month, she called and said two sentences, to which I responded with one word, and she slammed down the phone. Mercifully, that was the last I've heard from her."

"What were the two lines?"

"She said, 'Jodi died on that mountain. Now, thanks to you, I've lost her forever.'"

"What did you reply?"

"Finally."

Despite my distaste for Jill Wilde, I maintained my professionalism and confirmed three facts before we ended our conversation. First, the physical appearance of her mother matched that of the concierge at the Children's Academy. Second, her mother had moved to Colorado six months earlier. And most incriminating, after divorcing Jill's father, her mother had reverted to her maiden name, Sally Patterson.

I could hardly wait to pummel Lori Parks with this information.

Fortunately, Fran intervened before I had the chance. I met her and Donna at the house shortly before nine.

Lori had left for work hours earlier, unable to leave her post even in dire circumstances. Apparently, Donna hadn't attempted to conceal her disgust at her lover's priorities, which had led to another blowout. Fran had ended the rumble by reminding them the neighbors could probably hear their wrath.

Fran had made the best of unprecedented circumstances by assigning Lori tasks to perform at the Children's Academy, the most vital of which was to track down Sally Patterson's real address. In this pursuit, there was no need to mention Erica's disappearance. Sally's unexpected absence served as reason enough to inquire whether coworkers had visited her at home or heard her mention a neighborhood.

Meanwhile, Donna called in sick to her law office, no stretch of the truth, and made breakfast. I choked down scrambled eggs and toast, which Fran devoured.

Donna didn't swallow a bite but nursed a cup of tea laced with lemon. She held the mug tightly, her hands trembling.

I felt like bolting for the bathroom immediately following the meal, but I willed my intestinal tract to tolerate the necessary fuel. I couldn't function very well on no sleep and no food.

After Donna left the kitchen to phone friends and acquaintances she hadn't reached the night before, Fran scooted her chair next to mine. "Have an idea. Let's bring in a pooch, sniff out the culprit."

"A bloodhound?"

"Columbo. Success rate eight out of ten."

I shook my head in disbelief. "You know a tracking dog named Columbo?"

"Not personally. Met his owner, Kari, at Gay Bingo. Comes every week. Dog's her life."

"We can't bring in the police."

"Kari's an independent. Contracts with law enforcement agencies. Only a handful in Colorado have bloodhounds on the payroll. According to Kari, most departments don't give them due respect."

"Did I meet Kari the night we ran into Ruth and Janet?"

"Can't recollect. Squirt of a thing, mid-twenties, shirt too tight, bra a size too small, hair braided down to her rear?"

"That doesn't sound familiar."

Fran smacked her forehead. "Come to think of it, she was out of town that week. Flew to a breeder's in Ohio."

"Shouldn't we have called her in last night?"

"No loss. Hound can pick up a trail for thirty days. The trick is good scent material."

"Erica's clothing?"

"Better yet, a pillow case. Lots of aroma dander on it. People shed dead cells a million times a minute. Cells interact with bacteria and produce a gas. Smelly fingerprint. No two alike."

"Yuck. Good thing we can't smell it."

"Darn right. A bloodhound has scenting qualities three million times better than you or me. Just as well, all those body odors floating around, make you gag. Scent blows off the body, like pollen from a flower. Settles on vegetation, pavement, sidewalks, curbs. Hound can track the scent of someone who rode in a car with the windows closed."

"Closed?"

"If the ride came off the assembly line after 1978. All buggies made after that year are equipped with flow-through ventilation. Little invention that helped the bloodhound trade."

"How do you know all this?"

"Lots of dull moments at Bingo. Chitchat livens it up. Never thought I'd put the tidbits to use, but there you have it."

"Do you think we have a chance?"

"Cool weather, little humidity. No wind to scatter the scent and confuse the pooch. Couldn't ask for better conditions." Fran looked at me eagerly.

"Okay," I sighed. "What do we have to lose?"

Within the hour, Kari and Columbo arrived to pick up Fran and the scent. They took Erica's pillow case and left in a hurry.

I spent the morning with Donna, alternately comforting her and pursuing lines of inquiry by phone.

At one point, I couldn't help noticing her fingernails matched mine, bitten to the quick. And the dark circles under her eyes seemed to pull down her cheeks. She wore the same outfit from the day before—the pantsuit she'd worn to work. Wrinkled and stained with sorrow, her clothes gave off the sour scent of body odor.

We both reacted with a start when a phone rang in the afternoon.

Unfortunately, the noise came from my cell phone, not her home phone.

It was Rebecca Ramirez, returning my call after I'd left a message for her hours earlier.

I spent a considerable amount of time apologizing for the fake job ploy and assuring her Lori Parks would give her a superlative recommendation and a monetary settlement before I could get her to believe my new, authentic story.

After I convinced her Erica Parks was in danger, she revealed Sally Patterson's legitimate home address near Colfax and Simms. Rebecca had driven Sally to work several times when her Buick Regal was in the shop, and she was certain she resided in Lakewood.

With address in hand, I bolted out the door.

Twelve miles later, I arrived at a nondescript, six-story brick apartment building. I pressed the buzzer for the manager.

I used truth, or a partial version of it, as means of entry. I told the manager Sally hadn't shown up for work that morning, and we were concerned for her welfare. The manager phoned the Children's Academy, confirmed my story with Lori, and let me in to search.

The job didn't take long.

As I raced through the two-bedroom apartment, my heart seized up in the front bedroom. Furnished sparsely in second-hand, mismatched pieces, the room paid perpetual tribute to a dead girl's achievements. Yearbooks, music awards, sports trophies, and photographs filled the shrine with the spirit of youth. Large, glossy photos covered one wall, capturing Jodi Wilde's radiance as she sailed, hiked, played tennis, swam, ran competitively, and attended the prom, with a boy.

Her sister Jill was nowhere to be seen, except in one family photo published in the *Hartford Courant,* the week after Jodi's death.

I found the snapshot and accompanying article in a scrapbook on a desk in the corner of the room. The binder bulged with newspaper articles, from Denver and Hartford, about the ski trip. I skimmed the words and studied photos of the family, the rescue team, and the trailhead. I could barely tolerate digesting the record of heartbreak one time. Judging from well-worn pages, Sally Patterson/Wilde had traveled through it repeatedly.

I moved on to the kitchen.

In a newspaper section lying on the counter, I saw Sally had circled a classified ad for a green Subaru Outback. Four-wheel drive, 60,000 miles, $10,000 or best offer. She must have exchanged the Buick for a more reliable, all-weather vehicle.

I had begun to rifle through cupboards and drawers when my cell phone rang.

In response to an earlier inquiry, one of Fran's acquaintances, a fellow who worked for a consumer credit counseling bureau, gave me the results of the credit check he'd run on Sally Patterson. One Visa, with a $20,000 limit. Paid off every month. The only charges in the last twenty-four hours: $72.39 for groceries and $23.15 for gas.

Both receipts came from Lakewood, close to the apartment, and neither offered a clue as to the whereabouts of Sally and Erica.

Ransacking closets, diving under beds, and upending couch cushions, I continued the search.

When I found an empty box in the bottom of the bathroom wastebasket, I started to curse wildly.

Sally Patterson/Wilde had thrown away a container that once held bullets.

I barely had absorbed the magnitude of this find when Fran phoned with an update. "Columbo's a beauty in motion, Kris. Gentle, friendly, drools buckets. 'Course aloof and stubborn, too, but what genius ain't? Kari wiped the scent from Erica's pillow on a gauze pad. Put it in a plastic bag. Gave Columbo a big whiff, and off he went. Nose to the ground, tail up. Keyed on that scent like nobody's business. Never seen such commitment."

"Where did the scent lead?"

"Kari, too. Good handling skills. Interpreted Columbo's every movement. Had as much energy as him. She kept barking, 'Find the prize.' That's her code for the body. Higher Columbo's tail, stronger the scent. Done wore me out. Weeds, pavement. Weeds, pavement. Proof Erica went in a car."

"To where?" I repeated.

"Can't say exactly. Lost the scent after fifteen miles. Resting up, tackle it again, double back after we get a bite to eat."

"How far did you get with the trail?"

"Ain't gonna like this, way out Sixth Avenue, intersection with I-70."

Goose bumps formed on my arms, and my mouth turned dry. "Sally's taking Erica into the mountains."

Chapter 24

A rugged car. A tank full of gas. A few days worth of groceries. Christmas time.

Sally Wilde had every intention of re-creating Jodi Wilde's death in Winter Glades, using the child of the person she perceived to be her daughter's killer.

Erica—bait to lure Lori Parks or the ultimate prize?

Neither scenario held promise.

I didn't hesitate to make my next move.

"I found Sally's apartment and searched it," I told Lori as soon as I reached her by phone at the Children's Academy. "There are pictures of Jodi everywhere and newspaper clippings about the ski trip."

"No," she said, an almost inaudible protest.

"I think she's taken Erica to Winter Glades, to your parents' cabin."

Silence.

"Fran's coming back to the house to stay with Donna, and I'm going into the mountains. You need to come with me."

"Why?"

"To apologize."

"I refuse to apologize. That woman took away the only person who ever mattered to me."

"Sally has your daughter, Lori."

"I have to get off the phone now. I'll call you back."

"When?" I barked, not caring if I blasted her eardrum.

"In five minutes," she promised.

An hour later, I hadn't heard from Lori Parks. Nor had Fran. Nor had Donna. Nor had anyone at the Children's Academy, from which she'd apparently fled immediately following our call.

To hell with her, I headed west.

Near Genesee, ten miles outside of Denver, I hit light snow and a little slush. No big deal. I continued at full, highway speed. By Idaho Springs, however, thirty miles into my journey, the flurries had turned into a full-blown blizzard. Snow had covered the asphalt, and I started to see cars on the side of the road, twisted in helpless skids.

After I felt the back end of my Honda slip, I slowed down to a virtual crawl and moved to the right lane. Better to get there eventually than not at all. I flipped on my hazard lights to warn drivers following at full bore.

I successfully navigated the turn from I-70 to Highway 25, more from memory than clear vision.

Because I couldn't see ahead more than ten car lengths, I shut off the radio and concentrated on the stripes in the road. By now, snow seemed to attack the windshield from all directions, swirling me into confusion. I tested the traction every few miles, applying the brakes gently to see if I would come to a clean stop or an ugly skid.

Four o'clock in the afternoon, and the storm had brought on early darkness. Headlights on cars coming toward me bounced their light in spooky configurations.

Gripping the steering wheel tightly with both hands, I debated turning back but couldn't bear the thought of subjecting Erica to another night with Sally.

Ten miles up the approach to Kennison Pass, I stopped seeing other cars. None in front, none behind, and none on the other side of the two-lane road. All tracks had disappeared as well. Had the cars turned off somewhere? Was I headed in the right direction, over Kennison, toward Winter Glades?

Maybe the cars had fallen off the side of the road. No, I couldn't let myself go there.

Terror began to choke me.

For distraction from the danger, I talked out loud, pointing out reflective poles that marked the sides of the pavement and curves ahead. Every minute or so, I supplemented my car's pitiful defrost system by wiping the inside of the windows. My feet felt half-frozen, but I didn't dare divert heat to the floor.

I had to take it a mile at a time. String enough together, and I'd soon rescue Erica.

That's what kept me going through the next three hairpin turns. My talk with myself now included reminders about which side represented the mountain and which guaranteed drop-off to injury or death. Twice, I came to a complete stop when a wind burst brought such a flurry of snow I lost all sense of direction. No point in moving if I couldn't make an educated guess where to go.

I urged myself to hug the mountain, at the risk of being on the wrong side of the road. Weighing scenarios, I opted for a slow-speed, head-on collision in lieu of an end-over-end tumble.

Guardrails would have been nice, but they seemed in short supply.

I had nothing but my wits to protect me. Scant consolation when they were frayed to a nub from stress and sleep deprivation.

Would I ever get over this wretched pass?

"Back in the horse and buggy day, you had three classes of passengers who made it over Kennison Pass. First class rode inside the carriage. Second walked along side over the steep parts. And third class—"

My host looked at me expectantly. "Pushed?" I guessed.

"Too true," Brian Savant said, laughing easily.

This guy was my new best friend.

I'd bumped into him two hours earlier. Not literally, thank God. On one of the open stretches of Kennison Pass, my Honda had come to rest behind a pair of taillights, a sight so beautiful, I started to cry.

I'd hopped out of the car, desperate for company, and knocked on the driver's window of the van. Not startled in the least, Brian had rolled down the window, explained that the highway department had closed the pass, and invited me to join him in the wait for it to reopen.

I didn't have to be asked twice. I dashed back to my car, loaded up snacks I'd packed for my reunion with Erica, and returned to the comfort of the fifteen-passenger van.

Driver of the Winter Glades Express Shuttle, Brian looked fifteen but claimed to be twenty-three. He had a high-pitched, nasal voice and a shaved head and goatee. A passionate telemark skier, he lived in Winter Glades full-time. In the winter, he drove the commercial van from Denver International Airport to the resort, and in the shoulder seasons and summer, he worked construction.

We spent our time together playing gin rummy and eating chips, candy bars, and fruit rolls. Twice, I had to jump out of the van to pee. Fortunately, Brian lent me a pair of snowpants, which made the experience of voiding into a waist-deep snowbank a fraction less unpleasant. I came back from both forays with frozen nose hairs and eyelashes laced in snow. My companion must have had a champion bladder, strengthened, no doubt, from Kennison Pass closures, because he never exited the vehicle.

"Didn't they talk about building a tunnel through Kennison Mountain a few years ago?"

"Forget about that."

"You were opposed?"

"If two million people from the Denver area could get here in less than an hour, we'd lose everything that's awesome."

"You must be one of those transplants who wants to be the last one in, then close the gate."

His eyes flickered, but he said genially, "I'm fifth generation in the valley. Ranchers and cattlemen."

He spent the next four hands detailing his family's rich history in Winter Glades. I did my best to stay interested, but the sides of the van began to feel as if they had contracted.

I fidgeted in my seat. "How much longer do you think the pass will stay closed?"

"Who knows? Before you got here, I radioed one of our other drivers, coming this way toward Denver. He said he's stuck behind Beaver Gulch. At least once a year, snow comes down that chute. Last season, it buried a buddy of mine, one of the county snowplow drivers. They managed to dig him out, and he tells the story to every girl who comes to town. I've heard it about fifty times."

"That must get annoying."

"I'm usually too drunk to care. Plus, we all do it, spin lies. Another of my good buddies, local super boy, tells the ladies how he shot himself. His story's so ill, he doesn't have to add anything."

"How did he manage that?"

"A couple seasons back, we didn't have much snow. The crazy-ass bastard thought he'd shoot a bullet into the snowpack at the bottom of the mountain, to see if the ski area was telling the truth about the thirty-inch base."

"Were they?"

"He never found out. He said the snow was so icy, the bullet ricocheted off the top and hit him in the leg. When he's had enough brew, he'll drop trou and show the scar on top of his thigh. He's frickin' nuts."

"You guys have too much time on your hands."

"Sometimes," Brian said agreeably.

"We could be here all night," I said, depressed. For entertainment, I blew on my hands. Brian started the engine and heater every ten minutes, but the compartment never reached a toasty state.

"Not that long. This road is the pipeline to the ski area. They have one of the best full-time road crews in the state to make sure tourists can get in safely with their wads. This is the big week, Christmas to New Year's, the one that makes or breaks most locals."

Before I could comment on the state of tourism, a sonic boom went off.

I ducked in my seat. "What was that?"

Brian grinned. "They're blasting for avalanches."

"They cause them intentionally?"

"Little ones, to prevent them from becoming big ones."

"I don't know how you drive this pass every day."

"Twice a day, but only four days a week. Plus, I love it. I'd much rather be on Kennison than I-70. This mountain forces people to slow down. That or they go over the edge."

"That was my fear." I nodded in assent. "How come you don't have any passengers tonight?"

"I took a full load down on my 2:00 run and was supposed to bring back a charter group, but they had their flight canceled. They're stuck in Chicago with bad weather."

"It could be worse," I said, aimlessly sketching figures in the frost on the passenger window.

"Too right. I'd rather be sitting here than at O'Hare."

"Me, too," I said, unenthusiastically, staring into the darkness. The snow seemed to have let up, but my assessment may have come from wishful thinking. I felt as if I were hallucinating, as if I'd sat in this van for a week. "How many inches do you think we'll have by morning?"

"Enough to close the lumber mill. A bunch of my buddies work there. It's the best job in town, except for mine. If it snows four inches or more, they don't have to come to work until noon. They get first lifts and track out all the trails, kickin' it."

"Will you ski tomorrow?"

"Hell, yeah! I'll be pushing those amateurs out of my way in the lift-line. It could be the best day of the season."

Suddenly, I couldn't avoid talking about my plight.

"I lied earlier when I said I was passing through to Steamboat Springs," I said quietly.

Brian looked at me with increased interest.

"I have to get to this cabin as soon as possible. It's owned by the Parks family, and the waiting is killing me."

"What's the hurry?"

"A little girl was kidnapped last night, and I think she's in Winter Glades."

"Are you a cop?" he said, flabbergasted.

"A friend of the family."

"That's weird you're going to the Parks cabin," Brian said, deep in thought.

"Why? You know something about it?"

"Sure. It's owned by the parents of one of the four girls who went on that ski trip back in the '80s. The family almost never uses it, but someone's been up there recently."

I felt excitement and fear mount. "How do you know?"

"There are fresh tracks on the private road."

My heart rate zoomed. "You remember that ski trip?"

"Only because the locals keep recycling stories. I was three when it happened, but my uncle helped on the rescue. With the girl dying and Switz getting injured, that trip still ranks as one of the worst in the county."

"Have you been to the cabin?"

"I go by it all the time. Farther down the road, there's a B&B, the Backwoods Inn. Lots of their guests take the shuttle. That road's a mother to negotiate. Parts of it never get sun, and it stays icy for five months."

"Don't they plow it?"

"Plow and dump gravel, but once that first layer sets, it freezes and melts all winter. Do you have studded snow tires?"

"No."

"You'll never make it in that Honda."

"You're sure?"

"You'll fishtail right into a snowbank. Then you'll have to call Smiley Towing, and those pricks will charge you two hundred bucks for ten minutes of work. I have another idea."

"The van? It wouldn't attract attention if you do it all the time."

"Better yet, a dogsled. It'll get you closer."

I looked at Brian skeptically. "You're joking."

"I'll hook you up. My buddy Kirk runs an outfit, the best in the county. It's a family business, but he acts like it's his. He's built the kennel up to a hundred-twenty-five dogs, all Alaskan Huskies. Man, those dogs fly. He gets them up to twenty miles an hour, and that's pulling a five-hundred-pound sled and two riders. Kirk has a special forest permit and access to a thousand acres. He's mushed out almost thirty miles of track. He talks a lot of shit, but he knows what he's doing."

"And one of the trails is near the Parks cabin?"

"Less than a hundred yards from the back door."

"Could we approach without being noticed?"

"Those dogs are loud. They bark and howl constantly, but Kirk takes them out on three tours a day. Coming with you shouldn't look unusual."

"But I've met the kidnapper. She'll recognize me."

"Not when you're wearing a parka with a wrap-around hood."

"Good point."

"Plus, Kirk always bundles the guests in blankets. Most come from Texas or Florida, and they don't tip worth crap if they freeze their asses."

"I don't have to drive the sled, do I?"

At this, Brian laughed uproariously. "He'd never let you. Those dogs are his life. He treats them like members of his family. Trains them all summer, takes them to the vet whenever he hears a cough. He'll barely let me take a team out. And when he does, he's right behind me, bitching at the way I steer. I have a tough time managing six dogs, and look at these pipes."

Brian took off his jacket and flexed his biceps, which I duly admired. "It's that hard?"

"You'll see when you meet Kirk. He's a bruiser, and he struggles sometimes. He's broken both thumbs on sled motions, twisted his back a few times. He's got nothing against women. He thinks they're double-dope, but his family's never let one drive a team."

"How early can we go?"

"If you want to stick with his usual schedule, first groups go out at eight."

"I'll be there," I said, before slapping down my cards and proclaiming, "Gin!"

Two hours later, road crews opened Kennison Pass.

As I exited the van one final time, Brian grabbed my arm. "Follow my taillights, and I'll get us down. You can hang with me tonight."

"I couldn't impose," I protested.

"My roommate went south for the holidays. Dude's in Mexico now. This is Christmas week. You can't touch a reservation. The town's been booked for two months. It's not the Hilton, but it's better than sleeping in your car."

My face fell. "You're serious—there's nothing in town?"

"Not a closet. When we get back to my place, I'll call Kirk, get you hooked up with a morning ride."

"You're sure I won't disturb you?"

"Not in the least. I'll sleep good, dreaming of all that snow I'll thrash tomorrow."

"Okay," I said, smiling at his love of powder.

He certainly had resilience after driving and sitting in it for the past seven hours. If I never saw another flake, I wouldn't complain.

Traveling behind a county plow, Brian and I made it to the top of Kennison Pass and down the other side, safely, in about an hour.

Shortly before midnight, I breathed deeply for the first time all day.

When Brian had called his friend to set up the dogsled ride, Kirk had passed along news that a green Subaru Outback had been parked outside the Parks cabin all day.

Sally and Erica were there, in Winter Glades.

Despite my relief and my host's best efforts at hospitality, I didn't sleep that night.

Not one wink for one minute.

All I could think about was how I could continue to follow the advice Brian had given when we resumed our trek over the pass.

"Keep it safe," he'd said, as if intention alone could bring about a desired result.

Chapter 25

In the morning, I couldn't move.

I had long underwear, a wool sweater, thermal socks, and thick snow pants binding me. By the time I added mittens that extended past my forearms and parka coveralls with a hood, I could barely flex a muscle. Toe heater patches warmed my feet, though they seemed like overkill given the pack boots I'd borrowed were rated to minus-seventy degrees.

I was dressed in all black and stood out like a scarecrow in mourning.

I had to remove my hood to catch the conversation. "Brian explained it, but let me get this straight: You want me to run you to the Parks cabin, close as I can get on the trail. From there, you'll snowshoe to a door or window. I'll head north, around the bend. You'll call on the two-way radio when you're ready for me to come and get you. If you can't talk but need help, you'll flip the radio button three times as a distress call, and I'll page the sheriff. Cool?"

I nodded. "That's it."

Kirk Rorbaugh, owner of Dogsled Wilderness Tours, had inspired from our handshake greeting on. A few years older than Brian, he commanded respect from his animals, employees, and guests. I'd arrived at the kennels off County Road 92 shortly after dawn and watched idly as guests cut through a screened-in porch to register in the main room of an A-frame cabin. As they milled about waiting for dog teams to assemble, they warmed themselves next to a firepit in the middle of the parking lot, snacking on complimentary cocoa and homemade banana nut bread.

Pre-dawn, the flames had cut through darkness, but gradually, the sun had peeked over the nearby mountain range. As I'd waited, fidgeting, I witnessed the morning ritual of caring for the dogs along four rows of low-level huts. The dogs consumed barrels of food, and seemingly expelled an equal amount of feces. Muckers scooped up the waste with full-size shovels, threw it into wheelbarrows, and carted it around the bend into a dense grove of trees.

"How long will it take to get to the Parks cabin?" I asked.

"It's about five miles out. I could run the dogs in thirty minutes, maybe less."

"Is that your usual time?"

"Shoot, no. We string out the tour so we can charge more. We stop and view the Continental Divide, take pictures. We slow down in the meadow to check out wildlife tracks—moose, fox, coyote, hare. Tourists get stoked for that shit."

"When do you typically get to the Parks cabin?"

"Forty-five, fifty minutes."

"Let's do the same, in case they noticed your routine yesterday."

"It's a plan." Kirk handed me a pair of snowshoes. "Have you done this before?"

I shook my head.

"It's as easy as walking. Slip them on and practice a few steps while I gear up the dogs."

Kirk exaggerated a bit. To the background noise of howling canines, I stumbled around on snowshoes. Twice, my right foot came out of the binding mid-step, and once I pitched forward when the front of one shoe clamped down on the back of the other.

Those blunders aside, the experience wasn't all that graceful or effortless. I'd imagined gliding across the surface of the snow in light, delicate steps. In reality, each foot sunk about six inches through soft-hard layers of powder-crust and required considerable muscle to pull up.

My form, as awkward as it felt, must have met with Kirk's approval, because on my third lap around the kennels, he gave me a hearty slap on the back.

In no time, he had eight of the Alaskan Huskies strapped into individual harnesses and attached to a central wire that connected to the sled. Sensing our impending departure, the dogs intensified their cries.

Kirk situated me on the wooden seat, looking forward, and bundled me in a blanket and goggles. He climbed on the platform behind and called out a command to the two lead dogs. With a jolt, we sprang into motion.

We rode the first fifteen minutes in relative silence, across makeshift bridges spanning little creeks and ditches, through dense forests and alpine meadows. The scenery was breathtaking.

Pine trees with caps of fresh snow were set against the backdrop of jagged mountain peaks. The bright blue sky was as clear as if it had been washed. The sun burst through billowing clouds and pushed its rays across the horizon. Snowscapes, draped in sunlight, resembled fields of diamonds.

When we stopped to rest at Kirk's customary spot, the midway point to the cabin, I found the stillness almost devastating in its power.

For a moment, as I watched Kirk feed the dogs strips of bacon, a fuzz of the ears and a solid pat on the side accompanying each treat, I heard nothing but the sounds of the forest. The cackle and crowing of birds, the creaking and swaying of trees, and the trickle of a nearby stream were almost deafening. In the distance, I had an unbroken view of the Continental Divide and the Winter Glades ski area.

I couldn't fathom how this pristine environment had killed Jodi Wilde and permanently injured Liz Decker and Paul Switzer, nor how twenty years later that trauma continued unresolved.

Kirk's voice broke through. "We'll approach from the south. Stay away from the west side—a trail right by the Parks cabin leads into one of the most avalanche-prone chutes in the county. Perfect angle, thirty-seven or thirty-eight degrees."

I shivered.

"I'll stop the dogs behind the shed. There are no windows on that side of the cabin, so you should be able to get to the back door without being seen. You going to be okay?"

I nodded numbly.

"Don't forget to use the radio."

Those were the last words he spoke. Three turns later, we exited the forest and came to a cleared area. At the sight of the green Subaru Outback, I felt myself start to gag but fought the impulse.

From that point on, everything happened at warp speed. Kirk paused the dogs behind the shed. I clambered off, and in my last view of him, his considerable girth masked the blanket arrangement. He'd tried to prop the blankets as if there were a body underneath, but the masquerade looked patently obvious.

I could only hope Sally Wilde wasn't near a window.

I buckled my snowshoes and crept around the side of the cabin, hugging the wall for support and cover. I took my time with every footstep, not daring to make a sound.

I'd come within a leg's length of the back door when I stepped on a branch, buried beneath the snow. My weight broke the wood with a sound that ricocheted around the cabin.

I paused, holding my breath. Reverting to childish instinct, I shut my eyes.

When I opened them, Sally Wilde had a gun pointed at my temple.

She ordered me up the icy stairs, and I kicked off the snowshoes and scrambled to obey, but I tripped.

I came down the wooden stairs on my back, each step jarring my spine. Sally must have thought my fall was a ruse, because she expressed no sympathy and jabbed me in the side with the gun to speed my entry into the house.

"Is Erica here?"

She replaced my question with her own. "Did Lori send you?"

"Yes."

"Is she worried?"

"Terribly. And so is Donna. May I see Erica?"

"She's in the other room, asleep."

"Is she all right?"

"Of course she is. What kind of mother do you think I am?"

I looked at her closely. "I think you're a mother who suffered an unbearable loss."

Sally gestured for me to sit on the brown leather couch, below a mounted moose head. I complied as she occupied the rocker across from me, her feet resting on the head of a bearskin rug. A small fire burned in the moss rock fireplace, and a needlepoint "Welcome" sign next to the picture window mocked our situation.

Dressed in fleece-lined black jeans, a white turtleneck with gold snowflakes embroidered on the sleeves, brown bootie slippers, and a festive holiday vest, Sally looked the part of a mountain cabin hostess. Except for the firearm pointed at my chest.

If I stared at her at just the right angle, her head seemed to be part of the Parks family portrait hanging behind her. A massive photo, the setting reflected earlier times. Big hair, long sideburns, mom, dad, Lori, two brothers, and a golden retriever. One happy family, yet behind Lori's pubescent smile lay a hint of sadness, as if she could foretell tragedy.

As though chilled, I eased my hands toward my jacket pockets—and the two-way radio. I needed a sheriff, and now, but I never managed to send the distress signal. Sally cut short my movement with a threatening wave of the gun and a warning to keep my hands in plain sight.

A wave of despair came over me, not at her command but at the realization I'd lost my lifeline. I had shifted my jacket far enough to discover the empty pocket. The radio must have tumbled out in the fall, and I had no realistic shot of retrieving it from the powdery snowbank without Sally's notice.

I was on my own, and I'd never felt as alone.

Sally looked at me suspiciously, her face gaunt. "You know about my daughter Jodi?"

"Yes, and I can't begin to express how sorry I am for your loss."

Her features relaxed. "No one can understand the anguish, the waiting, the hoping."

"I can't imagine what you went through, but—"

"No, you cannot. Do you know what I prayed for? I prayed for the safe return of my daughter. When rescuers told me they'd found the girls, and three were alive and one was dead, I prayed for Jodi. I looked right into the eyes of those other mothers, and I prayed one of their daughters had perished.

"But they hadn't. The one who died belonged to me. And she died in the worst way possible. Alone, thousands of miles from home. I never wanted Jodi to come to Colorado, but she was stubborn. She said she'd always wanted to see the Rocky Mountains, that she was excited to try cross-country skiing. I knew my daughter was growing up, that I had to let her go, but this would be the first Christmas our family spent apart.

"I wondered what went through her mind those last nights on the mountain. When I was safe and warm while others searched. I wondered if she cried or if she knew she was about to die. I wondered about her last words and if anyone heard them. I wondered if she knew that I'd come to Colorado, that I was only five miles from her, but helpless. I wondered if she knew the hole in my heart grew with every hour."

All color had drained from Sally's face. "I wondered if she felt as naked as she looked, if she needed my touch, the embrace the authorities denied. I had to see her one last time. I knew I'd never have the strength to go to the funeral, to see her lying still in front of all those people. I had to do it now. My husband told me not to look. He tried to spare me, but I wouldn't listen. I knew she had frozen to death, but I never expected to see her looking like that. With her mouth open and her beautiful face twisted, as if she'd died in the middle of a scream. I thought she would look serene, as she had when I used to lay her to sleep in her crib. I never wanted to believe she'd died in agony. I knew in that instant I'd never allow an open casket. No mortuary could erase such pain. I had to touch her, but I couldn't. I wondered if she knew how much I wanted to hug her, to protect her from everything that had happened."

Sally Wilde continued, in a trance-like tone. "The hours went by in a daze. When I got home, I couldn't see anyone, couldn't speak of it, couldn't stop feeling the cold. I wondered if she forgave me for not going to the funeral, for not being strong enough to see the final sign of her life on this earth, for wanting to lie in the coffin with her.

"I went on with my life—for her sake—as well as I could. I lost her father because I lost her, but I made the best of it. I stayed busy, I prayed,

I made little things matter every day. I never made sense of it, but I came to accept it, in small steps, inches every year. I came to a peace with it."

Sally stopped speaking, and after a long pause, I said gently, "Then your other daughter called you."

"Yes," she said, not the least surprised by my intrusion or access to inside information. "And she said vile things about Jodi, which at first I didn't believe."

"And Jill kept calling."

"She wouldn't stop. And I couldn't make myself not listen. I'd come home and see the light blinking on the answering machine. I'd play the message and cry. Over and over, the words and the tears. This went on for hours, for nights, for weeks. I sobbed until I was out of breath, until my sides hurt. I pulled a muscle and displaced a rib, the doctor told me. It hurt to breathe. How did this happen, he asked. I never answered. If he couldn't see the grief in my face, the shaking of my hands, and the shuffle in my walk, he wouldn't understand."

"You had lost your daughter."

"Again."

"But you hadn't," I said quietly.

"No?" Sally's face contorted.

"I know those letters disturbed you, but—"

"You can't begin to know what was in them."

"I have an idea. They were love letters, from one young woman to another."

"They were wrong. They weren't love, they were evil. They were confused. They were against everything good and natural. I knew they were, and I knew I had to do something."

"That's when you decided to come to Colorado and track down Lori Parks?"

"I came on a visit. I never planned to stay. I wanted to meet this woman who had taken my daughter, to tell her I knew. I didn't set out to harm her or anyone else. I wanted to talk, nothing more."

"When did that change?"

"When I visited the Children's Academy and met her daughter."

"You saw Erica?"

Sally nodded. "I knew that woman didn't deserve to have a daughter when mine had died. I knew she didn't deserve to carry on as if nothing had happened. I knew she didn't deserve to have a family with another woman, no matter how many lies she told to preserve that right. I knew she didn't deserve to wake up every day without grief."

"That's when you decided to kidnap Erica?"

"Not then. I just wanted to scare her mother, to put her on alert, to make her live with worry. I wrote the notes and left the winter clothes and the picture of Jodi. But nothing affected her. She didn't say a word. She didn't change her behavior. She continued living as if nothing bad could happen, as if sorrow belonged only to others."

"You wanted Lori Parks to pay attention."

"Yes. When I drove Erica home Monday, I kept driving. At first, I thought I'd take her out for pizza and bring her home, claiming an innocent mix-up. I'd frighten her mother for a few hours. But once I started driving, I couldn't stop. I couldn't bring her back, no matter what."

"Do you think I could bring her back?" I asked tentatively.

"No," Sally Wilde said. "Not alive."

I felt my anger rising, and I forcibly checked it. "You know Erica's innocent, don't you?"

"My daughter was, too."

I tried a different approach. "Do you love Erica?"

"You spend enough time around someone, you come to care about them a great deal."

"You couldn't harm her."

"It would be difficult, but yes, I could."

"Could you live with yourself?"

"I died in Colorado the day I saw my daughter pulled out of these woods. Nothing could be worse than that."

I switched tactics again. "Would Jodi be proud of you—would she want you to do this? To trade a child for a child?"

"Jodi's dead," Sally said stolidly. "She died last year."

"When you found out about the love letters from Lori Parks?"

"Yes."

"She didn't have to die then. You'd loved Jodi faithfully all those years after she was gone. You can still love her today."

"No, I cannot. I cannot remember giving her a bath or walking her to school. I cannot remember helping her with homework or teaching her tennis. I cannot remember the way she played the piano or how she sang. I cannot remember the thoughtful notes she left on my pillow or the ease with which she made friends. I cannot remember the sun shining in her hair or the comfort of her laugh."

"All you can remember is that she fell in love with another woman," I said, dejected.

"I've lost all those memories. When they died, she died. And now," Sally Wilde said deliberately, "we'll die with her."

Chapter 26

I had hoped Sally Wilde meant she and I, not Erica. How naïve.

Sally kindly described our death to me. At gunpoint, she would march me and Erica straight into the path of an avalanche. She would trigger it, and we would die in a casket of snow. She would then turn the gun on herself. The same mountains which had claimed her daughter's life would welcome her home.

The day before, she'd scouted the trail behind the cabin and admired the deadly cornice hanging precariously on the top of the slope. She'd located the avalanche chute Kirk Rorbaugh had labeled one of the most dangerous in the county and had deemed it suitable for Erica's death. My unexpected arrival presented neither bonus nor burden.

After Sally had explained her strategy, she began to implement it systematically.

She went into the other room and brought out Erica, barefoot, clad only in a dress with flower-print. The little girl rushed to hug me, but

Sally halted her with a vicious tug on the arm. I gave Erica a slight wave and winked at her when Sally wasn't looking.

Holding on to the bow on the top of Erica's dress, Sally dragged her into the front foyer and returned with two sets of cross-country ski boots. She looked on solemnly as we struggled to get into the gear. The women's boots were gigantic on Erica, and the men's boots fit me like galoshes, but I tied our laces as tightly as I could.

When I knelt down to help her, Erica clutched my hair tightly, her stare never wavering from the barrel of Sally's gun.

"Where's Mom and Mommy Donna?"

"At home, honey. They asked me to come and see you because they know we're such good friends."

"I miss my moms."

"You'll see them soon," I whispered.

I started to outfit Erica with a coat, gloves, and hat from nearby hooks and baskets, but Sally nixed that.

Without a word, she forced us out the door, where we buckled into skis that looked as if they hadn't been touched in two decades. I had to show Erica how to glide—a rudimentary lesson that, surprisingly, Sally allowed.

All the while, I engaged a separate part of my mind, trying to determine how I could avert doom.

For starters, I needed to get Erica away from Sally. After my brief instruction, I wiped away the lone tear traversing Erica's cheek.

"Get going, both of you," Sally commanded, gesturing in the direction of the avalanche chute.

I leaned toward Erica and said in a low voice, "I need you to start moving."

"Without you?" she said, stricken.

I nodded. "Just a little ways."

The squawk of a two-way radio made all three of us start.

Sally turned quickly and began moving around the corner of the house, toward the sound, glancing back at us over her shoulder and trying to keep the gun on Erica.

I spoke again, my lips barely moving, "Go, Erica."

"But I've never skied before. I don't know how. I won't be good at it."

"You'll be fine. I'll be with you in a second."

"But what if I fall?"

"It won't hurt. The snow's soft."

"But I don't want to," she moaned.

"Nothing's going to happen. Can you please start skiing? Go over to that big tree and wait for me." I pointed toward a pine directly below the cornice's overhang.

"I'm cold."

"We won't be out long. Trust me," I begged.

Erica clutched me tightly and began to whimper. "No, please don't make me."

I kissed her cheek and gently pushed her forward on the skis. "It's the only way. I need you to be brave, as brave as you've ever been. I'll be right behind you."

"You promise?"

"I promise."

"Is Sally going to shoot us?"

"She might try, but I'll bet her aim's bad. She'll miss."

"Yeah, she's stupid. She can't hit us."

"Exactly."

That thought seemed to give Erica the reassurance she needed to start skiing. "Love you," she said, almost out of habit, looking over her shoulder.

"I love you, too, Erica," I said softly, then adding, "Push hard with your poles."

Halfway out, Erica fell. She looked back at me expectantly, her eyes begging me to ski out and rescue her. Instead, I gestured for her to get up and gave her a thumbs-up sign when she struggled to her feet.

Sally came back, fiddling with the two-way radio I'd lost near the cabin door. My heart missed a beat when she removed the batteries and threw them into the deep snow, tossing the radio in the other direction.

She stared at me wordlessly.

With Erica out of earshot, I pleaded with Sally. "You don't have to do this."

"Get going," she said briskly. "Follow her."

"I'll leave in a minute."

"You'll leave now."

"You may not like or respect Lori Parks, but you have something in common."

"What?"

"A love for Jodi."

Sally shook her head vehemently.

"You both lost someone you loved. Lori's love may not meet with your approval or match your definition of what's right and wrong, but that doesn't make it any less real. You can kick and shout and get millions of narrow-minded people to agree with you, but nothing's going to change. You can't stop us from loving each other. No matter how much you pile on the ridicule, you won't win. Not in this lifetime or the next. Your hatred can never outlast our love. Lori Parks is proof of that. She did grieve, and she has suffered. She goes through the motions but doesn't care about anything. Except your daughter. She, too, lives with Jodi's memory. Every day, she wakes up with her and goes to sleep with her."

I had begun to think my words had softened Sally, when her face twisted in fury.

"That woman does not, can not, will not ever sleep with my daughter," she screamed, and her body let loose a full-length shudder.

At that exact moment, a shot rang out.

At the sound of the blast, all panic vanished, and I acted with clarity and speed.

I skied out to Erica and in a giant embrace picked her up and turned her around. She held on to my pole, and I dragged her three hundred feet as fast as I could, with superhuman strength.

Out of harm's way, we both collapsed, struggling for air.

Moments later, we heard a loud boom as shelves of the cornice fractured and raged down the steep slope. The tree where I'd told Erica to huddle was uprooted instantly and caught in the wave of snow.

The avalanche debris and slurry spread over a great distance but stopped short of the area where Erica and I crouched. Mercifully, it did cover Sally Wilde's body and the surrounding blood-stained snow.

Regrettably, the violent pieces of nature came too late to erase an image that will forever haunt me. Sally's suicidal gunshot had successfully obliterated her lower face, yet left her eyes untouched.

And in them, I saw the etching of eternal grief.

Chapter 27

Christmas day, I woke to the sound of honking.

I looked out the window and gasped when I saw a Hummer idling in front of the house. Not the yuppie H2 version, but the original military monster, in camouflage green.

I hurriedly threw on an outfit from a discard pile next to the bed and ran into the street, stunned at the sight of Fran Green at the wheel.

Fran hopped out, ran around the Hummer's great length, and shoved me into the back before returning to her chauffeur's perch. Her haste made it hard, but not impossible, to make out this day's T-shirt: "My boss is a lesbian carpenter."

"Check out these wheels," she said, giddy with excitement.

"Are you authorized to drive?"

Fran emitted a huffy sigh as she pulled out her wallet and extracted a Colorado driver's license. "Not the best shot, but the gal at the bureau refused to take more pics after the fifth one."

"Where did you get the Hummer?"

"Belongs to Leonard. Let me borrow it for the day, in light of our important mission. Gotta take the fella home," she said, pointing at the wooden baby Jesus belted in the passenger seat.

"You cracked the case," I said grudgingly. "Where did you find him?"

"Stashed in the Crumplers' basement."

"Leonard didn't do it, did he?"

"No, siree."

"Who would have thought he almost took the fall for Eunice Crumpler?"

The smirk on Fran's face vanished. "You knew?"

"It occurred to me as I lay in their bushes, the night Sally kidnapped Erica."

Responding to her crestfallen look, I quickly added, "But you can fill me in. Why did Eunice steal from herself?"

Fran brightened noticeably at this tiny encouragement. "More like lifting from the sister. Took the pieces, stashed 'em in a locked room in the cellar. Only place in the house Leonard couldn't access, and Clarice can't manage the stairs. Didn't stop us. Me and Leonard picked the lock last night and retrieved this little devil," she gestured affectionately at Jesus. "Get the rest later. Slowly, without raising suspicion. It'd tear Clarice apart if she found out the hoodlum's in the family."

"Why did Eunice do it?"

"Started ten years ago. She came home after the mother died, felt it wrong of Clarice to keep the lights on, but her sister wouldn't budge. Eunice got mad when Clarice acted like the display was a tribute to their mother's memory and kept making it bigger. Whole mess got out of hand. Well, you've seen it."

"Every bulb," I said wearily.

"Eunice thought she'd have a little fun. Not too funny, ask me."

"Me neither," I agreed, the memory of hours spent on the cold ground still fresh.

"Went over this morning and gave Eunice a good talking-to. She promised she won't take anything more. Told her I'd rat her out in a cat's flash if so much as a piece of tinsel goes missing. Should be the end of it."

"What will we tell Clarice?"

"Someone in the neighborhood confessed. No one she knows. You, me, and Leonard'll haul the loot up the steps tomorrow when she's napping. Case closed."

"You can lie this effortlessly?"

"Without soiling an armpit."

"How about stealing?"

Fran raised an eyebrow. "Depends."

"I need a quart of pickles to give to Florence Bailey, the next-door neighbor. Did you notice any in the basement?"

"Never seen so many pecks packed in one place."

"Could we discreetly take a jar?"

"Good as done. Vanish without a trace."

I leaned back and spread my arms wide. "I can't believe Leonard let you drive his Hummer."

"Man has faith. Told me I'm the most careful driver he ever taught. 'Course, didn't see me take out that row of newsstands a few blocks back."

I smiled. "You didn't."

"Might have nicked 'em. Who can tell in this tank? Should get me one of these."

"You can't be serious!"

"Why not?"

"How much do they cost?"

"Start at fifty."

I sat up straight and took another look around. "Thousand?"

Fran nodded. "Who cares about sticker price? Got nothing more pressing to do with my ducats."

"I can't believe they're that expensive."

"Sucker'll go twenty miles on four flats."

"And exactly why would you need that feature?"

"Always try to prepare . . ." Fran said, an echo of Sally Wilde's threatening notes, and we both laughed, a long overdue expulsion of relief.

"Windows leak, though. Noticed that. And brakes touchy. Have to use the gears to slow down properly."

Fran had started to scare me. "You can't be serious."

"Nah. Got my eye on a Ford Ranger. Check out the car ads next week."

"Speaking of parking, I've talked it over with Destiny, and we'd like to have you move in permanently, if you want to."

Fran frowned deeply. "Appreciate the offer, but it's pretty loud on the second floor. You gals do too much walking in big shoes on three."

"We could cover the hardwood floors with rugs."

"Never have sex. Not natural for two girls starting out. Me and Ruth, in our prime, you couldn't pry us out of bed with a forklift."

"We have sex," I said hotly. "Just because we choose not to share it with the neighbors doesn't mean we're not active."

"Never cook. Me, I like to come home and smell something in the oven. In my day, we traded recipes. Now you youngsters exchange names of fast food places. Burritos, noodles, Thai food, none of that can replace a good casserole."

Before I could respond to this slur, she threw in another. "Destiny parks too close to the fence, hard to reach around and scrape the snow off her car."

My scowl had deepened to canyon-like proportions before Fran burst into a wide smile and slapped me on the knee. "Pullin' your leg, kiddo. Don't take lightly what you two have done for me. Roof over my head when I needed it most. Can't think long-term, but value the invite more than you know."

Fran clasped my hand tightly, before adding, "Let's go wish Destiny a merry Christmas. Can't wait for dinner. Up at the crack preparing for this feast we're having at Lori and Donna's."

"What did you make?"

"You name it, we got it! Ham, mashed potatoes, green beans, yams, pecan pie. Think those two can go a day without fighting?"

"Hopefully. It is a holiday."

"How's the little one doing?"

"Erica's hanging in there. On the drive home from Winter Glades, she didn't talk much. It may take time."

"Time we got," Fran mused, before adding emphatically, "We should take her snowboarding."

"She'd love that."

"Might do you some good, too," Fran said, studying me, almost looking through me.

How could Fran Green know what the experience had done to me, when I, too, had revealed nothing?

Maybe I would snowboard.

Maybe, just maybe, I could touch fresh powder again and not think shattering thoughts.

Later that afternoon, on our way to dinner, Fran, Destiny, and I stopped to run an errand.

In the south manger at the Crumpler estate, we dropped off the baby Jesus, tenderly tucking him into his straw crib.

It's not something I'll ever put on a resume, but we did put the Christ back into Christmas.

Publications from Spinsters Ink

P.O. Box 242
Midway, Florida 32343
Phone: 800 301-6860
www.spinstersink.com

DISORDERLY ATTACHMENTS by Jennifer L. Jordan. 5th Kristin Ashe Mystery. Kris investigates whether a mansion someone wants to convert into condos is haunted.   ISBN 1-883523-74-5 $14.95

VERA'S STILL POINT by Ruth Perkinson. Vera is reminded of exactly what it is that she has been missing in life.
ISBN 1-883523-73-7 $14.95

OUTRAGEOUS by Sheila Ortiz-Taylor. Arden Benbow, a motor-cycle riding, lesbian Latina poet from LA is hired to teach poetry in a small liberal arts college in northwest Florida.
ISBN 1-883523-72-9 $14.95

UNBREAKABLE by Blayne Cooper. The bonds of love and friend-ship can be as strong as steel. But are they unbreakable?
ISBN 1-883523-76-1 $14.95

ALL BETS OFF by Jaime Clevenger. Bette Lawrence is about to find out how hard life can be for someone of low society standing in the 1900s.   ISBN 1-883523-71-0 $14.95

UNBEARABLE LOSSES by Jennifer L. Jordan. 4th in the Kristin Ashe Mystery series. Two elderly sisters have hired Kris to discover who is pilfering from their award-winning holiday display.
ISBN 1-883523-68-0 $14.95

FRENCH POSTCARDS by Jane Merchant. When Elinor moves to France with her husband and two children, she never expects that her life is about to be changed forever.

ISBN 1-883523-67-2 $14.95

EXISTING SOLUTIONS by Jennifer L. Jordan. 2nd book in the Kristin Ashe Mystery series. When Kris is hired to find an activist's biological father, things get complicated when she finds herself falling for her client.

ISBN 1-883523-69-9 $14.95

A SAFE PLACE TO SLEEP by Jennifer L. Jordan. 1st in the Kristin Ashe Mystery series. Kris is approached by well known lesbian Destiny Greaves with an unusual request. One that will lead Kris to hunt for her own missing childhood pieces.

ISBN 1-883523-70-2 $14.95

THE SECRET KEEPING by Francine Saint Marie. The Secret Keeping is a high stakes, girl-gets-girl romance, where the moral of the story is that money can buy you love if it's invested wisely.

ISBN: 1-883523-77-X $14.95

WOMEN'S STUDIES by Julia Watts. With humor and heart, Women's Studies follows one school year in the lives of these three young women and shows that in college, one,s extracurricular activities are often much more educational that what goes on in the classroom.

ISBN: 1-883523-75-3 $14.95

A POEM FOR WHAT'S HER NAME by Dani O'Connor. Professor Dani O'Connor had pretty much resigned herself to the fact that there was no such thing as a complete woman. Then out of nowhere, along comes a woman who blows Dani's theory right out of the water.

ISBN: 1-883523-78-8 $14.95

Visit

Spinsters Ink

at

SpinstersInk.com

or call our toll-free number

1-800-301-6860